Praise for other books

Struck:

available in the series:

Stung:

'Action unfolds at a dizzying pace.'
- Sally Morris, *Daily Mail Online*

'Plenty of action along with a great mystery.'
- *Feeling Fictional* Blog

'This fast-paced action thriller is well written,
with charismatic characters and
an exciting plot.' - *Armadillo Magazine*

'A really gripping book through and
through . . . not a boring moment in it.'
- Rocky Williams, *Teen Titles*

Shaken:

'Plenty of exciting moments and some great action-
packed chapters.' - *A Dream of Books* Blog

'Romance and thrills with plenty of action to keep you on
the edge of your seat, and glued to the book!'
- *Reality's a Bore* Blog

For Steve and Susie Bagnall
and
with thanks to teachers and social workers
everywhere trying to make a positive
difference in the lives of young people.

OXFORD
UNIVERSITY PRESS

Great Clarendon Street, Oxford OX2 6DP

Oxford University Press is a department of the University of Oxford.
It furthers the University's objective of excellence in research, scholarship,
and education by publishing worldwide. Oxford is a registered trade mark of
Oxford University Press in the UK and in certain other countries

British Library Cataloguing in Publication Data

Data available

ISBN: 978-0-19-274596-5

1 3 5 7 9 10 8 6 4 2

Printed in Great Britain

Paper used in the production of this book is a natural,
recyclable product made from wood grown in sustainable forests.
The manufacturing process conforms to the environmental
regulations of the country of origin.

SCORCHED

Joss Stirling

OXFORD
UNIVERSITY PRESS

Chapter 1

Ember Lord was used to people being scared of her but she had not expected this to include the social worker and policeman who accompanied her to the detention centre. Both avoided her eye, chatting to each other about neutral subjects; neither wanted to risk attracting her attention.

Being on remand facing the charge of killing your own father must really mess with how others saw you, thought Ember.

The prison van took a sharp turn and slowed.

'Nearly there,' said the policeman with false cheer.

Ember took his word for it because there were no windows in the back of the vehicle.

'We don't normally deliver our clients so late at night,' the social worker said apologetically. 'We had to wait until the documentation came through, and then there was a mix-up over transportation.'

After a pause, Ember realized the woman had been addressing her. 'It doesn't matter.'

'You'll find Lockwood Youth Training Centre a good place to wait for your trial,' the social worker continued. 'You'll have your own room, a peer pal to help you settle, and of course your solicitor can have free access to you so you can discuss your defence.'

Ember swallowed against the nausea she had been

1

fighting since leaving Snaresbrook Crown Court in East London. She had never been a good traveller, and definitely not in the airless back of a police van. 'I said it doesn't matter.' Nothing mattered but protecting Max.

'You can have visitors at least once a week.'

Ember shook her head. She wasn't expecting any of those.

'And you'll be referred to as a trainee.'

The hypocrisy of that fanned her temper. 'Not inmate or prisoner? What a joke.' Ember opened her eyes in time to see the woman toss her head at the policeman in a 'what can you do?' gesture.

The case worker looked embarrassed to be caught revealing her true feelings about her charge, and her tone became snippy in response. 'It's not jail, Ember. You're in a secure centre pending trial.'

Ember was spared the need to answer when the van stopped. After a pause, the rear doors opened and a blessed breath of fresh air entered the vehicle. Ember could smell damp grass. Finally, she could be sure she wasn't going to humiliate herself further by throwing up. That was the first good news she had had in some days.

'All right, Ember. Time to get out,' said the policeman as he exited the vehicle first. He stood at the rear door to steady her as she stepped down. Having her hands handcuffed made such simple manoeuvres more difficult. They had arrived in a pool of light in front of a low-rise brick building, which had to be a contender for the Most Boring Architecture prize. Beyond lay the two rings of floodlit fence, and further off the darkness of the fields and woods that separated the youth prison, sorry, *training centre*, from ordinary unfettered life. A soft rain fell, misting Ember's face and chilling further her already cold skin.

Two members of staff were waiting just inside the building to greet her. Ember was shown into a reception room as yet more paperwork was filled out. The policeman removed her handcuffs without a word.

'Any trouble?' asked a motherly-looking woman who appeared to be the senior person on duty.

'None,' said the social worker. 'Ember's been very quiet.'

Ember directed her gaze away, retreating to the place inside herself where the real Ember lived. She'd been quiet since her emotional collapse on finding herself standing over her father's body. She hadn't known she had such an out-of-control person inside her. It had been like discovering she shared Bruce Banner's weakness, a panicked Hulk waiting to erupt and smash everything in its path.

'That's good. Ember, welcome to Lockwood. I know it must all be very confusing and frightening for you.'

'Not really,' Ember muttered. The authorities had treated her much better than her own father had ever done. No need to duck a fist or careless slap.

The woman pursed her lips. 'Right. So. My name is Kelly Bishop and I'm one of the unit workers on the girls' side. This is my colleague, Tom Forest. He normally works with the boys but drew the short straw tonight for the late shift.'

Tom, a big man with an unhealthy pallor, nodded and returned to his conversation with the policeman. They seemed to know each other quite well, joking about the latest manager to get the boot in the Premier League. In fact, everyone here knew each other, except Ember.

Mrs Bishop turned back to the social worker. 'Was she searched?'

'At the police station and again before her court appearance this morning.'

'And she's been in your custody all that time?'

'Yes, myself and a colleague were with her throughout.'

'Excellent. That means we can just do a brief pat down

then let Ember get some rest. If you two gentlemen wouldn't mind leaving us?'

The policeman and Mr Forest left the room.

'Ember, if you could just stand up with your arms and legs spread.'

Ember knew the routine. It didn't matter. Ember wasn't here. A shell Ember was letting this woman check her pockets for drugs and weapons. Mrs Bishop paused over Ember's necklace, a thin gold chain with a puma pendant. She hummed as she considered the thickness of the chain then dismissed it as a danger.

'Do you have any concerns over her state of mind?' Mrs Bishop asked the case worker.

'No, she's not shown any signs of distress since entering police custody.'

'Ember, how are you feeling?'

They were asking her if she was feeling suicidal, Ember realized. She was feeling desperate but definitely not that. She had to survive to make sure Max was looked after. 'I'm OK.'

'Then I don't think we need keep you from your bed any longer.' Mrs Bishop checked her watch. 'One-thirty. Not ideal for the usual orientation talk. I'll come by tomorrow and explain how things work. For the moment, I'll take you to your room and you can settle in. You can say goodbye to Miss Nevis now.'

Ember hadn't remembered that was the social worker's name until then. She had probably been told at some point but the information had not lodged in her mind, with so many other things competing for attention. 'OK.'

Miss Nevis gave a weak smile. 'I'll be in touch to see how you are getting along.'

'Whatever.'

'Nevertheless, you'll hear from me, probably later in the week.'

4

'Right.' Ember realized that, even though she didn't need the social worker, Miss Nevis might end up being her only link to her old life. 'Would you . . . ?' It was so hard to ask for anything. She'd always been ordered not to show vulnerability.

'Yes?' Miss Nevis looked up from the document case she was zipping closed.

'Would you check that Max is all right?' The words came out in an awkward tumble.

'Of course, Ember. I'm pleased you asked. I won't be dealing with him as I'm in the juvenile offenders' branch but I can ask my colleagues dealing with special case minors.'

'He won't manage on his own.'

'His needs will be fully assessed, never you worry. We hope to reunite him with Mrs Roe as soon as she's out of hospital and they are cleared to return to their home.'

Ember swallowed, then nodded. She still felt shaky when she remembered Nanny Roe had collapsed with chest pains on seeing the police put handcuffs on Ember. 'OK. You'll let me know they're both OK, won't you?' Surely no one would want to hurt Max, or Nanny?

'I'll see what I can do. Speak to you soon, Ember.' The social worker left to return to the van that had brought them here. Mrs Bishop led Ember in the opposite direction.

'Max is your brother? Older or younger?' she asked, making conversation to fill the silence.

'My twin.' Their separation came as a physical pain. It felt as though her ribcage was crushing her heart. Where was Max now? Did he even understand what had happened on Wednesday night?

'Will he want to visit you?'

Ember shook her head. 'No.' It would kill Max to see her in here. She hoped he believed her message that she was fine, just staying at a training centre—only someone as innocent as Max would fail to realize it was prison.

Mrs Bishop paused outside a white door. It looked reassuringly ordinary, no locks on the outside. 'You mustn't be embarrassed to ask him to come. Families are encouraged to keep in touch.'

Ember knew she had to nip in the bud any interest in Max. 'Mrs Bishop, I'm charged with killing my own father. Do you really think my brother will want to see me?'

The woman covered her fluster by opening the door. 'Here's your room, Ember. It'll be yours for as long as we have you as a trainee at our centre. There's a small ensuite through that door in the corner. You can add your own posters and personal touches as long as the material is approved by a member of staff.'

The narrow room was bare at the moment, just a bed, thin cupboard, chest of drawers and a desk. Ember tried to tell herself that it was no better or worse than some of the university accommodation she'd seen online when she'd been dreaming of taking a degree rather than taking over her father's business as he had expected. Uni had only ever been a daydream, of course, as she'd never taken GCSEs, let alone A levels.

'OK.' Steeling herself, accepting the price she had to pay, she crossed the threshold. A set of night clothes and basic wash stuff had been left on the plain blue cover.

'I'll send your case along as soon as it's been cleared. You need anything else?' From her hovering by the door, Mrs Bishop clearly wanted to dole out more words of encouragement and advice. 'Don't feel ashamed of asking. We understand this is a difficult time for our trainees, the first night.'

Ember bit her cheek to quell an unexpected wave of emotion. She couldn't show any softness, had to power on through this hell. The only way out was through.

'No, I don't need anything,' she said shortly. 'Just to be left alone.'

'Right then. Goodnight.'

Ember didn't respond or turn round to thank the woman for her attempt to reach out. If she did, Mrs Bishop might glimpse the tears in her eyes, offer yet more comfort, and then Ember might have a meltdown. That was unthinkable.

The door closed and Ember got her wish to be on her own.

Ember hadn't slept so she was awake when someone tapped on the door at eight. When no one came in but just tapped again, she realized she had to give permission. It wasn't like the police cell with people barging in all times of night and day.

'What?'

The door opened and a blonde girl of her own age put her head round the edge. 'Hi, are you Ember?'

Ember stood up with her back to the radiator and window, a fist clenched around her necklace pendant, letting the front legs of the puma dig into her palm, rooting her in the here and now. 'Yes.'

'Hey, your case is out here.' She put it inside the room. 'I'm Kate, your peer pal.' The blonde came in and took a perch on the empty desk, watching Ember with cool interest. This gave Ember time to assess the newcomer for threat potential. Kate was slim, agile looking; something about her nodded to street-wise, with her multiple piercings and gang tat of a scorpion on her wrist. 'Do you want to know what a mentor is?'

'I can guess. You've been asked to hold my hand for the first few days.' Ember uncurled her fist and dug her hands in the front pocket of her shapeless hoodie, prison issue.

'That's about it.' Kate rubbed her tattoo as if it bothered her. Why have one if she didn't like it?

Ember knew the number one rule of prison was to establish from the first that you were tough or they'd take advantage. 'Well then, you can eff off. I don't need hand-holding, got it?'

'I see.' Kate put her head to one side, considering.

'I don't need anyone. Just forget I exist.'

'Cool. I'll leave you to non-existence then.' The girl gave a couldn't-give-a-damn shrug. 'Breakfast is in the kitchen down the hall. It's help yourself and clear up after you've finished. We share out duties.' She walked out, no doubt muttering something unflattering.

Ember let out the breath she had been holding now the stranger had gone. Though shameful to admit, she had been scared that Devlin had put up an inmate to attack her on her first day; it was the kind of thing she had to expect. Even though they'd done their deal, Devlin was unpredictable, like a forest fire that could suddenly swing back and cut you off. He might well have thought that softening her up with a beating, making sure she knew he could reach her even inside, would keep her scared and compliant.

Ember forced herself to move from the window. It was tempting to stay in her room for the rest of her life but that wasn't really possible. The longer she put off meeting the others, the worse it would be. Dressing quickly in her own clothes from the case, she followed Kate and found the kitchen with no difficulty. Six girls sat round a table, passing the cereal and milk bottle between them. One was feeding a baby in a high chair. Their happy chatter stopped as she came in. Kate, who had only just taken a seat, ignored her as requested. Ember took the nearest empty chair and filled a bowl with some cornflakes. She didn't actually like the taste but it had been the closest packet. She could feel the looks of the other girls like sunburn. The silence became unbearable and inevitably someone had to blurt out what they were all wondering.

'Are you Ember Lord?' asked a girl with a high brown ponytail. She was wearing jeans and a T-shirt and looked much better than Ember, who was keenly aware that she looked more suited to a day shopping in Monaco than hanging out with her fellow prisoners. This wasn't by choice: when she opened her case she found it had been filled with items from among her designer collection, not the casual stuff she would've preferred. The social worker had a lot to answer for.

'Yes.'

'We read about you in the newspapers.'

'Lucky you.'

'Did you really off your old man?'

The five other girls stopped eating, waiting for her reaction to this blunt question. Even the baby seemed to be watching her with curious blue eyes.

The rage was so strong Ember could taste it, a bitterness on her tongue. *Clamp down on it; don't let it control you again.* 'That's none of your business.' She picked up her bowl and took it with her back to her room, not slamming the door, as that would give the girls the satisfaction of knowing they had got to her so easily. Besides, she didn't want to scare the baby.

Leaving the bowl of cereal to go soggy on the desk, Ember went to the window, looking out over the fence and the fields beyond. She thumped the frame with the ball of her hand. She wanted to scream; she felt so trapped. She let out a hissing breath, dragging herself back into command. It was a dreary scene out there; trees still bare, fields more mud than grass. There was a hint of distant hills but with the rain-bearing clouds it was hard to make out the horizon. She placed her palm on the cold glass. A few minutes and a single terrible choice had made all the difference in her life. In fact, hers was effectively over. All she could do was carry on so that the one person she cared for would come out of this OK. That was her plan; now she just had to stick to it and not let anyone break her down.

'Tough as nails,' she muttered. 'Mean as a snake. Chip off the old block.' Her father had been a useless individual alive, but now his personal mantra might be the only thing that could help her.

Chapter 2

Joe Masters decided that it was a kind of punishment to play Nathan at table tennis, considering the mood his friend was in. They were passing time in the old common room of a local secondary school, waiting for their colleagues to report in from their undercover mission at Lockwood Training Centre, a few miles away near Milton Keynes. The Centre minibus was due to deliver the girls at ten, for what their fellow internees thought was the community service part of their sentence.

'You think Kate will be OK?' Nathan asked, missing the stroke with a wild swipe. He brushed his dark hair out of his eyes as he bent down to retrieve the ball. He lacked all his usual coordination thanks to his preoccupation with Kate's wellbeing.

'Yes, Nat, she'll be fine,' Joe said easily, as he had on the previous six occasions when Nathan had asked the same question. 'She's with Raven. Those two make a good team.' He had no doubts about his colleagues' skills, even though both of their boyfriends were like bears with sore paws when their girls were on a mission.

'But she's in with a tough crowd.'

'Well, it is prison, my friend.' Personally, he thought Kate, with her background surviving a year-long pursuit by one of Indonesia's most deadly gangs, was probably the most lethal person inside the girls' unit. Nathan, however, persisted in seeing his girl as a damaged butterfly he wanted to protect. That annoyed Kate no end.

Kieran was less visibly concerned for his girlfriend, Raven, just frowning at the desktop, but Joe had a shrewd idea the data on the computer screen was taking a beating. Either his best friend was kicking ass in some game he had mastered, or hacking a global network that needed taking down: both were distinct possibilities when it came to the Young Detective Agency's resident genius.

With a very un-undercover toot, the minibus turned into the school carpark. Nathan chucked his bat aside, Kieran pushed back his chair, and they rushed to the window to watch the girls get out. Joe stood a little apart. He got that his friends were hopelessly devoted to their other halves but often he thought they overdid the concern.

'They look OK, don't they?' Nathan said softly, eyes following the little blonde head into the building.

Kieran dug his hands in his pockets, shoulders hunched. His jade-green eyes were fixed on a mass of spiralling black curls. 'Both are ambulatory and exhibiting no signs of distress.'

Joe bit back a grin. Kieran was unconsciously funny when he went all high-falutin' on them. 'What he means, Nat, is "yes, they're absolutely fine," and I think I should point out that they'll kill you if they find you've been fussing about them.'

Nathan looked at Kieran. 'He's right, Key. We've got to pretend we weren't worried or they'll think we don't think they're up to the job.'

Kieran nodded, a beat behind his friends but catching up fast. 'OK.' He grabbed a bat from the tennis table. 'The score's ten-eleven to you, Nat. Everyone, look relaxed.'

Joe started throwing darts at the battered dartboard. Nathan and Kieran took up their pretend game, long limbs taking lazy hits at the ball just in time for the door to open.

12

Fiendishly upping the tempo, Kieran placed a shot right in the left corner, getting past Nathan and bouncing on the floor for Raven to catch. 'Eleven all!'

She held up the ball. 'See, Kate, how hard they've been working while we've been banged up with thieves and murderers?'

Kieran grinned, his unruly chestnut hair flopping forward over his eyes. 'I've been told by someone that all work and no play . . .'

Raven ran and jumped up to hug him, legs round his waist. She ruffled his hair. 'You, Ace, are never going to be a dull boy.'

While Kieran and Raven were having their exuberant greeting, Nathan was taking care of Kate, giving her a hug and a kiss, murmuring what Joe guessed were private words of encouragement. That left Joe adrift, at least until their boss, Colonel Isaac Hampton, entered the room. Jan Hardy, mentor for the students in Joe's stream at the YDA, was by his side.

'Good, you're all here,' said Isaac. An ex-army man with piercing blue eyes and fair hair, he always held sway over any room, no matter the company. The YDA was his brainchild and he kept a close eye every time one of his students went out on a mission.

'Morning, Isaac, Mrs Hardy,' said Joe. 'Reporting for duty, sir, ma'am.' Mrs Hardy nodded. A no-nonsense former Metropolitan police officer, she ran a tight ship in C stream, Joe and Kate's division, for those who had the greatest aptitude for undercover work.

'Joe. Nice to see you are ready for the briefing, unlike some.' Isaac raised an eyebrow, silently agreeing with Joe that the air was just too full of romance. Isaac put two fingers in his mouth and whistled. 'Time to start, guys.'

On that signal, the couples sheepishly separated and came to attention.

'Let's sit down.' Isaac gestured to the beaten-up sofas by the window. St Bernard's School, which was run by a friend of Isaac, had lent them the old sixth form block for their mission. This wing was due to be knocked down and houses erected on the land now that the school had moved into its new buildings on the former playing fields. Sharing the site was perfect for headquarters. Their mission depended on them convincing their target that they were locals and therefore above suspicion, going about legitimate business in and around Lockwood.

'Let's get right to it. How did you get on with our subject?' Isaac asked Kate.

'She arrived last night, too late for me to meet her then,' Kate explained. She pulled her knees up to sit cross-legged on the sofa next to Nathan.

'I was hoping you'd get to her while she was feeling most vulnerable,' said Mrs Hardy, their expert on human psychology. 'How did that happen?'

Kate shrugged. 'Some bureaucratic delay. I called in this morning first thing but Lord had already put up all her shields. Told me she didn't need me, didn't even want me to acknowledge her existence. It would've been out of character for my cover identity to push it, so I left. I've rarely met anyone so hostile. It's not hard to see her as the daughter of Mick Lord.'

'Raven? Do you agree with Kate that she's hostile?' Isaac turned to the second member of the inside team.

'I only saw her briefly at breakfast.' Raven's expression turned distant as she re-ran the scene in her head. 'One of the girls came right out and asked her if she'd killed her father. She walked out, more from pride than hurt feelings I'd say.'

'So she is unlikely to make friends while on remand, not in the time-frame we are working to?' asked Mrs Hardy.

'Doubtful.' Raven tugged at a strand of her hair, letting it spring back. 'I'm not sure she's so unreachable though. One of the trainees has a kid—seven months and cute as a button. There was something in Lord's eyes when she saw the baby, some kind of feeling, not sure what.'

'I guess even stone-cold killers might have a soft spot for a kid but, still, that's something to work on. Let's go over what we know.' Isaac called up his notes on his tablet. 'Ember Ann Lord, seventeen. Mother, Ann-Marie O'Malley, deceased eight years ago of an overdose. Father, Michael Lord, known as Mick, also deceased last week thanks to the knife in his chest. Brother, a twin, Maximilian Michael Lord, currently placed in a foster family in East London as his carer is in hospital after a suspected heart attack. Damien and Rose are undercover in his community to find out what they can from him. He's not gone back to school yet due to compassionate leave but they've met him while he was walking his boxer dog in a local park. They've borrowed Dr Waterburn's spaniel and are getting to know him as fellow dog-walkers. I'm hoping for more later today.'

Jan Hardy flicked through her own briefing document. 'We're not expecting Max Lord to have the information we require. He was always described as peripheral to Mick Lord's operation. It was the daughter Mick was said to be grooming to take over.'

Joe rolled his shoulders, feeling in need of a run in the fresh air. He'd only seen school photographs of the subjects, but had been annoyed to find himself approving of the way the girl rocked her school uniform. Ember, with her sleek long black hair and shuttered light-brown eyes, looked disturbingly like his favourite fantasy avatar, the one he picked as his adversary when he played warrior to her demon goddess. Whereas her twin Max, with his elfin blond looks and vulnerable happy smile, seemed to belong to a much more innocent world. Hard to credit that they were related. 'Are we sure about that? Isn't it more usual for guys like Mick Lord to train up their sons?'

'That's true, but Ember Lord appears to be the exception,' said Jan. 'She turned out to be the dominant one in that nest and pushed out the other baby bird. Max has been living mainly with the carer, known as Nanny Roe, in an annexe, separate from the big house, while Ember and her father ruled the roost. Word is that Max is a nice boy, not too bright, maybe a little simple, but no trouble at school. It's always been Ember who's made the waves. She got expelled from her last elite girls' school for getting into a fight with another pupil on the hockey field, an incident that left the victim needing stitches.'

'Not so jolly hockey sticks,' muttered Kate.

'She rapidly picked up a reputation for being as tough as her father. Her schoolmates—we found no friends—all said they were scared of her and weren't surprised she'd been charged with murder.'

'OK, so we know she's violent, but it's still a leap to murder. Seeing how her behaviour escalated, do you think she's psychotic or suffering from another mental illness?' asked Raven. 'I mean with a father like that you have to come out all sorts of messed-up.'

'The prison psychiatrist will be taking a close look at her and it might be part of her defence, but my understanding to date is that she's regarded as dangerous, but basically sane. Bear that in mind when you have dealings with her.'

'And don't let her near any sharp objects,' said Nathan, pressing Kate's hand where it rested in his.

'Not funny,' replied Kate.

'It wasn't a joke.'

'We'll give it a few more days, but if she's not responding to the girls' attempts to make friends, maybe she'll open up to a boy? Or at least brag to one of you. She's been surrounded by men all her life so she might respond better to a male.' Isaac put his tablet back in his messenger bag. 'In view of this, I think we should go ahead with the second part of the plan. Jan, is your contact still happy to lead the way?'

Mrs Hardy gave a wry smile. 'I'd say he was embarrassingly eager. The idea of putting on a play in a juvenile prison appeals to his belief that Shakespeare is the cure for all ills, including criminal behaviour.'

'I would've thought a playwright who depicts regicide, fratricide, rape, mutilation, and murder with alarming frequency would have the opposite effect,' Kieran murmured to Joe.

Nothing got past Isaac. 'You'll be pleased to hear then, Kieran, that the chosen play contains none of the above. *A Midsummer Night's Dream*. The authorities vetted it carefully and agreed that, as a whimsical comedy with fairies and forests, it would have a therapeutic value for their young charges. Boys, you'll be going in with Jan's good friend, the renowned theatre director, Henry Rawlings, posing as his helpers and actors as required. You are doing it as part of your gold Duke of Edinburgh scheme while appearing to study here in the sixth form, understood?'

'Yes, Isaac,' said Joe.

'I didn't know I was registered for the award.' Kieran frowned.

'You're not, cupcake. It's your cover,' said Raven.

'No point in wasting it though. I'll register us all and we can beef up our CVs for Uni.' Kieran opened up a page on his laptop browser.

'If you do that then you also have to do a four day expedition in the Brecon Beacons carrying everything you need on your back,' added Nathan. 'Camping. Wet socks. Lugging backpacks up mountains. No wifi.'

'Oh. In that case.' Kieran closed the laptop.

Joe rather liked the sound of the outdoor challenge. 'Call it up again. I'm all for it, Key. Let's do it.'

Kieran shook his head.

Raven patted Joe's arm. 'It's not the camping Kieran doesn't like. Cut my guy here off from the Mother Ship and he doesn't know what to do with himself.'

'You won't have time, I'm afraid, for any extra-curricular activities over the next month,' said Isaac, ending the banter. 'We need you to be focused on getting the information from Lord. It's a top priority for all of us.'

'Any news on the whereabouts of the weapons?' asked Joe. None of the mission team could sleep easy knowing that there was a cache of high-tech arms and ammunition, taken from NATO-trained troops in the conflicts in the Middle East, and now washing around the seedier parts of Europe.

'We don't think Lord's death put much of a hitch in their stride, unfortunately,' said Mrs Hardy. 'The shipment is now rumoured to be reaching the end of the pipeline—intended destination, the streets of London.'

Isaac gave a grim nod. 'With so many weapons flooding onto the black market in the capital, a whole new round of gun violence will kick off and the guns could possibly fall into the hands of home-grown terrorists.'

As an American, one of the things Joe appreciated about living in the UK was gun crime being so much lower than in his homeland. He thought sometimes that he would fight twice as hard as his colleagues to keep his adopted country that way. 'Then we'd better make sure Ember Lord tells all.'

'We hope she'll talk in exchange for a deal on her case. She'll know that criminal gangs don't stop just because one of their number is eliminated. Mick Lord's second, Seamus Devlin, has stepped up and it's business as usual in the East End underworld.'

'You think Ember Lord was expecting to take over?' asked Joe.

'Probably, eventually. She still might be thinking along those lines. That's the problem about getting her to make a deal. There's no guarantee the court will convict her and she could be walking free in a few months, back to take over from Daddy.'

'But she was found alone at home with the body. No sign of a break-in.'

'I know the facts, Joe, I'm just saying that juries don't always reach the verdicts you expect.'

Ember leafed through the battered library copy of Shakespeare, pausing at favourite scenes. Romeo and Juliet on the balcony. Portia arguing for mercy in the trial scene in *The Merchant of Venice*. Viola getting horribly muddled in love while pretending to be a boy in *Twelfth Night*. It was Ember's secret. With her school record, no one expected her to read anything other than celebrity gossip magazines, and even then they thought she merely flicked through to look at the pictures. She had blended in with the women who hung around her father's gang—that had been her survival technique. Ember had done everything she could privately to defeat the cliché expected of her, to build up an Ember whom she could like and respect, as the external one was seemingly so horrible. While Mick had presented her at his famous party weekends for clients as the spoilt princess interested only in fashion, boys, and money, she had been working away at educating herself in everything he hated or didn't understand—theatre, classical music, literature—the most bizarre kind of rebellion quite deliberately chosen. It had made him furious but he couldn't completely stop her despite his best efforts to make her conform. She hadn't done it because she liked that stuff, but because it would take her out of his reach, but a liking had developed as she pressed on. Some of the things she had got her hands on she didn't understand and probably only read because it was high-minded material other people rated, but parts had got through to her. Funny how such old writers had words to sum up how she felt now.

Her fingers wandered to the last play in the volume. *A Winter's Tale*. It was January outside and she did indeed feel like Hermione, the wrongly accused wife who masquerades as a statue in the final scene. Frozen—and not in the Disney sense. Did the queen suffer all those years waiting, or had she turned off the tap of emotion to be like marble? Was that what that last image meant? Was it even possible not to feel? Could she learn to do that?

Oh God, the horror was creeping up on her again. Her hands began to shake. Deep breaths. Hard as nails. Count to ten. Living was just a question of surviving one moment and going on to the next.

Kate, the peer non-pal, and her partner in crime, Raven, came into the library. Ember quickly pulled the copy of *Hello* over the book she'd been reading. Over the last few days, these two had been the most persistent in their attempts to talk to her. The others had quickly learnt to give her a wide berth. For once the two girls didn't try to be friendly.

'It sounds so lame—a play,' groaned Raven. Where had she picked up that American accent, Ember wondered. The two girls were in here for drug running offences, some stupid gap-year decision that had gone horribly wrong. They were lucky not to be executed in the Far East where they'd been caught. Amateurs.

'But we get to work with someone from the outside and the guys from the local sixth form—makes a nice change from staring at the same old faces day in day out,' argued Kate.

'I suppose so. Are there any good parts?'

'I don't know. Let's look it up.' The girls went to the classics section expecting to find the reference copy of Shakespeare but came upon a big gap instead.

'It's been nicked. Who would bother?' mocked Kate.

'It's not stolen. It's here.' Ember pushed the book out from under her magazine.

'You thinking of auditioning too?' asked Raven, grabbing the book from her. 'Is there a part where the girl gets to kiss a guy? If so, I'm so all over that one.'

'What play?'

'Oh yes, you don't come for the morning talk, do you? You snooze, you lose.'

Ember never joined in with any of the optional activities. She ignored Raven's dig.

'There's a theatre director coming in to work with us on a production of a play called *A Midsummer Night's Dream*,' explained Kate, perhaps remembering her neglected peer pal role. 'Some guy called Henry Rawlings. They made it sound a big deal.'

Ember struggled to hide her burst of enthusiasm. She had seen Rawlings' seminal production of *Julius Caesar* at the Globe last year, having sneaked out without permission and queued up to stand among the groundlings. The best ten pounds she had ever spent. 'He's coming here?'

'You've heard of him?' Kate exchanged a look with Raven.

Ember got up to go. 'It doesn't matter. I'm not interested in acting.' She spent her whole life pretending to be something she wasn't. Why would she want to act by choice?

Kate frowned. 'I think it's going to be compulsory that we all do something towards the production.'

'I'd like to see them make me do something I don't want.'

Ember reached the door. 'If you want to be kissed by someone, try out for Bottom.'

Her retreat to her room was pre-empted by Mrs Bishop. 'Ah, Ember, just the girl I was looking for. Miss Nevis is waiting for you in my office.'

'I didn't know she was coming.' Ember wondered if she could refuse to see her.

'Apparently she was seeing one of her clients on the boys' side and decided to call in. She said she had a message from your brother.'

'Oh.' Ember abandoned all thought of crying off the meeting and hurried to the office at the end of the hall. She tapped on the door.

'Enter.' Miss Nevis was updating her files at the desk. 'Ember, so glad you agreed to see me.'

'You've news from Max?'

'Yes. A letter. I hadn't realized.' She held out the folded piece of A4. Ember could already see that Max had lavished upon it his very best pictures but his writing gave away his educational challenges. 'Do you know if he ever had an assessment for special needs? My colleagues can't find any trace.'

That was because Mick Lord would never agree to let any do-gooder look at his idiot son, as he termed Max. Ember had wanted to kill her father many times for calling Max that to his face.

She shrugged, pretending ignorance. 'Can I have the letter?' She held out a hand.

Miss Nevis held it back. 'Please sit down. I'll give you this, I promise, but we need a chat first.'

Don't lose your temper, Ember told herself. *She might not bring any more letters if you do*. With bad grace, she slumped into the chair that she had briefly imagined flinging across the room. Such displays of temper had been more her father's thing, though; not wanting to be like him, she'd always tried to turn her own fury into other less violent channels. She didn't always succeed.

'Mrs Bishop says you aren't joining in.'

'I'm not the joining-in type.'

'It will help you, I think, if you do. Time must pass very slowly. It will be months before your case goes to trial.'

That didn't matter.

Miss Nevis sighed. 'You'll want to write back to your brother, won't you? What will you have to tell him? That you sat in your room doing nothing?'

Ember curled her fists. It was true. Max expected her to entertain him with stories of what he thought was her glamorous life, most of it a fiction.

'Mrs Bishop mentioned the director they have coming in for a few weeks to work with you. Why don't you give that a try? I see you're studying English in the tutorial sessions they offer here, hoping to take a GCSE one day. This will help.'

Ember's formal education so far had been a joke. Every time her father had sent her away from Max to a school where she couldn't be with him, she had made sure she was expelled. At the last, she hadn't even had to try very hard. Chloe Norris, the daughter of one of her dad's rivals who knew her a little from the Essex social scene, had been put in her games set. Claiming Ember had disrespected her, Chloe had attacked with a hockey stick, aiming for the face. Ember had retaliated and drawn blood. Sitting outside the head teacher's office, hearing the threats to sue from Chloe's gorgon of a mother, Ember realized she'd been given the perfect opportunity to get herself chucked out. She had willingly taken all the blame. Put back in her old school, she'd deliberately failed tests to be in all the bottom sets with Max, helping him disguise his slowness. It wasn't that Max was stupid—far from it—he just moved at a different pace to the rest of the world and didn't have a mean bone in his body. How would he cope now she wasn't there to stand between him and everyone else?

'Ember, are you OK?'

Ember found she had screwed her eyes shut and was taking breaths through her nose. 'I'm fine.' Her voice came out half-choked.

'Panic attacks are quite normal for someone in your situation. I can ask your doctor to prescribe something to help you keep calm.'

'I'm. Fine.'

'Right. Well. OK. I won't push it, but do consider the play. Here's the letter.'

Ember snatched it from Miss Nevis' hand and bolted from the office. Back in her own room, she spread it out on the desk and read it six times at the first sitting. Max's handwriting was hard to decipher but the brilliant pictures told the story: he liked his temporary foster parents, no one from their old life had bothered him, Patch was doing fine with lots of long walks in the local park, he'd made friends with some people with a spaniel called Jellybean. He'd drawn jellybeans around the edge just in case she didn't get the reference. He told her Dad was dead and had been buried with lots of flowers piled on top of his coffin. Nanny Roe had sent one from him and Ember with DAD spelt out in carnations, which had looked pretty cool as everyone would know who sent it. He wasn't sad Dad was dead but he was sad that they were still talking to Ember about how he died and that she had to stay at her training college. That wasn't right. He ended by asking when she was going to see him and when he could come home.

I will not cry. Ember held the letter to her chest, head bent. She took up a piece of blank paper to write a reply. How could she match the stories of parks and spaniels? Miss Nevis was right: she was severely short on material. The baby. Max would like to hear about Simone's seven-month-old and how he always smeared Weetabix in his hair each breakfast. Ember went into the kitchen each morning hoping to catch him at it.

She sat back. A couple of lines weren't enough even if she sketched Johnny in his high chair. Perhaps she could do something small in the play, watch the famous director at work, so she could have something more interesting than 'I sat in my room' to write to Max? If she was going to be made to participate she might as well do it on her own terms.

Chapter 3

'Hello, everyone. My name is Henry Rawlings, but please, call me Henry.'

A younger boy in the front row of the gathered trainees sniggered. 'Yeah, right.'

Henry's very alert eyes speared him. 'You've an excellent high carrying tone, perfect for comedy. I suggest you try out for one of the fairies.'

The boy flushed and sank further down in his chair. Joe hid a grin. The slight white-haired man with the goatee beard might look a pushover but no one dared laugh at the director after that.

'I've been invited into your centre to put together a performance of *A Midsummer Night's Dream*. To grease the wheels, so to speak, I've got with me a team of volunteers on their Duke of Edinburgh Award community service from St Bernard's—that's the local comprehensive school for those of you who are new to the area. As they are also drama A-level students, they'll help fill the major roles and coach those in the cast how to speak the lines. You see, the play is a little old and some of the language might strike you as strange. However, I've pared it down to the bone for ease of understanding and when we start rehearsing you'll see the themes are completely relevant. You'll soon acclimatise to the language if you give it a chance.'

Joe sought out Ember Lord's face among the crowd. He couldn't see her and worried that their plan might come to nothing. Girls and boys were housed in separate buildings but came together for classes and some social activities in the education centre, where the rehearsals were being held. All the boys had arrived on time but the girls had taken a while to drift in. Kate and Raven had warned that Lord might not turn up, despite surprising them all by putting her name down on the list. Then he spotted his target standing at the back of the room, a row of empty chairs separating her from the nearest trainee. Dressed simply in a sharp-cut white shirt and designer jeans, she still managed to look catwalk-gorgeous, just as her photograph had suggested. Joe found something inside him stretch and purr. Geez, what was wrong with him? He forcefully reminded himself of what he was looking at: a manipulator. Long legs, slim frame, long dark hair, he wondered cynically if she knew the power of her beauty and whether she used it to good effect when she was in her father's circle? Joe could imagine all those East End guys not knowing what to make of her, like a racehorse hitched up to a string of trail mules. Her face was petal-shaped, emphasised by the loose straight hair, and her cheekbones pronounced, though more often than not they were hidden under a curtain of hair. There was no sign of anything but stillness in her expression, reminding Joe of a cat waiting to hook a goldfish from a pond. He wondered what had made this controlled creature resort to murder. Had she done it in the same aloof manner that she used for listening to the director's lecture, or had she struck in anger?

'This morning I'd like to see each of you individually and hear you read a section. While I'm doing that my volunteers will explain the play, show you a few video clips of past productions, so you know what you're getting yourself into. Trust me: it comes alive once it leaves the page.' Henry checked his list. 'Right, I'm going to set up camp in classroom A. Stay here until you're called. I'll audition you in alphabetical order. Akwan, you're up first.'

Joe assisted Henry, reading in the other parts while Henry made notes on each person. Some of the candidates had trouble with the language so Henry allowed them to recite something they knew by heart instead, which resulted in a bizarre range of audition pieces from rap songs to a jingle for a popular brand of bread. Henry didn't mind, in fact he seemed positively to relish the change from his usual routine.

Auditioning the likes of Dame Judi Dench, Benedict Cumberbatch, and Sir Ian McKellan must get so boring after a while, thought Joe, keeping his smile to himself.

'Now once more, Graham. Forget the jingle. Make me believe this is the best sliced loaf ever!' Henry beamed at the kid who had been the one to snigger during his introduction.

Losing his embarrassment the boy broke into a very impressive sales patter.

Henry made a big tick on his notes. 'I don't suppose you have any experience of sales?'

Joe thought that might be a dangerous question for a boy inside for drugs offences.

'Dad works on the Whitechapel market,' the boy replied, gaze dropping hungrily to the tick of approval.

'Ah, that explains it, the natural delivery and persuasive tone. I'd say you'd make a fortune alongside him when you leave here if you choose that as your career.'

The boy left the room with his head held high. Joe thought Henry had probably done more good in five minutes than months of visits by probation officers. Henry had already explained his ethos. He knew that he wouldn't reach or impress everyone in what was a tough audience, but the occasional comment might get through.

'Who've we got left? Ah yes, Miss Ember Lord.' Henry glanced up from his list.

She hadn't come when her name had been called for the first time so they'd pushed her to the end. Joe looked out into the hall to where Kieran and Nathan were briefing the candidates about the play. 'She's still not back from wherever she went.'

Henry sniffed. 'Normally I'd leave her if she can't be bothered to wait, but I understand she's of particular interest to you all.'

'I'll fetch her.'

Trainees weren't allowed to leave the educational centre without an escort to their units, so Joe quickly established that Ember was still on site. He hunted her down to the library where she sat with a book on her knee, her left hand running a pendant up and down her necklace, lost in thought.

'Henry's ready for you now.'

'OK.' Ember put the volume back on the shelf. Glancing down at the title, Joe was surprised to find that it was a volume of Emily Dickinson's poetry. What on earth had she wanted with that?

She walked beside him along the corner, arms folded, but Joe had the distinct impression she wasn't really with him, but travelling in her own bubble.

'My name's Joe, by the way.'

She flicked a glance at him.

'You might be wondering about the accent. I'm from New York, but I've been here for a few years now.'

'I wasn't wondering.'

Joe had a humorous vision of his attempt to make conversation being shot down in flames. 'Suit yourself.' He opened the door to the audition room. 'Here's the lost sheep, Henry.'

'Ember, come on in. Now what would you like to read for me?' Henry gestured to the photocopies of the various female parts in the play. 'Helena, Hermia, Hippolyta? Shakespeare was definitely in an "h" mood when writing this play.'

'She missed the briefing outside. She won't know who any of them are.' Joe took his seat next to the director, leaving Ember hovering by the door. Without a word, Ember strode forward and grabbed the print-out with 'Titania' written in black felt tip across the top.

'Ah, Queen of the Fairies,' said Henry. 'Very well. Joe, you read in for Oberon.'

With a grimace that this might become very embarrassing, Joe gave Oberon's cue. 'Ill met by moonlight, proud Titania.'

Her reply was the longest speech given by the fairy queen, a challenge for any actor. No one had chosen to audition with that piece, as it looked far too daunting. Regal and taunting, she delivered it flawlessly, scratching away at her spouse in their dispute about ownership of one of their followers. She waved her arm to emphasise a point and Joe had to remind himself not to clasp her hand, not to try to stroke claws to paws as Oberon might as he bargains with his wife. Ember didn't pause until she reached the end, only then did she recall where she was. 'I just want a small part. Cobweb maybe.' A prisoner once more, but still regal, Ember slammed the sheet back on the table and walked out.

Henry rocked back in his chair as the door banged shut. 'Well, that was a surprise. Short on charm but long on talent. Where did she learn to speak blank verse?'

Joe quickly scanned the part she had read. There was no mention of the names of the other fairies who attend the queen in the play. 'She knows the story already.'

Henry shrugged. 'She must've seen a production.'

'Unlikely with her background. The father kept his children close to home and he was known more for his interest in Formula One than the Royal Shakespeare Company.'

'School then?'

Joe shook his head, not if her school reports were to be believed, but he dropped the subject. Another mystery to add to the enigma that was Ember Lord. He would prefer to find out the answers from the source rather than speculate. 'Will you give her a small part?'

Henry chuckled. 'You have to be joking, dear boy. We've found our Titania. I can't imagine a better casting.'

'And Oberon?'

'I don't think any of the boys we've auditioned are quite up to snuff, do you? How about you taking that role?' His eyes twinkled. 'Good luck with charming information from your Titania. It's a play about a bitter marital dispute between the king and queen of the fairies, with only a patched-up reconciliation to look forward to. Still, there will be plenty of excuses to run lines together.'

Joe collected in the scripts. He knew he was at risk if he got closer to Lord—his reactions just to being near her for a few minutes were unprofessional, and he had no desire to put himself in a position where he was battling a stupid and distracting chemical attraction while trying to stick to a mission. He could take one for the team if necessary but he would much prefer it if another of his friends were put in the role. Yes, that would be safer all round. 'Henry, you know that Nathan or Kieran could do it.'

'Casting decisions are the director's prerogative,' was all Henry would say.

Joe felt a looming sense of doom. 'Are you by any chance a mischief maker?'

'Oh yes. I'm a Robin Goodfellow at heart. Like that sprite in the play, I'm quite ready to make mayhem among the young cast. I think Kate and Nathan as Hermia and Lysander, and Raven and Kieran as Helena and Demetrius, don't you?'

31

The lovers whose affections get amusingly swapped by Puck on the application of a magical flower to their eyelids. 'I'm going to love watching that.'

'Excellent. Akwan will make a passable Mustardseed, Simone Peaseblossom.' Henry went through the rest of the parts, distributing them among the trainees. 'All in all, very satisfactory. Shall we go break the news to the cast?'

Ember stood shocked to the core on hearing the announcement just made by her hero. Henry Rawlings wanted her as Titania. But that was unthinkable.

'I can't do it,' she blurted out.

All eyes in the room went to her. It was the first time many of the male inmates had heard her voice.

'Of course you can, my dear.' Henry carried on as if she hadn't spoken. 'First rehearsals will be tomorrow. Look over your parts—'

Ember took a gulp. 'I won't do it.' She walked out of the room. She knew the value of a rapid exit; it had saved her from her father many times. She hurried to the staff desk in the lobby. 'I want to go back to my room right now.'

The member of staff on duty, Tom Forest of the first night, got up with a weary sigh, leaving a half-drunk cup of coffee on the desk. She'd nicknamed him Dogberry in her mind after another Shakespearian character not known for his intelligence. 'And I don't suppose Miss High-and-Mighty wants to wait until I escort the others back to your unit?' She'd learnt that Forest got a kick out of making sly digs at his charges when other members of staff weren't around. Normally she wouldn't ask him for any favours.

'No, I don't want to wait.' Ember clenched her hands together.

'Have it your way, Miss Lord. It won't be like that much

longer, not when you get in a real prison, not like this holiday camp.'

As he turned to unlock the door, Henry Rawlings' helper ran down the stairs two at a time. 'Hey, wait a moment!' The sixth-former reminded Ember of a young Othello with his military bearing and warm smile. She could well imagine him charming a Desdemona—totally gorgeous—but she reined in her brief flight of fancy by reminding herself just how that relationship went in Shakespeare's play. In her experience, love ended in disaster both on and off the stage.

Mr Forest paused. 'Joe, wasn't it? With the St Bernard's lot?'

'That's right, Tom. Sorry about Arsenal last night.'

Mr Forest groaned. 'What a complete spectacle they made of themselves! At least I didn't waste my money on a ticket, though I'd thought about it.'

'Can I have a quick word with Ember?'

The man glanced back at his coffee, then out at the rain falling. 'You can walk back with us if you don't mind getting a little wet.'

Ember dug her hands in her pockets and hunched her shoulders against the shower. Her plimsolls quickly got drenched in the poorly drained courtyard.

Joe strode along at their side as if it was as sunny as the Caribbean. 'Henry sent me with a message. He heard what you said but he wants you to think about it overnight. Here's the copy of the cut-down play.' Joe tried to hand her the script but she wouldn't take it. Sneakily, he rolled it up and shoved it in her back pocket.

'Hey!' She tugged it out but didn't want to throw Shakespeare in a puddle. She kept it rolled up in her fist like a truncheon, wondering what the penalty would be for hitting him with it.

Perhaps he caught an inkling of her irritation because he danced out of reach, jumping over a particularly large pool of rainwater. 'Really, Em, you gave a good audition. Don't throw it away because you're scared.'

'I'm not scared,' she said automatically. But of course she was, utterly terrified.

'You'll take the part then. Great. I'll let Henry know.'

Before she could protest, Joe ran back into the education centre.

Almost as quickly, Tom left her just inside the girls' unit to return to his coffee.

Ember didn't quite know how that had come about. Somehow that boy had wrong-footed her. 'And I'm not called Em,' she told her bedraggled reflection in the glass doors.

The following day, Ember's court-appointed solicitor turned up for an initial interview. With a short cap of dark hair and Roman nose, Ms Pierce looked ready to take on the lions on behalf of her client. Pity her skills were wasted here, thought Ember, as she had no intention of mounting a robust defence.

'Ember, I'm pleased to meet you at last,' Ms Pierce began, indicating that Ember should take the seat to one side rather than opposite her. Ember ignored the invitation and sat down across the table, keeping her distance. 'I've read your statement, such as it is. Was this given freely? Do you think it accurate?'

Ember couldn't really remember what she'd said during that horrendous morning. It had been a blur of people and blood and knives and her, the zombie, moving through the horror show. She pulled the statement over to read it, noting that she had already signed at the bottom. She only had a vague memory of doing that. Her account had been sketchy. An argument that evening overheard by Nanny Roe. Waking up with a sense of dread. Looking frantically for Max. Next thing she remembered clearly was standing on the trailing bedcovers in her father's room, his body sprawled in front of her on the bed. His already dead, cold body. She had hated him, fantasized about getting rid of him, but that hadn't meant she ever wished to see him like that. It hadn't felt like revenge, more like some horrible inevitability, the solution to the long equation that had been their dealings until then.

She dropped the statement. 'It's OK.'

'It doesn't say very much.'

'No. I don't remember what happened.'

Ms Pierce nodded and made a note. 'Shock can distort memory, but you really must try and remember. The prosecution are going to make much of the fact that you were the only person in the house with your father and that you were discovered with the body. What about your brother and Mrs Roe in the annexe: were they in the habit of coming and going freely?'

'No, absolutely not. My father wouldn't allow it.'

'So you were the only one in the house, the only one by the body?'

Ember said nothing. What was there to say? She knew what it looked like. She had had blood on her and had been hysterical.

'But the usual house security had been switched off. Despite there being no signs of a break-in, there might have been an intruder. Your father, I'm afraid to say, had plenty of enemies.'

Ember clenched her hands in her lap. 'You've done your homework.'

'I have. You realize that everything you tell me is covered by client confidentiality? If you give me the fullest picture you can, I will do my best to get justice for you.'

There was nothing just in her situation. This was about deals and promises. 'I appreciate that.'

'So, let's start by trying to fill in some of the picture. What was the argument about—the one you had with your father?'

Ember swallowed, gaze going to the window. 'He was going to send me away.' She gave a harsh laugh. 'To finishing school in Switzerland, like I was some kind of minor royal.' She would've liked to have seen more of the world, but not under those conditions.

'And you didn't want to go?' The lawyer's pen hovered over her notepad.

'No.' Ember didn't add that she couldn't go because there was no place for Max in the school. Her father had said he was going to put Max in a home for retarded children. Horrified that he really meant it this time, she'd screamed at him that such places no longer existed, that had been the horror of his own childhood when perfectly good kids were labelled as failures and locked away in institutions. She'd threatened that he would remove her and Max from the house over her own dead body. Not his. She hadn't made that threat as far as she knew.

'Mrs Roe is very vague about the details of the argument.'

Nanny Roe was well paid and loyal. She knew not to betray Max. 'She might not have heard much over in the annexe. She turns off her hearing aid when things get tense.' That was perfectly true.

Ms Pierce hummed and made a note. 'That's good. Makes her witness statement less reliable as a result.'

'Why good?'

'She says she heard you both shouting. You threatened each other.'

Had they? Ember's memory was so hazy she could not be sure she'd gone that far, but maybe she was misremembering? She could recall being absolutely furious with her father. It

36

wasn't until she had to swear to give an account of traumatic events that she realized how plastic her own recall was, bending to her mind's suggestions of how things happened. Reality was very different from the neat accounts given in fiction. 'I don't remember doing that.'

'Still, a dispute about going to school abroad is hardly a motive for murder. The prosecution will have trouble arguing that.'

Ember couldn't quite suppress a burst of hope. Her deal with Devlin had been that she would submit to the trial, take the sentence if found guilty without casting doubt on her own guilt. It didn't stop others arguing to make her look innocent. 'So what do you think they'll claim is my motive?'

'My guess is they will either say you are emotionally unstable and struck out in anger—that's manslaughter and carries a lighter sentence. Alternatively, they might deem you mentally ill and then the goalposts shift. Or they will argue that it was a calculated move and that you were trying to take over from your father at the head of his . . . er . . . business. That fits the facts more closely as your father was found dead in his own bed, no sign that he was awake when the killing blow was delivered.'

Ember rubbed her temples. She didn't want to think about that.

'Ember, some of the questions I have to ask, and that will be asked in your trial, are very difficult ones so I apologize in advance. I'm asking because I genuinely think the answer will help your case. Why did you go into your father's room that morning?'

'He was late. He hated being late.' Ember felt as though she was floating, part of her mind detached like a helium balloon released from a careless grip.

'And you went to wake him?'

'I think so.' It was a blank but she knew that wasn't quite right. Bits were coming back to her, like feeling seeping back into numbed fingers. It was painful to remember. *Why couldn't she remember that morning?* 'I don't know.'

'You don't know your intent when you went into the room?'

Ember shrugged.

'And why were your prints found on the knife?'

'Because I'd held it.'

The lawyer's eyes widened.

'Not like that. I mean, I used it. It was from the knife block in the kitchen. I did a lot of the cooking. I'm . . . I'm vegetarian and he wouldn't let the staff prepare veggie meals for me.' A daughter of Mick Lord wasn't allowed to be a tree-hugging, kaftan-wearing hippy, according to Father.

'I see. So even though you have staff, it was natural that your prints should be found on kitchen implements?' Ms Pierce noted this down then tapped the paper with an emphatic full stop. 'Good. That's something the prosecution will not know at this stage. It undermines their reliance on forensic evidence to convict you. And what about other members of the household? Your brother. Nanny Roe. Why weren't their fingerprints found on the kitchen utensils?'

'They have their own kitchen in the annexe. My father didn't want outsiders in his house.'

'Outsiders? That's a funny word to use about your brother and the woman who has looked after you both for seventeen years.'

'My father was a funny man.' Something crumpled inside her. Father was dead. She'd been bricking off her feelings about that fact but sometimes the wall failed to hold. 'I've had enough. Can we break here?'

Fortunately, the lawyer was as astute as she looked. 'Of

course, Ember. But meanwhile, I'd like you to write down everything you recall before we meet again. You'll find the act of remembering will help the details come back.'

Ember gave a jerking nod and fled before she succumbed to the shivers. She got back to her room in time to lock the door and hide under the duvet. Mick Lord had been an appalling man but he had still been her father. Now he was dead and there was nothing she could do, no fix to the situation as she hadn't had time to arrange one. Max had always counted on her to find the solution; short of letting herself go to prison for decades, she had no answers. The racing car was already in the skid and she was just steering to try for the softest landing for Max. As long as he stayed free, she would pay whatever price was demanded.

'After watching the excerpts on the video, I expect you've come thinking this is a play about fairies and foolish lovers.' Henry prowled up and down in front of the cast members gathered for their first rehearsal. He'd arrived hot-foot from London where he had a professional play in rehearsal, so hadn't a minute to waste. His new recruits were an eclectic bunch, the majority from the boys' unit, as was to be expected since there were only eight girls and forty-nine boys in Lockwood. Joe saw Raven and Kate sitting with a freckle-faced girl bouncing a baby on her knee. No sign of Ember. From the boys' belligerent expressions, Joe guessed that the news that they had been cast as members of Titania and Oberon's fairy court had gone down badly.

'I'm not dressing up as a fricking fairy,' muttered one guy, a big lad with a barbed wire tattoo running around his bicep. Henry had cast him as Cobweb.

Henry grinned. 'And believe me, I know better than to ask you, Raymond. No, *A Midsummer Night's Dream* is usually played as the clash of two worlds, Theseus's court and that of the otherworldly fairies. But that's been done to death. Our production is taking those old ideas and shaking them up. If you strip away the tinsel elements, what is the story really about? Oberon, the king of the underworld, "the king of shadows" as he is called by Puck at one point in the play, is supplying vision-changing drugs to a number of innocent teens, as well as his wife, all part of his belief that he controls his territory and has every right to test out his merchandise as he sees fit.'

'So he's like a what? A Mexican drug lord? Mafia boss?' asked Cobweb Raymond.

Henry clapped his hands in delight. 'Exactly! In our production, the forest is going to be his centre of operations, a nightclub. Our young lovers are people outside his cartel who have foolishly wandered in to live on the wild side for an evening. He gets his henchman, Robin Goodfellow, nicknamed Puck, to interfere with them out of plain old arrogance. Bottom the weaver, the man who gets the ass's head, well, he goes on one weird trip, as does Titania, Queen of Fairies. Read the text with that in mind and you see how it can play.

'Speaking of which . . . where's our Titania?' Henry scanned the ranks of his actors. 'If there's one thing I can't abide it's tardiness. Anyone seen her?'

Raven put up her hand.

'Yes, Helena?'

'She had a meeting with her lawyer this morning but we've not seen her since. She didn't come to lunch.'

'Yeah, and she was on washing-up,' grumbled Kate.

'Joe—or should I say, Oberon?—can you see if you can find our elusive fairy queen?' asked Henry.

Joe tapped his forehead in salute.

'The rest of you, we'll begin blocking the first scene. Theseus, Hippolyta, you're up.'

Escorted by a female member of staff, Joe made his way over to the girls' unit. Kate and Raven had said the accommodation wasn't too bad, a bit like staying in a cut-price hotel where you had to clean up after yourself, and nothing like the horrors of Victorian prisons as depicted by TV dramas. Some of the staff were disengaged and demotivated, but most were honestly attempting to help their young charges through this difficult experience. Passing along the lemon-scented corridor, he noted that most bedroom doors stood open during the day, giving a glimpse of posters of favourite bands or dream holiday destinations, bright touches of cushions and photos on display.

The staff member who had accompanied him knocked on Ember's door. 'Ember? It's Mrs Gardener here. Did you forget your rehearsal?'

There was no reply. Mrs Gardener tried the handle. 'It's locked. She must be in there. Ember? Ember? Are you all right?' She waited a few moments, concern visibly growing. 'I'll have to use my master key. There's a privacy lock but it can be undone from outside in case of emergency. I have to report in first and get another member of staff to assist. You'd better go.'

Joe picked up on the woman's alarm. Her mind had clearly gone to some drastic scenario where Ember had hurt herself but he didn't think the girl had that in her. Too tough to take that way out was his analysis. 'Let me try.'

'Please do. I'll just call Mrs Bishop.' The woman turned away to get out her walkie-talkie.

'Hey, Titania, it's Oberon. Get a move on. Henry'll think you've chickened out.' He held up a hand to Mrs Gardener to indicate that he could hear movement inside the room. 'She's coming.'

41

The bolt slid back and the door opened. An ashen face appeared in the gap. It crossed Joe's mind for the first time that maybe Lord did indeed have emotions; either that or she had gone down with the flu. 'I haven't chickened out.' Her voice was tense, barely a whisper.

'Then why aren't you at rehearsal?'

She turned away but left the door open as she straightened the bedding. Her room was completely bare apart from the regulation-issued furniture.

'Ember, you had me quite worried there for a moment,' admitted Mrs Gardener.

'I was asleep.'

'Yes, I see that now.' She patted her chest. 'Good. Right, let's take you over to the education centre.' Mrs Gardener was quick to buy the explanation but Joe wasn't so sure. Lord looked distraught, not sleepy.

Ember ran a quick brush through her dishevelled hair and checked her reflection with a grimace. Another surprise. Joe had been expecting her to preen; instead she seemed, well, the word that came to mind was *weary* of what she saw.

She's sad, Joe realized with a flash of insight. And bone-achingly tired. Could he use that? Get her to open up to him?

'Hey, Em, glad you finally woke up. Can't do my part without my queen,' Joe said cheerfully, covering the rather awkward silence as she got ready.

'Rawlings has cast you as Oberon?' It was the first question she'd directed towards him, a slight show of interest.

'Is that a problem for you?'

Her eyes flicked over him as she grabbed her sweater. 'No. You'll probably be good at the part. But I don't think I'm the right choice for Titania.' They started the walk over to the education centre, industrial carpets of the interior giving way to wet tarmac of the car park.

'Henry thinks you are and he's directed the cream of the acting world in famous productions of the classics, so I'd accept it as a compliment if I were you.'

'But you're not me, are you?' Her spark of interest appeared to have been snuffed out by the fresh air.

No, thank God, Joe thought. He wouldn't want to be in her shoes for anything. The press were crucifying her as they continued to report on the sensational murder of the gangland boss. They made her sound like a character from some Greek tragedy rather than one of Shakespeare's comedic heroines. If you believed what was written about her, she was a harpy with iced water running in her veins.

But she also might be the key to rounding up the weapons before they reached the wrong hands.

He decided to plough on with his attempt at friendly banter. 'So, Em, Oberon, Titania: we share a couple of big scenes. If you need a hand with running the lines, I'm your man.'

'I'm not called Em and I don't need help.'

'Then maybe you can help me?'

She met his eyes. 'I very much doubt that.'

A thrill of something ran through Joe, awareness of her as a person rather than a mission target. She was so much cleverer than he had expected and her eyes suggested depths he and this team hadn't even begun to guess. She wasn't going to be an easy case. It was like working on an unexploded bomb with no manual to the wiring. He decided to disarm her with a cheeky grin. He didn't think many people dared flirt with her but he couldn't help himself. 'Don't doubt it, Em. You've got a lot to offer.'

She blinked, then remembered herself. 'You're wrong.'

'Bet you I'm not.' Joe could see Mrs Gardener was smiling out of Ember's eye-line; the prison guard was enjoying watching someone take on the unit's ice queen.

'That's a stupid bet.'

'No it isn't. It's one you can't lose. Either you're proved right and win, or wrong and I prove there's much more to you than people think and you win again.'

'I'm not talking to you.' She picked up her pace.

'That's so obviously not true. We've got to spend the next hour arguing in blank verse.'

'You always have a comeback for everything, don't you?'

He tilted his head to one side, delighted he'd got her to the point where she would say something personal about him. It felt a moment to high-five himself. He had to remember that this was for the mission, not because he loved a challenge. 'We'll have to see. Oberon wins the argument with Titania, but it doesn't mean to say that I have to win all our conversations, does it?'

'You call this a conversation?' She stalked off, going ahead into the rehearsal room.

'Ouch.' Joe laughed.

Mrs Gardener shook her head. 'That's the first time I've seen her behave like a seventeen-year-old girl. You have the magic touch.'

'I'm the king of the fairies, what do you expect?' With a wink, Joe followed his angry queen into the education centre.

Chapter 4

Hungry and out of sorts, Joe checked the pasta. Still needed a few minutes. 'How's the cheese coming along?' he asked Kieran.

His buddy was studying the grater, the sort that had a little revolving cylinder and handle. 'Fascinating. Much more efficient than the usual sort.' Kieran had been playing with the odd collection of kitchenware in their rented house since Joe started dinner. Someone had stocked the drawers with spare utensils left over from the sixties and seventies. Joe's money was on a yard sale being responsible.

'Yes, chef, but what about the damn cheese?'

Kieran sliced a block of cheddar into cubes calculated to fit the machine and began grating. 'So you're not enjoying the mission, Joe?'

Joe was surprised Kieran of all people had noticed his irritation. He was usually the last to catch on to someone's emotional state. No, that wasn't fair, Joe corrected. Kieran used to be that way until Raven brought his attention to focus on the outer rather than his inner world. 'Sorry. I guess it's more difficult than I anticipated. Lord is a hard nut to crack.'

'You can say that again,' said Nathan, coming in from his trip to the recycle bin. 'She's impossible.'

Joe glanced out the kitchen window at the depressing view at the rear. He could see Nathan had parked the bin out the back gate next to the identical blue wheelie bins of all the identical houses in their road. This estate, no longer so new, had probably looked good on paper forty years ago but had missed out on soul when it was built. English suburbia. Stirring the red sauce, Joe speculated that a movie maker would make this location a start to an alien invasion or a horror picture just to shake up the ordinariness. He had plenty of material for the blood splatter right here if they wanted to make a beginning tonight.

'Raven's pretty depressed about it,' said Kieran. 'And if she's down then there's something very wrong.'

'Kate said they're finding every attempt to make friends rejected.' Nathan grabbed some fizzy water from the fridge and poured them each a glass. 'It's like trying to cuddle up to a porcupine. We've had two weeks now, eight rehearsals, and zilch to show for it. You're the only one who's made any headway, Joe.'

'I wouldn't call it that.' Joe switched off the hob. 'I get her to do things by challenging her. It's more like we're rivals than friends. She knows her lines, barks them at me, and barely smiles at the part when we're supposed to be reconciled. Though I have to say, in Henry's gangland version, the Oberon-Titania deal does feel more like a battered wife giving in to the bullying husband than a joyous reconciliation.'

'So what do we tell Isaac?' asked Kieran. 'That we should try something else?'

'What "else" is there?'

'The brother?' Kieran heaped the thin strings of cheese into a blue and white bowl.

'She doesn't mention her family at all,' said Joe. 'I've tried talking about mine while we're rehearsing—my sister, her kids, a little about my parents—but I might've been reading her the telephone directory for all the interest she showed.'

Nathan got out the plates and carried them to the stove. 'Damien says that he and Rose see Max Lord at least once a day. He's always cheerful but doesn't go beyond dog talk. Rose thinks he might be a little young for his age, you know, kind of vulnerable? She's not happy at the idea of using him for information.'

'And what does Damien say?' Joe expected a tougher line from their Cobra friend. YDA students were divided into four streams nicknamed Owls, Cobras, Cats, and Wolves after their respective skills of intelligence, cunning, undercover work, and hunting. Damien had a hard edge that his Owlish partner lacked.

'He agrees, but for a different reason. He thinks they're wasting their time with someone who's basically an innocent. The sister is going to be the one in the know. That's what we suspected from the start.'

Joe plated up the meal and put the first serving in front of Kieran, who went on to decorate it with cheddar, aiming for even coverage.

'The thing to wonder,' said Kieran, 'is whether her silence on the subject of her brother is a sign of indifference or the opposite?'

Such an insight was especially interesting coming from Kieran. 'What do you mean?' asked Joe.

Kieran avoided Joe's eyes by pretending interest in his meal. 'You'll remember that I didn't tell Raven about my family until it was almost too late for our relationship?'

'Yeah, man, I remember.' Joe also recalled how he had shortly afterwards let his buddy down by partially succumbing to the brainwashing techniques of the criminals they'd been investigating at an elite school. He still had nightmares about that.

'I didn't speak because it meant too much, made me feel

exposed to acknowledge my mother.' Kieran's parent had a serious issue with alcohol and had made his early years a nightmare until Isaac rescued him and brought him into the YDA family.

'We all get why you did that, Key. You can't be blamed for it,' said Nathan. He'd also had a rough start in life, being abandoned just after his birth. The two were a complete contrast to Joe with his wonderful and involved parents who would've happily adopted all his parentless friends as extended members of their family.

'It's not about blame but about what I could or couldn't do at the time,' admitted Kieran. 'Whatever brought Lord to the point where she stabbed her father must've been intense. She has to be afraid she's going to lose her brother now and he's all the family she has, isn't he?'

'You don't buy the heartless killer explanation then?' asked Joe.

Kieran rolled his shoulders, a sign he was feeling awkward. He usually left the people side of things to his friends. 'No one has said she's a psychopath, and I've seen no evidence of that in rehearsals, so the probabilities from human behavioural studies suggest that she wants family like the rest of us. I had a sister with special needs too and I'd've done anything to protect her. Just because I never spoke about things, didn't mean I didn't care about them. I'm extending the same logic to Ember Lord.'

'You think I should ask her head-on about her brother?' Joe ground black pepper over his pasta.

'If she does feel protective towards him, she'll want to see him, won't she? Maybe she'd cut a deal on the information she has for a sentence served in a prison near his home? Isaac could probably swing something like that.'

'She's not been convicted yet, Key.'

'I've read the Crown Prosecution file.' *Hacked it* that meant. Kieran was nothing if not thorough in his preparation for a mission and there was no computer system that could keep him out. 'Evidence all points to her and I can't hear her making loud protestations of innocence, can you? She's going down unless some new evidence comes to light.'

'It's hard to feel sorry that a guy like Mick Lord has been taken out of circulation.' Nathan flicked through the file of tabloid cuttings Jan Hardy had sent them that morning. The papers were still milking the Lord story, going on about how much he had spent on his daughter, paying for a privileged education she squandered and clothes she rarely wore more than once. 'But I do feel a little sorry for her despite everything she's done. That kind of upbringing would smother you, twist you up inside.'

'To me it sounds like he was killed by his own kindness: spoiled the princess and then she turned on Daddy when he didn't toe her line.' Joe studiously ignored the file, not wanting his appetite ruined by thinking about work during what was supposed to be their down time. Ember Lord was tying him up in enough knots during the day as it was. He hated what she represented, deplored her crimes, and yet he found himself flirting with her and attracted by silly stuff, like the curve of her cheek or the flick of her hair. He wanted to give himself a kick in the butt. Their mission was everything; Ember was the means to a very important end: he had to remember that.

'According to the papers and a very leaky police source, the last argument was about some chalet school deal,' said Nathan, his Wolfish nature making him less ready to give things a rest. He liked to chew over and worry things until he'd ex-tracted the marrow. 'Maybe Daddy didn't want to stump up the cash for Ember Lord's idea of what she deserved?'

'That's not right. According to the statement I read, she

didn't want to go to Switzerland,' corrected Kieran. He frowned, winding his spaghetti round and round his fork in a neat coil. 'In fact, there's a pattern now I come to think of it.'

'Oh? What pattern?' Joe hoped that Kieran's formidable brain might be able to provide them with their much needed breakthrough.

'If you look through the dates you'll see that the times before the stabbing when she came to the authorities' notice for bad behaviour came shortly after her father's attempts to get her out of the house to boarding school or abroad. She rapidly did her utmost to get expelled, or ruined her application by falling foul of some minor law, like smuggling in alcohol to one dorm, or bashing another girl with a hockey stick.'

'That's not making me feel any sorrier for her; just sounds like she needed firm parenting rather than Mick's bribes and giving in when she threw a tantrum.' Joe didn't like the way Kieran was suggesting there could be more to Ember's actions than met the eye. It was bad enough being attracted to her, he couldn't start excusing her. He thought how his own parents would have been horrified if he'd tried Ember's methods to get his own way. He'd've been grounded for life and on kitchen chores for a year if he'd got himself expelled, let alone arrested. 'I guess she didn't want to leave the nest in case she lost her place in his organization.'

'I'm not sure that's it. My hunch is that it's worth exploring. There's something there we're not seeing.'

'OK, I'll add it to the mix when I next speak to her.'

The doorbell rang and Joe jumped up to answer. 'Hey, Isaac, you're just in time for dinner.'

The YDA boss took off his motorbike jacket and put his helmet on the side table, rain still beading the visor. 'Great. I'm starving. Been in meetings all day. Don't get up. I'll just pull up a chair and dig in.'

Joe wondered what this unannounced visit by their leader could herald but knew Isaac wouldn't keep them waiting unnecessarily. Once he'd brought his plate to the table, Isaac began.

'Thanks for the reports. They're not why I'm here. I've just been passed some very alarming intelligence which came in from our American friends.'

This couldn't be good. If Isaac was worried then it was ultra serious. 'What's happened?'

'The intel has raised red flags all over Whitehall and the security services. That cache of weapons is now rumoured to include some nuclear material from a defunct Central Asian atomic programme, the kind of radioactive waste that could be used to make a dirty bomb.'

'Way to put us off our food,' said Joe, pushing his plate from him.

Isaac nodded. 'Yes, I know. It's only rumoured, but the source in the Bulgarian mafia is credible and usually reliable. That means that we're no longer talking about conventional weapons. Let off a bomb containing nuclear material in a city centre and you could change the fate of that country for decades, if not longer, through land denial, not to mention the casualties and subsequent illnesses.'

'And this radioactive material is headed our way?' asked Nathan.

'Yes.'

Nathan pulled a grim face. 'Then maybe we should crack out the thumbscrews?'

'That's rather the spirit in which I'm here, I'm afraid.' Isaac was usually inscrutable but his face tonight registered his conflicted feelings about the situation. 'I'm giving you new orders, and these are from the top. You've tried developing a friendship with Lord and that's failed. We want you now to break

51

her down quickly through any means you judge potentially fruitful, short of thumbscrews, naturally.'

'I don't understand.' Nathan looked to Kieran and Joe.

Isaac sighed, not liking giving his orders any more than they enjoyed receiving them. 'Strong emotional pressure. Use anything you can to get her to tell us what she knows. Just get through to her.'

'We think her brother's a weakness,' said Nathan.

'Then we'll use that too—get him out here, look at how they interact. But you've been given Ember Lord to interrogate while the police and MI5 go after the rest of Mick Lord's operation. They're going to be monitoring them so if they sneeze, the intelligence services will know. But the secrets are here. She's the main course, the rest are merely side orders. The spooks judge the daughter to be the weak link as she's the only one already in custody with serious charges hanging over her. That gives us leverage. If you make no progress after a week, they'll take matters into their own hands and interrogate her themselves. Believe me when I say that the YDA would be a much kinder and more effective option for her.'

Joe jiggled his leg under the table, a nervous habit he hadn't been able to shake. This was wrong. 'I'm not comfortable with bending someone like that—quickly with no finesse,' said Joe. 'It's against our training.' And too much like the brainwashing he himself had experienced, a really ugly scar that was still to heal from his recent past. Anything that hinted at brain manipulation was like brushing against a live wire for him. 'You've told us not to get emotionally involved with our mission subjects.' He made an effort to still his leg but Nathan had noticed and gave him a sympathetic look.

Isaac's expression was grim. 'You're absolutely right, Joe. I've always said you shouldn't, but the rule doesn't extend on this occasion to the person we are targeting.'

The penny dropped. 'You want us to get her to fall for one of us, enough to confide in us?'

'Yes.'

'You mean me, don't you?'

Isaac nodded. 'I'm sorry, Joe, but from your reports I think you're the one with the best chance here.'

'It sounds like you're asking me to romance or bully the answer out of her.'

'It does sound like that because those are your orders. All I can say to make you feel better is that we'll all feel a hell of a lot worse if the centre of London becomes a fallout no-go zone because we didn't try.'

Wednesday was free of rehearsals thanks to the director having an engagement in Paris. Ember found she almost missed them. They'd given her days a purpose and her letters to Max had been much more amusing as a result. Rawlings' interpretation of Oberon and Titania as rival gang leaders competing for turf was audacious and original, as she would've expected from the award-winning director, and doubtless more than the prison authorities bargained for when they let him loose on their charges. Though the talk of gangland cut close to the bone, she had to admit it made sense. Innocent-sounding lines took on a whole new importance. She had spared Max the specifics but her brother had loved her drawing of Jamie, a fellow remand prisoner from the boys' unit. She had sketched him wearing the ass's head in the comedy role of Bottom, and Max said he had giggled over her description of her painful attempt as Titania to pretend to be in love with the half-man half-donkey while under the influence of a drugged spell. She knew she was much better at the argument scenes than the comedy. Henry was probably regretting casting her as he had already complained she didn't have a funny bone in her body.

She'd wanted to laugh at that accusation, as most of her existence had been one big joke, but she had instead kept in character and walked out with a slammed door. She was expecting the director to sack her at the next rehearsal but until he gave her the boot she'd carry on learning her part.

There came a quick knock then Mrs Gardener opened her door. 'Ember, you've a visitor.'

Ember slid Max's letter into her desk drawer. 'Who is it? Not another social worker?'

'Someone from home, he said.'

It had to be Max. She had told him not to come but it would be like him to ignore anything he didn't want to hear. 'Is it my brother?'

'No, I don't think so. A man. Said he was your godfather and guardian. A Mr Seamus Devlin.'

Ember's heart sank right down to her toes. He was one visitor she could not refuse to see. 'OK. I'm coming.' She quickly brushed her hair, drawing confidence from the fact that it still lay sleek and shiny on her shoulders despite not having a trim or any conditioning treatments for over a month. Her face was hopeless though: drawn, pale. She pinched her cheeks, trying to raise some colour, and tucked her necklace out of sight. That would have to do.

Seamus Devlin looked fully at ease in the visitors' lounge, arm stretched out along the back of the cheap orange sofa. His dark brown hair was slicked back, grey-green eyes taking in every feature of the room as if assessing its resale value. Two members of staff stood discretely by the doors making sure no one passed the inmates any contraband and to intervene if anyone got out of hand. Ember took a steadying breath, picturing her walk across the room to sit on the seat at Devlin's left hand, the corner of the coffee table separating them.

It's just like your first entrance as Titania, she thought. *Don't show him you're scared.*

'Uncle Seamus,' she said briskly. 'I didn't expect to see you here.' She hadn't seen him since their deal was struck over her father's body.

'Ember.' Devlin stood and leaned in to give her a kiss on the cheek but she sat down quickly before he could make contact. 'I have to say I never expected to see you here either.' He pulled a face of mock regret. 'How are you?'

'I'm fine.'

'Are they treating you OK?'

'Yes.'

'Are you still refusing the solicitor I recommended?'

Confide in someone deep in Devlin's pocket? No way. 'The court-appointed one suits me well.'

He shrugged and settled back on the cushions. 'I looked her up. Inexperienced but, still, it's the barrister that makes all the difference when things go to court. I'll send you some names to approach.'

She nodded. It was pointless saying she would use the list as a guide to whom to avoid. They both knew that but this conversation was all about appearances.

Seamus took a sip of the coffee he had helped himself to from the vending machine. 'Foul stuff. You missed your father's funeral.'

That bald statement hit her like a slap, no doubt as Devlin intended. 'The police advised me that the press wouldn't leave me alone. I didn't want that for the family.' The last thing she wished to see was a picture of her and Max in the papers. So far they'd not written much about Max, other than to say she was the bad twin to his good. They'd dug up an old school photo with them both pictured together, his innocent face next to her scowl. That had sealed the image and, as the interpretation of their two characters sounded like a fairytale, the reporters had loved that angle.

Devlin scratched his chest lazily. It couldn't be that his heart was paining him as he didn't have one. 'You're a good girl, Ember. Well, apart from the obvious.'

Ember didn't want to discuss that with him of all people. 'How . . . how is everyone? Maeve? Bernie and Harry?' she asked, naming his wife and his two sons.

'Grand. They send their best wishes.'

She very much doubted that. 'Thanks.'

'And you're remembering our deal?'

She gave a sharp nod, eyes sliding to check the guards weren't in earshot.

'It's for the best, you know. We both realize that Max would never survive in a place like this, whereas you will probably be running it after a few months.' He looked around the room. 'Not a bad prison, this. I've been in far worse ones. Maybe you can serve the first part of your sentence here, while you're underage.'

Ember dug her nails into her palms. 'You said if they don't convict me, then our deal still stands?'

He rubbed his chin. 'As long as you don't start throwing about accusations, shifting the blame, leaking information, then yes, the deal stands.'

'And you'll leave Max out of it?'

Devlin leaned forward, eyes sparking with temper. 'Remember your place, girl. I gave you my word, didn't I? Don't push it.'

Nausea rose in her throat as she remembered the brief horrid meeting over her father's dead body where they had struck their deal. He was now parroting her father's favourite line. The one benefit of her father's death had been that she thought she wouldn't ever have to hear that again, but here was Devlin coming up with the same old refrain. 'I'm sorry, Uncle Seamus.'

'That's better. Show me respect and you'll be OK. If not, well then, places like this have dark corners and people ready to be bought for the right price. You're not naive. You know I can reach you in here.'

Ember wasn't intimidated by threats to herself. She was used to them. This must've shown in her face because Devlin felt obliged to extend the warning. 'And your brother loves that fat dog of his. I'd hate to see something happen to it—or to the owner.' He swirled the coffee in its plastic cup. 'Still, parks are public places and you get all sorts hanging about there.'

'If you hurt Max, then the deal is off,' Ember hissed. 'And if you ever want access to the Swiss accounts you'll have to be a hell of a lot nicer to me.'

Devlin put down the cup and stood up. 'You're running out of road, Ember. You may have had your father's protection at one time, but you don't have mine. Think on that, won't you?'

Her father hadn't protected her, he had found her useful. His ego had been invested in training her up, not his affection. The problem was that to Devlin she only had limited use: her knowledge and her silence.

'I do, Uncle Seamus. All the time.'

His manner changed again, returning to the bluff family friend of the introduction. 'Good girl.' He raised his voice for the staff to hear. 'Keep your spirits up and it'll soon be over.'

Ember knew what he expected of her. She stood, arms folded protectively against further attempts to hug or kiss her for the cameras. 'Thank you for coming to see me.'

He patted her shoulder. 'Can't say when I'll be able to come again but you can expect me to drop by unannounced from time to time to check on you.'

'I can't wait.' He just wanted the bank account numbers, but they were the last card she held.

With a smirk at her irony, he walked out.

Sitting in the old sixth-form common room with their canteen lunch on a tray, Joe and Nathan reviewed the footage taken from the visitors' lounge at Lockwood.

'What do you think?' Nathan asked. Sadly there was no sound, just the video.

Joe narrowed his eyes, trying to lip-read. 'It doesn't look like they are very fond of each other, does it?'

'Bit of an understatement there, Joe. Mortal enemies is my guess. From the body language, I'd say that was an exchange of threats and he knows he has the upper hand.'

'I would've thought Devlin was thanking his lucky stars she got rid of the one thing standing in his way of assuming command.'

'Make that two things. By taking out Mick Lord, she also removed herself from the picture. A massive miscalculation on her part if she did it as part of a power struggle.'

Joe froze the picture on the expression of violent dislike on Ember's face as Devlin walked out. 'How much hate do you think you'd have to have to cold-bloodedly drive a knife into your father's chest while he slept?'

'Do you think she has that inside her?'

'I really don't know. But if I were Devlin, I wouldn't turn my back on her.'

'How are you going to get her to open up to you?' Nathan kicked back in his chair, looking through his script as one of the lovers caught up in the mix-up of affections.

'No idea. Suggestions?' Joe picked up some oranges from a fruit bowl and began juggling them. He'd learnt the trick from a circus performer who had trained the YDA students one summer, and he found it helped him focus. He grabbed a sharp little penknife he'd used to open a packet and added that to the mix, then his spoon.

Nathan, familiar with his friend's skills, ignored the juggling. 'Looking at that interview, I'd say she was well used to intimidation. How about trying kindness?'

Joe added a banana to his revolving fruit and cutlery. 'That seems worse somehow.'

'You're a decent guy asked to do something underhand. You're going to feel bad whatever approach you take. But it's got to be done quickly.'

He let the fruit drop back in the bowl, the spoon to the tray and threw the knife at the dartboard where it sunk into the bullseye. *'If it were done when 'tis done, then 'twere well it were done quickly.'*

'Come again?'

'That's Macbeth justifying assassination. Not a good omen.'

'Do you really like all this Shakespeare stuff?' Nathan had already confessed that he was struggling with remembering his lines. He had always been more interested in art than literature.

'Like? Not sure. It's more like I find it unsettling how he's said it all before. Must've been an unnerving man to meet.'

Nathan's phone buzzed with a text, doing a little circle on the table top. He snatched it up. 'Right. We're on. Isaac's explained the situation to the senior warden at Lockwood and they've agreed to give us more access to Lord. She is scheduled to come out with Raven and Kate on a supervised visit to use the sports facilities here. The gym's been booked for us. I suggest we get downstairs and make it look like we should be in there.'

The boys took up positions at a weights bench, Joe doing the lifting while Nathan spotted for him. Through the glass window looking on to the pool they could see a whole class of younger students standing on the edge of the water taking instruction on life-saving. Putting his frustration with this mission into the exercise, Joe had time to work up a sweat before the girls came in. When the door opened, Nathan greeted Kate with convincing surprise.

'Hey, Hermia, fancy meeting you here!'

The three girls were accompanied by a guard who took a seat at one side of the room and got out a newspaper, keeping only the lightest supervision on them as arranged.

'Lysander, ill met by artificial lighting,' Kate quipped.

Joe got up from the bench and wiped his face on a towel. 'Stealing my lines now? Kate, isn't it? I think we spoke briefly at rehearsals.'

'Yes. This is Raven, and you know Ember?'

'Sure. I didn't expect to see Titania down a gym.'

Ember didn't reply but went over to a running machine and programmed a tough course.

Kate rolled her eyes. 'Sorry about her. Ember likes being the mysterious silent type.' She opted for a cycle machine.

'They let you out of Lockwood?'

'Yep. They think it's good for our rehabilitation. Gets us ready to rejoin society.' Raven wandered over to a rowing machine. 'Any idea how this works?'

Nathan went over to help, though Raven knew full well how to use the equipment as the YDA had its own, much better-equipped gym. They were clearing the way for Joe to talk to Ember. With an internal groan, he went over to the running machine.

'Need any assistance with that?'

'No.' She had already run half a kilometre.

'Want to make it more interesting?'

'No.'

'Aw, come on, Em. You against me. I'll give you a head start.'

'I'm not interested in silly bets.'

'I am. First one to reach five K.' He started up the machine next to hers.

She'd plaited her hair before coming so the braid dangled down the line of her spine. As she ran, it swung like an angry cat's swishing tail. 'And what do I win? A promise that you won't bother me again?'

'If you like.' He quickly changed the setting to maximum. If he lost he would completely balls-up the mission in a single stroke.

'OK then.' She upped the tempo.

Joe was grateful he was already warmed up. He began pounding the track, keeping an eye on her distance counter as well as his own. The silence between them became fiercely competitive. She was serious about winning her privacy but he was even more determined to stop her. Two kilometres in for her, he had made up some ground, reaching 1800 metres. His legs were starting to burn. Ember's eyes flicked to his dial and she punched up the speed. He was already at maximum and could do nothing but hope she didn't have the stamina to go all the way to five K like that. He could feel his friends discretely watching them. Just in front of them through the glass windows, a whistle sounded and a group of students wearing pyjamas jumped in the pool. He could do with cooling off himself. Was she going to beat him after all? Glancing sideways, he could see she was now struggling, teeth gritted. Though how she managed to look attractive despite running flat out, was a proof the universe wasn't fair. He was sure he was dripping with perspiration and she only had a healthy glow. Wasn't she ever going to give up? Joe pounded on, beginning to worry he'd blown it big time. When the counter reached four and half kilometres, she finally cracked, angrily reducing the speed to her original pace, then dropping it still further. Trying not to smile with relief, Joe ran on, reaching five kilometres two hundred metres before she did.

Slowing the machine to a jog then a walk, he jumped off.

'That was fun. You almost had me.'

Ember scowled. 'I'm out of condition. Been sitting around too much for the last few weeks.'

He held out his hand to shake hers. 'Still, it was a good match. Thanks.'

'Glad to amuse you.' Reluctantly she took his palm in hers and gave it a brief shake.

A shiver of pleasure ran from Joe's fingers right through his body. He firmed his grip before making himself let go. 'Amuse? Hell no. You almost kicked my butt and Nat would've never let me forget it if you had.'

Ember went over to the water machine and helped herself to a cup. Pausing, she offered it to him. 'You might need this.'

It was the first generous gesture he had seen her make but he didn't let his surprise show. 'Thanks.'

She filled a second cup for herself. 'What do you win? We forgot to make your part of the bet.'

How could he get through to her? Kindness, Nathan had suggested. 'Oh, nothing. That was just to get you to play. Winning is enough for me.'

'So you don't want anything from me?'

Only information. 'Like what?'

'Money. Or some kind of forfeit.' She seemed confused by his refusal to take advantage.

'Relax, Em. It was just a game.'

'Oh.'

Joe sat down on the bench, stretching his long legs out in front of him. 'Take a pew. You must be beat too.'

She gingerly took the gap beside him, not too close but not the other end of the room either.

He looked for uncontentious subjects for a conversation. 'You like keeping fit? Did you use to go running, you know, before?' He gestured to the room, in a motion that took in everything that had happened to her in the past month.

She rubbed her calves. 'Only in the gym at home. My father didn't allow us out alone and he wasn't the running type himself.'

It would be too obvious to leap on the first mention of Mick Lord. 'That's a shame. Nothing beats going for a long run in the countryside. Or on a beach. That's my favourite.'

'Sounds nice.'

He'd not heard that wistful note from her before, but again it would be foolish to show her he had noticed. 'It is. I went on some great vacations with my folks in New England. You can run for miles along the beaches there. Have you been anywhere you really enjoyed?'

'No. We never left London.'

He hadn't picked that up from the briefing, had assumed that family holidays were too ordinary to be mentioned. A normal sixth-former would surely find that surprising too. 'What? Really? Not even to France?'

'Yes, really.' Ember got up and dragged over her head the Versace sports top she'd taken off for the running machine.

He was losing the brief chink of insight into the real Ember he had earned with his bet. 'I apologize. That was tactless of me. Not everyone gets to travel. I realize I'm very privileged.'

'Yes, you are. You with your nice parents and your big sister and her kids: sounds too good to be true.'

So she had been listening to his chatter about his family. 'And you? You've a brother?'

'I guess you read that in the papers?' she asked bitterly.

He shrugged, not wanting to go into where his information came from. 'But they don't always get things right.'

'In my experience, they usually get things wrong.'

'So you don't have a twin?'

'What I have is a private life that stays private.'

He held up his hands, palms towards her. 'OK, OK, sorry. I was just making conversation.'

'Then don't.'

'Geez, Em, you are one prickly fairy queen.'

'At least I'm in character. Oberon isn't friendly. It doesn't suit him.'

He stood, finding her head reached his chin. She'd always seemed so sure of herself that he'd made her into an Amazon in his mind. Standing right by her like this, so close he could smell her light perfume, his instincts were screaming a very different message. He wanted to pull her to his chest and tell her things would be OK. 'I'm not him, Em.'

'No, you're probably just a cash-strapped drama student who plans to sell his insider knowledge of the infamous Ember Lord to the nearest tabloid journalist.'

He clenched his jaw to bite down on his anger. He'd been having stupid soft thoughts about her while she'd been entertaining such a low opinion of him. He was so frustrated by his performance on this mission; he was messing up badly. 'I wouldn't do that.'

'Everyone I've ever known even slightly has sold their story, so why should you be any different?'

He reached out and caught her wrist just before she moved off. Her pulse leapt, way too high. She was not as resigned as her words suggested. Was this anger or something else driving her? 'You can trust me for two reasons. One is that we are in the same play. I wouldn't do that to a fellow cast member, not only because it would be wrong but because it would mess up the performance. The second is that I'm more interested in impressing Henry Rawlings in the hopes of getting a good reference from him for drama school applications than I am in making a quick buck. Bearing tales from inside his production would not reflect well on him, and by extension on me. Bang would go my chance of getting into RADA with a glowing report from Henry.'

Giving him a pointed look, Ember waited until he released his grip. 'I think I believe you. Still doesn't give you the right to push your nose into my business.'

'There's a difference between being pushy and friendly.' Right then Joe wasn't sure he'd got the balance right.

'Maybe. But I don't need a friend.'

'That's so not true. I've never met anyone more in need of a friend, Em. We all do and it's nothing to be ashamed of.'

Turning away to pick up his towel, he left it there. A seed had been planted. Now he just had to hope it grew very rapidly or he would be out of time with her and the intelligence agencies would take over. He hoped to pick the lock to her secrets; they'd prefer to smash their way in. If Ember had any sense of self-preservation, she'd better decide to trust him—and quickly.

Chapter 5

Sitting in a row on her own in the minibus taking the girls back to Lockwood, Ember couldn't shake off Joe's last words in the gym. *I've never met anyone more in need of a friend, Em. We all do and it's nothing to be ashamed of.*

She had never had a friend—hadn't dared take the risk. The important relationships in her life boiled down to her brother, Max, and the surrogate grandmother they had both found in their nurse, Nanny Roe. Even so, Ember had always felt that Nanny preferred Max, as he was so sunny-natured and uncomplicated most of the time. She didn't blame Nanny Roe for loving the fireside tabby Max, as opposed to the suspicious alley cat Ember had become once her father had started taking an interest in her. Ember didn't much love herself, knowing she was prickly, difficult, and a bit mean, so wasn't surprised when no one else warmed to her, apart from Max of course. She had deliberately made herself into someone it was difficult to like, let alone love.

What would happen if she was, God forbid, actually nice to Joe? It might be worth doing just to see how shocked everyone would be. She smiled at the thought, catching sight in the window of the unfamiliar expression on her face. Was that really her?

Whatever the outcome of the trial, she had reached a watershed. She would never be welcome back in East

London, no matter what happened. She would need a new start, practice at making friends, and Joe seemed interested enough to make an effort to get to know her. Most of that was in the spirit of making the cast get along, and now she knew he was serious about his drama aspirations she understood that better. Taking a starring role in an interesting production would do his CV the power of good and he had to get on with his co-star. She found she didn't mind that he had ulterior motives for friendship. Knowing he wasn't doing it out of the goodness of his heart made him more trustworthy.

Her mind went back to her own painful history of relationships. Joe's motives were better than the ones she had met with before, boys wanting to suck up to her father, or get their hands on the millionaire's daughter's credit card. All of them had been vetted by her father and quickly got rid of when he tired of a new face at the dinner table, part of the strategy games he was constantly playing with her as a pawn. And she had to admit that her thinking about Joe was probably influenced by the fact that she found him very easy on the eye. Ridiculously so, with his smooth dark skin that made her want to run her hands over him, and smiling eyes that broke down her defences. Despite all media reports to the contrary, she was only human. And he was gentle with her. It appeared that, despite her best efforts to toughen up, she was a sucker for anyone who treated her kindly.

The van turned into Lockwood and parked in the playground. Mrs Bishop hurried out to meet them, green sleeveless coat slipped over her uniform making her look more like a gamekeeper than a prison guard. Perhaps the jobs were more similar than Ember had realized: wild creatures to pen and protect.

'I'm glad you're back on time. Ember, you've got another visitor.'

Not Devlin so soon? 'Who?' she asked warily.

The answer was provided by a dog lolloping out from behind the education centre and arrowing towards her. Leaping up, the boxer lavished snuffling licks over her hands, wagged his stumpy tail, and barked ecstatically.

'Patch, down!' urged Ember, too stunned to react other than automatically.

'Ember!' Max ran along in his dog's wake, waving the lead. 'Surprise!'

Oh no, he was going to do this in front of everyone, she just knew. Bracing herself, she absorbed the thump as he collided with her and threw his arms around her for the Maximum Bear Hug.

'What are you doing here, Max?' Ember cast an anxious glance at her travelling companions but Raven and Kate were chatting with the female van driver, ignoring her.

'I came to see you, silly!' Her lovely brother beamed at her, hazel eyes shining from within the fur-trimmed hood of his winter coat. 'My new friends brought me.'

Ember felt a sickening lurch of apprehension. 'What new friends?' If the press had got to him, lured him here in hopes of a story, she'd raise merry hell with the press complaints authority.

'Damien and Rose and Jellybean. They're waiting outside. Damien can drive and he's only eighteen, can you imagine it!'

'The spaniel owners?'

'That's right. We got talking and they said they were taking Jellybean out for a long walk in the countryside today and did I want to bring Patch? I said no, as you told me, but then I said yes as Patch really wanted to come. They asked me if there was anywhere I wanted to go so I said here.'

This tumble of information was too much to unpick so Ember went for the obvious. 'Why aren't they at school? Why aren't you at school yourself?'

'My social worker—you don't know him, he's called Roger, he's got a cat called Jung and a goldfish called Mephistopheles—anyway he said I didn't need to go back yet till I've had a sessment.'

'An assessment,' Ember corrected him gently, tucking a strand of his blond hair back from his eyes. Maybe that was good. Now their father wasn't blocking the process, perhaps Max would get the learning support he needed. 'And your friends?'

'Oh, they don't go to school. They had the day off college. No lessons. So we escaped!'

Max looked so proud she couldn't bring herself to dampen his high spirits, but she wanted to meet these new friends of his most urgently. The powerlessness of being behind bars had never been more apparent. 'Why don't you ask them in?'

'They're not allowed. Only people on a list can enter. And I'm on the list. Patch wasn't but the man on the gate said that was OK. He said I could bring Jellybean too if I wanted but my friends said they thought she would be too much of a handful.'

She had a list of allowed visitors? Ember hadn't paid much attention to that part of the rules, not expecting to get a visit from anyone she wanted to see. Adults like Devlin, she understood, but surely the authorities would not want her brother associating with a murder suspect? Looking out beyond the wire fence, she could see two people walking hand in hand across a nearby field, a spaniel darting in and out of the hedgerow. 'Is that them?'

'Yes. They're wonderful, Ember. I can't wait for you to meet them.'

Were they really just nice people wanting to do a boy a favour, or were they in it for some other reason? She couldn't reach them to check so she'd have to make sure Max did what he was told. 'You won't talk about me, will you?'

Max shook his head and grinned. 'Uh-oh, big no.' She'd taught him that when he was little and he'd stuck to it.

'OK then.' This time she hugged him. 'It's lovely to see you, Max. Tell me all about what you've been doing.'

Mrs Bishop said it was fine to stay outside with Patch as long as Ember kept to the area in view of the staff desk in the education centre. Ember listened carefully to Max's news, rooting through the details in her mind to check he wasn't at risk and that Devlin had left him alone as promised. When Max had repeated much of what had already been said in his letters, he came to a stop and just looked at her. His mind might be a little literal in its grasp of the facts but it was a mistake to think he was stupid. That was what their father had never understood. Max was quite capable of seeing what was right in front of him and very clever in his own way.

'Why are you in here, Ember? I don't think you've told me everything. Why is there a gate and a fence? Is it a prison?'

She smiled bravely. 'It's a youth training centre. You saw the notice board on the way in, right?'

'Then what are they training you for?' Max shook his head. 'No, that's not right. It's a prison. My new friends said it was.'

'I thought you said you didn't talk to them about me?'

'I didn't. They had to look up the address. I heard them talking. What have you done?'

He would find out sooner or later. 'The police think I killed our father.'

'But you didn't. You wouldn't.'

She was glad he thought that. 'That's what the trial is for, to find that out.'

'Why don't you just tell them what happened?'

'That's not how it works.'

Max was getting agitated, tapping his foot like Thumper in Bambi, a bad sign. 'Why doesn't it work that way? That's the truth, isn't it? They can't keep you in here.'

'Please, Max.'

'No, Ember, this is wrong. You shouldn't be here behind these fences. You should be with me—at home. He's not there any more. We'll be safe.' His grip on Patch's lead made his knuckles white.

Ember covered his hand with hers. 'Sssh, love, yes, I know. I will be. Soon.'

He pushed her off. 'You said that in your letters. Weeks and weeks have passed. I don't believe you. You're going to leave me like Mum did. Like he did.'

He was getting worked up. Max was the sunniest-natured boy until he panicked, and then even Ember didn't know how to handle him. 'I won't leave you.'

'But you already have. I want to go home. Why can't we go home?'

The argument was going to go in circles as she had no answer. 'I'm sorry.'

'I don't care that you're sorry. I'm going to go back to my new friends now. They'll stay with me. Patch, come on!' With a whistle to bring the dog back from his exploration of the bins near the gate, Max stalked off. He was punishing her for failing him, Ember knew that. It wouldn't last and he'd regret it tomorrow but he needed to lash out at someone for making him feel scared. Ember was the only one left with whom he could do that. She waited until he'd joined his friends in the car park beyond the perimeter gates and climbed into the vehicle. One of them, a girl with dark red hair, looked over in her direction and gave a wave. What did that mean? That it was OK to go in, that they'd look after Max from here? Anyone who spoke to him longer than for five minutes would get

71

that he had special needs and required careful handling. Could she trust in the kindness of strangers?

She never had before. Being in prison was making her take risks that she had always refused to allow into her life. The bitter truth was she now had no choice.

At rehearsal the next day, Ember decided to put her new resolution into practice and try to make a friend, or at least an acquaintance, of her Oberon. He was safe as he would leave at the end of the session, not like the girls with whom she was having to live. She was just so tired of there being no one, not even Max it seemed, on her side.

Her decision matched one taken by Joe. He turned up in the rehearsal room with a little bunch of snowdrops tied with a piece of green gauze ribbon and a handful of different bars of chocolate. Henry was running the actors doing the play-with-in-a-play through their parts, the four lovers were rehearsing theirs, so Oberon and Titania were more or less alone at their end of the room. Joe gave a smile and a bow as he presented his flowers.

'Sweets for the sweet,' he quipped.

She took the snowdrops, not sure what to do with them. No one had ever given her a bouquet before. The gesture thrilled some secret part of her that had wanted romance but never dared hope for it. 'I'm hardly sweet.'

'For the fair Titania then. I thought you needed a consolation prize.'

Not romance then. A little part of her was stupidly disappointed, but it was better this way. She filled a mug with water from the drinks machine in the corner and propped the flowers in it. She relaxed now she understood he had brought them as a teasing way of reminding her of her failure. 'You're not going to let me forget I lost that bet, are you?'

'Maybe. Eventually.' He juggled the bars of chocolate. 'Which one do you want?'

She named her choice and he deftly threw it to her without breaking pattern. 'Where did you learn to juggle?' she asked.

'A special summer course at college one year. It was great fun—possibly the most fun I've had there, and right after I started school in the UK. Great way to break the ice. My friends and I all picked up different skills. Kieran is a demon with a bull whip.'

Ember choked on her mouthful of chocolate. 'That seems . . . unlikely.' The quiet Kieran with his jade-green eyes had always seemed so undemonstrative, the last person to start a lion-tamer routine.

'I know.' Joe's brown eyes twinkled with amusement. 'That's why it's so delicious.'

No, it was Joe who was delicious. *Ridiculous, weak thought.* Ember turned her gaze to where the four lovers were practising their lines. 'Your friend seems to be getting on well with Raven.' They were sitting very close, arms touching, while they went through one of the many muddles that beset the foursome as they wandered through the forest.

'You're right. I'll have to remind him.' Joe frowned.

'Of what?'

'That she's in here, and he's . . . not.' He shrugged a little awkwardly.

'Do you think being in prison means she'll never have a normal life again, can't date, that she doesn't deserve it?' Ember asked sharply.

'No, of course not.'

'You do. I can see it in your face.' There was definitely disapproval there. She felt disappointed that the guy she had picked on for her first experiment in friendship had fallen at the first fence, but in an odd way it was reassuring. He was living up to her expectations of people. 'You think that once we're in here we join some kind of underclass, that we don't deserve a second chance? That a boy shouldn't like someone who made a stupid mistake just the once?'

'Whoa, Ember, stop putting words in my mouth. I don't think that at all. I just meant that Kieran needs to take care he's not leading Raven to think there's more in the relationship than there is. Being in a play casts a temporary glamour over people, like a spring break romance.'

Joe was right but Ember still felt angry. The smallest thing seemed to set her off at the moment. She folded up the wrapper on the chocolate bar and tucked it into her pocket for later. 'You're here to practise. Shall we get on with our scene then?'

But Joe wasn't ready to move on yet. 'Hold a moment. I want you to know that I think everyone deserves a second chance. And I realize some people don't even get a first chance.'

That was very perceptive of him. Her life fell under that description. Perhaps she had been too quick to leap to conclusions about him? 'OK. I'm sorry if I accused you of things you don't believe.'

'That's OK. I get that it's tough being in here. I want you to know that, as your acting partner, you can let off steam with me if you need to. It must be hard, not being able to just walk out and tell people to go to hell if they annoy you, knowing you're stuck until someone else unlocks the door.'

Her temper dissipating, she gave a rueful smile. 'I still manage to tell people to go to hell quite effectively.' And she had never had any but stolen freedom at home either. She'd just swapped one prison for another. There weren't wild bursts of violence in Lockwood, at least, not that she had witnessed. The boys' side was rumoured to be more violent than the tiny girls' unit.

74

Joe smiled in response. 'I guess you do. Is there no one who doesn't annoy you?'

'My brother. He gets annoyed at me instead.'

'Sibling rivalry?'

She laughed and shook her head. Joe looked taken aback to see her act so spontaneously and his shocked expression added to her humour. 'You couldn't be more wrong.'

'I like it when you laugh. You should do it more often.' Joe snapped off a row on his chocolate bar and offered it to her. She took it as a peace offering. 'You look completely different when you smile. So why am I wrong?'

'He's more like a little brother I have to protect than a rival.' She wondered why she was telling Joe this. Maybe because Max's visit was still raw and if she didn't say something to someone she'd break down and do something terrible, like cry in front of people. 'He doesn't like it when I don't do what he wants and it's hard to explain that he can't always have his way.'

'But he's your twin? Isn't he old enough to understand?'

'He's my twin but he's . . . I guess you'd say he sees life in very simple terms: right, wrong, up, down. He thinks the best of people, especially me, and so can't understand why I'm in a detention centre.'

'He wants you home?'

She nodded.

'He must miss his father.'

Friendship only went so far. Ember stood up. 'Not really. Our father was a very unpleasant person and a worse parent. Neither of us are mourning him. Let's run the scene.'

Joe caught her hand. She looked down at where they were connected, his strong fingers a contrast to her slim ones. Not counting Max, Joe was the only person who had touched her, Ember realized, apart from the infrequent searches by staff, which were an intrusion rather than this offer of comfort. 'Ember, did he hurt you?'

Hurt was too ordinary a word for the screwed-up treatment she had endured. 'You have no right to ask me that.'

'Sorry, no. I just . . . just got caught up in worry for you. I wondered if you needed to tell someone your side of the story. If it were me, I'd explode if I couldn't offload to a person I could trust.'

'I have a lawyer, Joe. You don't need to stand in for her. OK, what's your line after I say "O how mine eyes do loathe his visage now"?'

'It's "Silence a while".' He brushed the tops of the snowdrops with a forefinger. 'Oberon's such a nasty piece of work, isn't he? There's a word for guys who set their wives up with other men for lovers.'

Ember grimaced. It was true. This hard-edged reading of the play had lost the magic. Oberon had only been forgivable as a creature from another world that played by fairy rules. As a very human mafia boss his behaviour just became vicious. 'I normally like Rawlings' productions, but I think he's got this one a little too real in an attempt to make it relevant to us.'

'You've seen others?'

'Yes. I went to his *Julius Caesar* last year.'

Joe leant back against a desk. 'So did I! The Globe's near . . . some friends so I get in to see most productions.'

'Groundling?'

'Of course. You?'

'I snuck out from home and stood for three magical hours.'

'Em, I believe I have identified a fellow thesp!' He pulled a comically dramatic pose. 'Are you thinking of studying English or Drama at college, or going to acting school?'

'I'm thinking of avoiding a life sentence and perhaps taking some GCSEs when life returns to normal.'

Joe was sweetly embarrassed by his *faux pas*. 'Sorry, I forgot. It's just that you're clearly so clever. You'll get those exams, no problem.'

His praise felt like sunshine pouring over a frosted landscape. 'Thanks. And I like that you forgot. The one thing that never happens to me is have someone treat me as just Ember, not Mick Lord's daughter, or the evil twin of the tabloid papers.'

'That's a heavy reputation to cart around.'

He understood. 'I'm just so tired of Ember Lord. I wish I could kill her off in this act and start with a new role.'

Joe toyed with the cord that raised the blinds. 'If you made a clean breast of what you know, maybe you could get a fresh start?'

'What? Like confession to a priest? I'm not a Catholic.'

'You could tell me. I wouldn't be shocked.'

She seriously doubted that. Her father had quite a few skeletons in his cupboard and she knew where some of them were buried. That was partly why Devlin was so anxious for her to keep her mouth shut, as much of it would wash back on him. He had often been the man to carry out what her father had called 'the household maintenance'. This conversation, however, had gone deep enough—way too deep.

'Thanks for offering, but let's get back to the play.'

He shrugged and stood up. 'OK, but the offer stands.'

'We could put some warmth back into the relationship if you like,' she suggested tentatively. She had been staging the play in her head during the long nights, imagining it taking a different course. 'We could make it more like the bet we had yesterday—a friendly rivalry where on the surface they seem keen to win but in the end both knowing each other well enough to realize that losing isn't so bad, as the other won't take advantage. They've been married a long time, it seems to me, so it could be how they spice up their relationship.'

Joe let her change the subject back to their roles. 'The text doesn't really support that, not how Henry wants us to deliver it.'

'But it ends in a dance, doesn't it? A picture of two people finally agreeing, finally in step with each other. I was thinking it could be like the one in *Dirty Dancing* where Baby stumbles upon the professionals dancing with each other after hours. She sees how they move in harmony, what real dancing is after the stilted steps of the amateurs—that they're so right together.'

'I didn't have you down as a fan of old dance movies, Em.'

'Thank YouTube. I wouldn't call myself a fan, but I have caught a few clips over the years.'

'Yeah, you keep telling yourself that. I think you really love it.'

Of course she did, but she wasn't going to admit it. *Nobody puts Baby in a corner*: best line in a film of all time. Her mother had adored that movie and shared it with her daughter. Ember would love to take a flying leap and be caught, soaring above everyone's heads just for a brief moment of glorious freedom like the character did. 'But do you get my point?'

'You mean let their body language do what the spoken word doesn't? Sounds a good idea. Thing is: can you dance?'

'Oh.' She hadn't really thought this through. She began fingering her necklace nervously. She was obviously about to make a complete cake of herself. 'I had some ballet lessons when I was younger until Mum died but I've not really tried since.'

'Lucky for you that I can.'

'Modesty, thy name is not Joe Masters.'

'No point being modest if it means missing out on a great theatrical moment. Let's talk to Henry and see what he thinks. Then we'll have to come up with the track.'

'Jailhouse Rock?'

'Was that a joke, Miss Lord?'

She smiled. 'I would think it could have been if it wasn't for the fact that I don't make jokes.'

He tapped her nose. 'That's a fib. I think you've been making them for years, just haven't shared them. There is far more to Ember Lord than is dreamt of in our philosophy.'

She chuckled. 'We keep misquoting Shakespeare. He must be turning in his grave.'

'Like a machine on spin dry. Come on, let's have a word with Henry.'

Henry listened to Joe with sharp interest. 'That's quite brilliant, Joe. I like it.'

'It's not my idea, Henry. Ember came up with it.'

'Titania, I have to commend you on your insight. Rather than making them common nightclub owners—the direction in which I was heading—we make them into stylish criminal lords and ladies. Raffles, the gentleman cat burglar, not the thuggish Kray brothers.' He began to pace, excited now. 'And the Forest can be a casino. Yes, yes, that fits with the lottery element of who gets the drugs squeezed into their eyes. Let's set it in the most infamous of all casino cities. Theseus and Hippolyta have come to Las Vegas for their nuptials and the play-within-a-play is like a floor show. It all fits! There's even Caesar's Palace in the real place which works with the antique names and talk of Amazons.' He swooped on Ember and gave her a hug. 'Quite, quite brilliant. Have you ever thought of directing?'

Blushing, Ember disentangled herself from his embrace, her long hair getting caught on the buttons of his shirt. Mrs Gardener took a step forward, probably worried Ember would file a complaint against Henry even though the gesture was clearly innocent and born of enthusiasm. Ember was very far from complaining, though. She was overwhelmed. No one she respected so much had ever praised her like that. 'Thanks for saying so, but it was just a little idea that you've developed into something much bigger.'

'Don't undervalue yourself. You have set the whole production off in a new and improved direction. I'll make sure you get a credit on the programme.' Henry beamed, having gone from thinking of her as his play's liability to regarding her as director's favourite.

Ember shoved her hands in her pockets, awkward under the praise of someone she admired so intensely. Making friends had done this. She looked up to find Joe studying her with a strange expression on his face.

'Are you OK? It was your idea too,' she asked.

He shook his head. 'No it wasn't, Ember. I'm fine. Let's go listen to some tracks together and see if we can pick a song to run past Henry. I'm not sure his music tastes go much beyond 1970.' He held out a hand.

Feeling like she was jumping off a cliff, she took his offered palm in hers. 'I'd like that, Joe.'

He squeezed her hand in recognition that she had finally used his name. 'I'd like it too, Ember.'

Back at St Bernard's sports centre, Joe smashed the squash ball against the wall. 'This. Is. The. Pits.' He hit the ball again and again, quite ignoring Damien, who had agreed to partner him when his other friends had refused. They had seen the mood he was in after rehearsal.

Damien, cool blue eyes amused, spun his racket on the ground, waiting for the storm to pass. He'd driven up from London to report on what Max said about his meeting with his sister, but he had to deal with Joe's crisis first.

Joe missed the rebound and threw his racket into the corner in a fury.

'I believe that's a violation of the rules.' Damien picked up the ball and tucked it into his pocket, clearly deciding Joe was not safe to leave with any form of missile.

Joe slumped against the wall and bashed his head against it. 'I can't do it, Damien.'

His friend slid down beside him. 'Tell me about it.'

'Isaac's orders—heavy application of emotional pressure. I'm leading that girl by the nose into thinking I'm her friend, sweet talking her into trust. I think she's even falling for me a little, getting flustered when I give her flowers and chocolate. They're classic moves and she isn't questioning them enough for a girl we thought was a tough nut.'

'That's a difficult position to be in.'

'I feel like I'm at Westron Academy all over again, but this time I'm the one brainwashing and feeding someone a load of poisoned crap to force her compliance.' The school had been subject of the mission when Kieran had met Raven.

Damien grimaced in sympathy. They all knew that Joe had taken a good six months to get over that operation. The damage hadn't been so much from the brainwashing but the knowledge Joe carried away with him that he hadn't been strong enough to withstand the abuse. 'It's not the same, surely?'

'Isn't it? What's even worse is that, with her softening towards me, it means my methods are working and I've no excuse to give up. I've only got a week to do this. With an upbringing like hers she's messed-up enough, and when she finds out I'm using her she's going to freak out. The damage will be severe.' He should know. He'd felt stripped to the bone by his experience, no longer able to rely on his own instincts about people.

'Toughen up, Joe. That won't be on you. You've orders—responsibilities to protect the public.'

He felt a spurt of anger at his friend's words. It was easy for

81

the smooth Cobra Damien to preach hardness, but for Cats like Joe their weakness and their strength was that they had to empathise with their targets to do their job. He knew too well what it felt like on the other side of this unequal relationship. 'I know I have my duty but it's not true that I'll be blameless. I don't have to do this. It's my choice to try stop that shipment this way.'

Damien tried another tack. 'You know, you might be helping her? She might want someone to talk to. Rose doesn't think that Ember's the cold-blooded person she presents to the world.'

'Rose is a sweetheart—always has been. But she hasn't met Ember. How can she know that?' Joe was also just starting to suspect that their target was more of a marshmallow than she let on, so it would be interesting to hear Rose's take. This worried him though. Was he looking for excuses to like Ember because he was finding himself attracted to her, or was there really more nice than nasty to the girl than everyone thought? Why couldn't he just see her clearly, like he always had every other target he'd ever been given on a mission? He was so furious with himself he wanted to bash his head against his racket.

'Rose will say it's enough that she's met the brother. Max studiously doesn't talk about his sister. It's like she's the great big elephant in the room none of us are allowed to acknowledge, but when manoeuvring around the subject he gives a lot away. She's the reason he's got that dog of his, and kept his old nanny on to look after him long after the woman should've retired. Max was plain terrified of his father. I think Mick was into old-fashioned clip-round-the-ears, and much worse, when his children disappointed him.'

'That I can believe. The fact that beating your kids is illegal wouldn't've stopped him as he never obeyed the law in any other area of his life.'

'Raven, Kate, and Mrs Harding who was driving the mini-bus, all agree that the two siblings were genuinely affectionate towards each other when he came visiting. Ember was seen tidying his hair, acting the older sister looking after a younger brother. It felt very natural to them, not put on for show.'

'So?'

'So if she does have a heart and some conscience, then she won't want a dirty bomb going off in the place where her brother lives, will she?'

'I guess not. If we had more time, maybe we could risk that approach, but I'm under orders and the intelligence services are breathing down our neck. We've only a few more days.'

'You're the only one who's got through to her.' Damien paused, correctly judging from his friend's silent misery that Joe wasn't convinced. 'You know when I tried dating Rose, telling myself it was excused by the mission, you came down on me like a tonne of bricks?'

'Yeah, I remember.' That hadn't been so long ago. He had thrown a wet flannel at his friend when Damien just wouldn't see what emotional damage he risked in making Joe's neigh-bour fall for him. The Cobra stream's weakness was that they were often too ruthless when going after their goal and Damien had made mistakes of that nature in the past.

'You were only cool with it later when you saw it was genuine liking on my part. How about trying to be a real friend to Ember, not just a fake one? Isn't there anything about her you can like?'

'It's quite hard to see past the murder part.' And he didn't want to admit to Damien that he'd already found plenty of things that he liked about her. He kept throwing up the mur-der charge just to give himself some defences.

Damien tested the strings on his racket, checking the tension. 'You might not have that violence in you, Joe, but I

83

know I've got it in me in the right circumstances. Good fortune and training has kept me from taking that fatal step. She's been unlucky and maybe she had no one to tell her better?'

'It doesn't excuse her.'

'Of course not, but it might help you understand.'

'Yeah, yeah, I know. Maybe I keep throwing that in the way because I don't want to start to like her. It's easier to do this if I think she's not worth worrying about, not when weighed against the possible damage she and her criminal pals might be doing.'

'That, my friend, is what they call being caught on the horns of a dilemma. Or even more succinctly, damned if you do, damned if you don't.'

'Sounds almost Shakespearian.'

'I bow to you, our resident expert, on that. Joe, you're tying yourself up in knots and that's going to get in the way of what you know you've got to do. Come on, let's play a proper game to work off some of your anger and then we can get back to the job.'

Damien was right, damn him. 'Fine. OK.' Joe got to his feet.

The concentration needed to play Damien at squash helped Joe settle. Damien didn't have quite his reach but he was fiendishly fast, so they were evenly matched. As Joe pounded the court, he revolved in his mind what his friend had said. Find things to like about her. There were plenty peeking through that hard shell of hers. He suspected she had a totally soft centre when it came to her brother, they had been right about that. She was showing a sense of humour and keen intelligence. Quite how she had got to seventeen without a qualification was a mystery. He desperately needed more information about her to hone his approach. Most of the questions about her would be resolved by understanding just what had gone on behind the closed doors of the Lord mansion in Chigwell. Maybe it was time to make a visit there and see what he could tell from the evidence the family had left behind?

Chapter 6

At the briefing following the squash game, the other boys enthusiastically took up Joe's idea that he visit the Lord mansion. Damien had the car so insisted he came along, and Nathan and Kieran weren't going to be left out of a little bit of breaking-and-entering after weeks of pretending to be ordinary sixth-formers. All of them were a bit stir-crazy being in institutions all week—school and prison, not much difference really.

They couldn't just follow their impulse without going through the YDA protocols. Joe took the idea to Isaac, who agreed it would help them make progress with the case. Isaac came back ten minutes later having got the green light from his police contacts, so technically it wasn't illegal, but that wasn't going to spoil their fun.

'It's a go. And there's no time like the present,' said Joe, once he came off the phone from Isaac.

'As this is, sadly, a very respectable break-in, we can at least add some spice by doing it in the dark,' added Nathan.

'I was thinking more that we should go now so that if any of Mick Lord's associates or nosey neighbours are watching the house, they wouldn't know we visited.'

'Good plan. Load up the snacks and let's get a move on,' said Damien, clicking his car key like a flick knife.

As the car ate up the miles of M25 separating them

from their target, it was at the back of Joe's mind that it was wrong of them to treat this more like an outing than a mission. He would have to remind them when they arrived that this was still a job like any other. He understood that for them it was a release from the frustrations of the mission to be doing something concrete that drew on their core skills. He felt it as much, if not more, than his friends. Normally he enjoyed going undercover, but this time pretending to be a drama student romancing an enigmatic girl felt like squeezing himself inside a pair of jeans a size too small for him, painful in ways that didn't bear thinking about. A huge part of the pinch was the knowledge that he wasn't being fair to Ember. Could he do anything to change that?

Damien took the turn off the M25 and into the leafy suburbia where Ember had grown up. Chigwell, a satellite village to the capital, was well known for its affluent inhabitants who had made good in the city and moved to the prettier surroundings of Epping Forest. The area the Lords had lived in comprised of large detached housing with expensive vehicles parked in the drives and elaborate security systems. The Lords' home, an ugly red brick Victorian mansion, formerly a vicarage with unnecessary gothic flourishes, was one of the largest as it also had an annexe and extensive gardens backing on to a golf course. Even if it was unattractive and like the cliché of a turreted haunted house in a Stephen King novel, it still had to be worth millions.

After driving by to check for lights or signs anyone else was there, they parked in a side road and went the rest of the way on foot.

'We go in through the yard,' said Joe.

'He means garden,' said Damien, pulling on a black beanie to disguise his fair hair.

Joe tugged the hat over Damien's eyes as punishment for

that bit of English smart-arse-ness. 'The house is protected by motion sensors and a security alarm. Key, can you deal with that?'

Kieran nodded, pulled out his phone and started hacking into the house's electronics. Ironically, the higher spec of tech a place used, the easier it was for him to bypass.

'I want a full search. Nathan, can you take the annexe and pool? According to the police, the nanny isn't due to be released from hospital until the end of the week, but take care in case she's discharged herself early. Damien, Mick's bedroom, bathrooms, and spare rooms. Kieran, the family rooms, cellar, and office. I'll take the kitchen and Ember's bedroom.' He didn't want anyone else invading her privacy; it was bad enough he had to do it.

'What are we looking for?' asked Kieran.

'I hope we know it when we see it.'

'That could do with a bit more detail, Joe,' said Damien.

Joe rubbed his face in frustration. It was difficult to put his gut instinct into words. 'I'm not expecting to find anything about the arms shipment, nothing on the criminal activities, as the police would've taken all the electronics and documents into evidence. I suppose I'm looking for answers as to who was actually running the show in this house. From the things that Ember has let slip, it wasn't her. I'm not sure any of us understand her yet and without that we won't know which buttons to push.'

Once Kieran gave them the all-clear that the system was down, they gave each other a boost over the high wall. Joe went last and was pulled up by his friends from the top. They'd brought a thick rubber mat to lay over the glass embedded along the brickwork, which had been cemented there as a defence to deter chance thieves coming off the golf course. Dropping down into the bushes, Joe had his first look at the rear of the house. It had a pretty garden, with a big lawn and the bare stalks of rose bushes promising much more for May and June. There was a small summer house with a dog bowl on the wooden porch. Looking through the window, he saw a garden chair, a couple of blankets, a pile of comics and graphic novels, and several mangled tennis balls: Max's shed he would guess. Nothing here suggested Ember used it.

Arriving at the door leading into the utility room, Nathan knelt down by the lock and got out his set of picks. Again, they could have borrowed the keys from the police, but that had the slight risk that word of their visit would leak, and finessing the locks made it more of a challenge.

'Getting old here,' teased Damien. They had a competition running between the four of them as to who could get into a building quickest. Nathan currently held the record.

'You're getting in my light,' he grumbled.

'Excuses, excuses.'

'And the master succeeds again. Open sesame.' With a grin, Nathan turned the handle and pushed open the door. 'I'll go deal with the annexe and leave you to have fun here. Don't break anything.'

Stepping into the kitchen, Joe noticed immediately the stale air which gave away that the house hadn't been open in a while. He took out his flashlight and made a quick survey of the room. They weren't going to turn on any overhead lighting just in case a neighbour was watching. His search found nothing out of place. All clear. His friends slid by him, no longer joking now they were intent on their mission. He went to the fridge and opened it, letting the light spill out into the room. The milk had expired two weeks ago. He found it sad that no one had cared enough, or considered that Ember wasn't going to return to her family home anytime soon, to come and empty it. So much for family friends and faithful staff—it looked like they'd all fled as soon as Mick was dead. The contents of the fridge were simple enough: a single expensive steak wrapped in white butcher's paper, a wide variety of vegetables, white wine, a chocolate cake going mouldy, and a special pack of cheese advertising that it was suitable for vegetarians. Following a hunch, he checked the recipe books on the shelf by the range stove. The most thumbed one was by a well-known chef who specialised in non-meat recipes. Interesting. If Ember was the vegetarian, that hadn't been in her file. Yet it didn't sound like Mick Lord, unless he was under doctor's orders.

Joe turned to the work surfaces, his flashlight catching on the black handles of a knife block. The gap where the largest blade should have been brought him up short. Had Ember stood here, contemplating taking the weapon, or had she just grabbed it in anger and run up to her father's bedroom? It would be revealing of her state of mind to find out how far that was from here, how long she would have had for second thoughts.

Following her imagined path, Joe left the kitchen, took the stairs up and went the short distance along the carpeted corridor to stand outside the master bedroom. He could see Damien moving around inside, making a thorough search as they had been taught.

'Everything OK?' Damien asked softly, turning round to find Joe hovering in the entrance.

The bed had been stripped, bedclothes taken away as evidence. The mattress however had a rust brown stain on the near side.

'It's about thirty metres from the kitchen to here. If you were running, it would still take you six or seven seconds. That's quite a lot of time for thinking.'

'You're wondering about Ember? Why she did it?'

'Yeah. They say he was asleep when he was stabbed. That sounds like premeditation, not heat of an argument.'

Damien picked up a framed photo and took off the back. 'The law can work against women in that respect. Being generally smaller and not as strong as most men, they can't lay in with their fists like an angry male would in an argument; instead they tend to fume then flip. There have been battered wives' cases like that.'

Joe nodded. 'Found anything?'

'It's what's not here that's interesting. Look at his photos.'

Joe joined his friend at the chest of drawers. There were five photos all picturing Mick Lord. Only one featured Ember looking cold in a white ball gown, her arm linked in his. The rest were either individual shots or had him with a variety of men in sporting situations. Joe recognized two with Seamus Devlin, one on a golf course, the other at a Formula One race somewhere sunny, Monte Carlo maybe. Ember might not have gone anywhere but it looked like her father had.

'There are none of Max,' Damien commented.

'Or their mother. We don't know much about her, do we? Or the circumstances of her death. I'd better check Ember's room now.'

Joe thought it revealing that Ember had chosen a bedroom the furthest away from her father's. It wasn't the biggest and had a view of the side of the house looking at the neighbour's brick wall rather than the garden or the street. He held up his flashlight to illuminate the area and had a moment's fear when it caught on the glassy eyes of a stuffed animal lying on the cover. No cuddly bear for Ember: this was a fairground tiger. Who had given her that? Or had she won it herself?

Her room was another surprise. Not a lavish princess boudoir but a quiet space with pale grey walls and shelves filled with books and CDs. He ran the light over the titles. Good grief: she was better read than he was: classics, modern

91

fiction, plays, poetry, even some collections of French writings. Intrigued, he turned to the CDs. She might have talked about modern bands when they selected tracks for the dance from a streaming service, but here she had gathered some famous recordings of Bach, Mozart, some opera, and a sprinkling of Irish folk. She even had a clutch of vinyl records tucked away at the end but no sign she had anything to play them on. Maybe she just liked having something rare to hand? The DVDs included *Dirty Dancing*—that made him smile—but mainly concentrated on boxed sets of critically acclaimed drama serials. The children's films were few but he spotted *Mulan* and *Pocahontas*, indicating that she was drawn to the older ones with strong female leads.

Joe paused, suddenly aware of what he was doing. Spying on her secrets. How would he feel if someone prowled into his bedroom at the YDA, and what would they find out about him if they did? He didn't think of himself as someone with anything to hide—well, apart from his undercover work of course. They'd see from the DVDs that he liked *A Game of Thrones* and *The Lord of the Rings*, which suggested a taste for the epic and a wish for magic. He had quite a few buddy comedies, including some with a gross sense of humour that Kate and Raven always moaned about. His music was all sourced online so there were no CDs but if they got into his playlists they'd find a wide selection of contemporary artists, heavy on the R&B. His bookshelves were half given over to fantasy and half to crime fiction, though he did have a small bedside table for some classics. An astute psychologist might be able to guess quite accurately what was in his bedroom from observing him. By contrast, Ember had done a good job of laying a false trail as to what really made her tick.

He opened the double doors of the fitted wardrobe, holding the light between his teeth. Now this was fascinating.

Half was what he would call princess clothes, the kind of stuff she'd been wearing in prison—designer, impractical, expensive, and from the looks of it, rarely worn. These fitted the tabloid version of her. The other side contained casual inexpensive outfits with high street labels, plain shirts, a few school uniforms from establishments she had only briefly attended. If he hadn't known she was the only person who used the room, he would have guessed she had a shy sister. He thought back to the clothes he had seen her wearing at rehearsal. He had assumed that the designer jeans and white top combination had been the true Ember, but maybe she was still hiding even in prison, saving another side for her private life?

Turning his attention to the photographs, he found a reversal of the situation in Mick's bedroom. There were many of her brother, some of Nanny Roe. There was a studio portrait of an attractive woman holding two babies on her knee. Her blonde hair and vulnerable wide blue eyes looked more like Max than Ember, but the lady had to be their mother surely? There was no picture of Mick, or anyone else for that matter. No smiling gaggle of schoolgirls or boyfriend. His own room was packed with photos of family and friends; Ember's world boiled down to two people. Aside from the baby photo, she didn't have a single picture of herself.

Joe sat down on the bed, thinking himself into Ember's shoes as he'd been taught to do at the YDA. What was it like to be Ember Lord? Grey walls. Neat room. Few personal touches. It felt bleak. Lonely. The people she loved were out in the annexe. So why didn't she join them? The evidence made no suggestion that she revelled in being Mick Lord's little princess, so why stay here in a modest room at the other end of the house?

Because she had to.

That was the only answer that made sense. What the compulsion was he could only guess: a domineering father's order, a desire for a quiet life, a deal struck? All were plausible.

Ember hadn't acted like a downtrodden mouse, though. The talk of her taking over her father's role in the fullness of time hadn't been just gossip. The spooks said she'd been seen with him at meetings, entertained his business contacts, and had been treated by Mick as a confidante. Kieran had said she always resisted any attempt to make her leave the house or country to go to another school. Why hadn't she jumped at the chance to get her freedom? Joe scanned the room. The answer was either she was secretly scared to leave Chigwell in case she lost her position in her father's company, or she was scared to leave her brother. He would have put money on it being to do with Max, as Ember had showed no sign that she missed her role in the business. That was unless she was a very cunning actress. Was he fooled by a pretty face that looked so heartbreakingly grateful for any kindness? He just didn't know what call to make. Nice or nasty?

Joe switched off the flashlight and let his night sight recover. The objects that made up Ember's sanctuary from the rest of her life receded to grey ghosts of themselves on dusty shelves. He had more pieces of the puzzle and was coming round to Damien's view that maybe there had been a snapping moment and that violence wasn't the norm for this private, complicated girl. He was veering towards the nicer person rather than the alternative. He suspected if he knew more he might even think that Mick had needed killing, horrible though it was to say that. He was a criminal boss used to getting his way; it was a logical deduction from the evidence here that he treated his own children as minions or even possessions. If Ember had struck out, it might very well have been like the kicked dog turning on its owner, not the spoiled princess Joe had assumed. At the very least Mick should have been arrested and put behind bars rather than been allowed to continue abusing his family.

Unfortunately Joe also had another answer. If Ember had stayed here unwillingly for the sake of her brother, the intelligence services could get any answers they wished from her and quickly if they appeared to threaten Max. Joe wouldn't need to continue to make her fall for him if they took that route. He would be off the hook.

But Max and Ember would be the victims again. She might think that bullying by the spooks was no better than by Mick Lord.

Damien appeared in the door. 'Time to meet up with Nathan and Kieran. Find anything?'

'A very complicated girl.'

'That's no surprise.'

'It's the way she's complicated that's the interesting part. I suspect she's been sacrificing herself for her brother for years. He's been her hostage for good behaviour.'

'You could tell that from her room?'

'Look where it is. It's the kind of room you'd give to an au pair or a less favoured guest. I counted two larger rooms with much better views on this corridor. Her belongings—the things that really are hers and not given to her—are all those of a clever girl wanting to immerse herself in culture to escape. She's hardly in this place at all—no photos, little in the way of grooming products or make-up beyond some expensive essentials, nothing personal. I can't find any jewellery worth mentioning and the only piece she has with her is that little necklace she wears—nothing by way of diamonds, silver, or gold.'

'I suppose expensive pieces might be in a bank vault?'

'But there are no papers, no diaries either, unless the police took them.'

'No, there was nothing like that listed in the evidence.'

'So too private even to write something down. My point is she hasn't left much trace of herself here. I expect she lived in her head most of the time, talking to no one, just like she does at Lockwood.'

'So was she or was she not part of Mick's inner circle?'

'Maybe that was the deal: Max gets the annexe, the dog, and the carer as long as she does what her father tells her, pretends to be the daughter he wants the world to think he was clever enough to raise—beautiful, sharp, ruthless like him.'

'And what is she really?'

'Sad, lonely, trapped.'

'Do we throw in furious? Furious enough to kill the old man?'

'I would have said yes, but then look at her bookshelf. I saw she had copies of *Testament of Youth*, Ann Frank's diary, *I Know Why the Caged Bird Sings*, *If This is a Man*.'

'Sorry, I'm not following.'

'They're only some of the most beautiful and brave books about human suffering. You couldn't use it as evidence in court but I can't imagine anyone who values those books would be capable of patricide, not unless it was self-defence, and the crime scene doesn't read like that.' The more he thought about it, the more it didn't add up. Joe led the way down the stairs. 'I think we need to go back to the forensic evidence and you should have another chat with Max. See if he can cast any more light on what happened that night.'

'That's a good idea.' They joined Kieran in the kitchen. Nathan was waiting for them outside, ready to lock the door behind them.

'Was there anything in the annexe?' Joe asked.

'A missing knife in the block on the work surface, white handle. I guess the police took that to eliminate it as the murder weapon.'

'I'll double check the list but I don't think so,' said Kieran.

'Let's follow it up. Beyond that, there's plenty of proof that Nanny Roe absolutely adores Max and Ember,' said Nathan. 'The place is stuffed full of drawings by them, hoarded since they were infants, as well as photos on every surface. I'm afraid to say Ember shows no promise as a potter but her pen stand is on Nanny Roe's desk nonetheless.'

Joe couldn't help the smile. 'Good.'

'How good?' Nathan gave the thumbs up that the door was locked.

'She has someone to love her. I was getting the impression that there weren't many candidates. What about Max?'

'His bedroom is neat but still full of toys rather than the paraphernalia you'd expect of a boy our age. He is seriously into dogs. Got a whole row of soft toy ones.'

'Any tigers?'

'What? That's a bit random, isn't it?'

'Ember had one on her bed. It seemed out of place. I wondered if they'd got one each from a fair or something. It doesn't fit the rest of her room.' Joe stopped, detective instinct kicking in. 'I want to go back.'

Nathan gave a groan and knelt down to reverse his activity on the door.

'Kieran, do you have your sweeper on you?' asked Joe.

'Yes. There weren't any bugs in the office.'

'It's not the office I want you to check.'

Kieran's handheld sweeper found the device in the belly of the tiger immediately. Joe ripped it open, spilling stuffing onto the duvet. It was an upmarket version of a baby listener, the light on the battery shining a pinprick of green to show it was still active. It was a model that only kicked in when a noise triggered it, thus extending the battery life.

'She was being bugged. In her own fricking bedroom,' cursed Damien.

The picture was shifting again: Ember moving further from suspect to victim, or maybe a combination of both? Joe used a gloved fingernail to switch the control to off. 'The problem is, so were we when we were having our little conversation just now.'

'Damn: you're right. Any way of finding out who was listening?'

Kieran took the listener and sealed it in an evidence bag. 'They won't be very far away as these things are short range. I'll dust for prints then see what else it can tell me. Let's check the rest of the room.'

'I take it you two weren't very discrete in your conversation?' asked Nathan, standing on a chair to scan the corners of the wardrobe.

Joe wondered how serious a reprimand they would get from Isaac. 'I never thought . . . why the heck didn't the police sweep the room?'

'Because they thought her the perpetrator, not the victim. Sloppy on their part.'

'And on ours.' Joe cringed as he reviewed his conversation with Damien.

'What did you say?'

'We mentioned some names—ran a few theories by each other: so no, we weren't discreet. We have to allow that maybe someone knows about us now, but how do we find out about them?'

'You'll have to ask her who gave her the tiger,' said Kieran.

'Not something you can casually drop into conversation, though, is it?'

'I suggest you find a way very quickly.'

Nathan cleared his throat. 'Guys, I think I've got a camera here too.'

Kieran ran his scanner over the buried wire with the tiny lens at the end and deactivated it. 'You do indeed. No audio. Welcome to the fishbowl. Was it her dad's idea, do you think, or is someone else still watching?'

'So everything she did and said was monitored?' said Damien. 'And now we've been caught on candid camera? Isaac's going to skin us for this. We know better than to talk about a mission in the middle of a break-in.'

Joe rubbed the back of his neck wearily against the oncoming headache. 'It's my fault, my op. I should have given you clearer orders.'

'You can't blame yourself, Joe. We all cocked up.'

Joe didn't agree. They were better than this. 'Just because the police knew we were here, doesn't make it acceptable that we dropped our guard. Let's get out before we make any more mistakes.'

Chapter 7

Saturday afternoon at Lockwood was official visiting time. As Ember had had two visitors already that week, she wasn't expecting anyone else to come, so she was taken aback when she got the message that Nanny Roe was waiting for her in the lounge. Just released from hospital with an all-clear, she had hot-footed it over to the prison to see Ember.

So much for keeping my nearest and dearest out of this, she thought wryly.

Entering the room, the first thing Ember noticed was that Kate and Raven were chatting with a light-haired man over by the window. She couldn't seem to turn round without the two of them being in her path, though to be fair they were here first. Their visitor had the keenest pair of blue eyes she'd ever seen. His gaze passed over her briefly before returning to the girls. She wondered what he was to the two drug mules? Legal adviser maybe? Simone was with her mother, who came faithfully once a week even though she could barely afford the fare from London. Johnny was sitting happily on his gran's knee, chewing on a rusk. Her own visitor was watching the baby with a fond expression on her face. Nanny Roe simply adored children and had been a little sad that her own charges had grown up so quickly. At least with Max she had someone who was always going to be a little bit of a child no matter what age he was.

'Sweetie, how are you?' Nanny got up from the low sofa with some difficulty. Ironically she had chosen the same place as Devlin, emphasising the contrast between them. Small, almost birdlike, she was reaching the fragile stage of old age when bones were brittle and health unreliable—another thing for Ember to worry about. Mentally, Nanny had become frailer too, becoming forgetful and muddled over simple things she used to handle with ease.

'Hello, Nanny. The real question is how are you?' She exchanged a careful hug, not wanting to squeeze too hard. Nanny's familiar scent filled her nostrils, sweeping her back to childhood. Nanny had been inherited from their father; when she was twenty-five, she had been employed to raise Mick and stayed on as housekeeper until he had his own family. The only good times in Ember's upbringing had been overseen by Nanny Roe in her domain of the nursery, elaborate games and craft activities, ideas taken from a bygone era. She really had been Ember's saving grace. Nanny had never interfered with Mick, though, not even when he struck his children. Brought up in an earlier generation where such things were normal, she had only tutted when she thought the discipline undeserved. Ember's wilfulness had needed curbing, she said, and Max had to learn somehow. A hiding now and then never harmed anyone, according to Nanny's philosophy of child rearing. It was one of the areas on which they never agreed, that and Ember's decision to go vegetarian.

'Oh, I'm fit as a fiddle. The doctors were just being cautious. And would you believe it, they ran a silly test on me and told me I'm getting a little—what did they say?—con-fused? The cheek! They want me to wait until Max comes home again.'

'Oh, I'm sorry.' To be honest, it had cropped up through odd things—lost keys, forgotten appointments—that Nanny wasn't quite as sharp as she once had been, but nothing out of the ordinary for a lady of her age.

'It'll be fine. We'll all be back together soon. You look better than I thought you would,' said Nanny in a pleased tone. 'Are you eating properly? Not living on rabbit food?'

How like Nanny to worry about what she ate when she was facing a murder charge. 'I'm eating well, thanks. We have a kitchen in the girls' unit and cook our own meals.' One of the other trainees was vegetarian so Ember hadn't had to make a point about her diet.

Nanny reached into her squashy bag and took out her knitting. She would never just sit and talk, and always had something to occupy her hands. 'I know you said not to come but once Max told me he had disobeyed I decided to join him. You can't keep your old nanny away, dear. You should've known better.'

'I do. It's good to see you. How is Max?'

'Cross with you.' Nanny pointed a knitting needle at her, causing the staff member standing on duty to tense. He had probably underestimated its ability to be an offensive weapon when he had checked her bag.

'You'd better put that down,' murmured Ember, amused.

'Oh pish! He doesn't really think you're in danger.' Nanny Roe threaded it back into the next row and resumed knitting. Ember noticed Nanny appeared to have lost track of the pattern as the garment was full of dropped stitches and odd colour changes. 'I'm cross too. You shouldn't be in here. Why on earth are you letting them think you did anything to your father? Max and I both know that you wouldn't hurt a fly.'

'They found me with the body.'

'So? You live in that house, don't you? Who else did they expect to find him?'

'And the knife had my prints on it.'

102

'Now that's just pure foolishness. I know about these things.' She dropped her ball of wool and tried to gather it back by pulling on the thread. Ember quickly scooped it up and rewound the wool. 'Thank you, dear. Now where was I? Oh yes, I've seen television documentaries like CSI about all this. The science is not as open-and-shut as they suggest. Get that lawyer of yours to challenge the forensics.'

Ember had a little private smile at the cop drama CSI being described as a 'documentary'. 'You told them I threatened my father.'

'I told them you were both shouting at each other, which you were. I could hear it even in my little kitchen in the annexe. Quite normal for the two of you and it never before led to any violence. I told them that too.'

Ember rubbed at the knot in her chest. What Nanny took as par for the course in a stormy father-daughter relationship the police read as murderous intent. 'But if they don't blame me, then who else will they look at?'

The knitting needles paused, her gaze suddenly alert. 'What are you afraid of, Ember?'

'Where was Max that night, Nanny?'

'In his bed.'

She lowered her voice, keeping her head down so there was no chance of anyone overhearing. 'No, he wasn't. I'm really confused about what happened that morning but I know I tried to find him so he wouldn't be late for school—I do remember that much—and that was before I went into Father's room. Max wasn't in his bedroom in the annexe, neither was Patch.'

The knitting started again. 'There you are: he was walking that dog of his.'

'But the bed hadn't been slept in.'

'Maybe he made it himself when he got up?'

Max never did that. 'He was very upset by the threats to put him in a home. Father said he couldn't take Patch with him. He might've panicked.'

'That doesn't mean he attacked your father.' Nanny clucked her tongue as she dropped her wool again. 'If your brother panicked, I think he would've come up with some half-baked idea of running away to join a circus. He would've got as far as the gate and stopped as he wouldn't have a clue what to do next. He'd be lost without us.'

Ember clenched her hands together to hide that they were shaking. 'I suppose so.' She just didn't trust the police to reach the same conclusion.

Nanny reversed her row. 'Did you check the summerhouse? You know he goes there when he's upset. He always has ever since he was little.'

'No, I didn't. I think I was in a hurry to get Father up in time for his breakfast meeting. I was going to look for Max after that.'

'So you're sitting in here letting them blame you because you think they might turn on your brother? Ember, that is the most foolish thing you've ever done. You will stop it immediately and instruct your solicitor to clear your name instantly.' Ember felt the old grey eyes scan her face, genuinely concerned for her.

'Don't look at me like that, young lady, like I don't know what's what. I brought you up to be a respectable girl, not a prison inmate. I expect better from you.' Respectable was relative in Nanny's world. She didn't count criminal activities of the sort Mick undertook. Bad behaviour was wearing too short skirts or swearing, anything that she judged as not being ladylike.

'Yes, Nanny.'

'And you'll do that? Clear your name?'

But she had a deal with Devlin hanging over her head. 'I'll try.'

'Don't try, succeed.' Nanny gave a firm nod, which was her signal that the subject was closed. The ball of wool rolled so far under the seat this time, the guard had to pick it up and return it. 'Thank you, dear. Now that's all settled, tell me how this play you're doing is going? Fancy our little Ember doing Shakespeare!'

'Ember, I've some excellent news for you.' It was nine-thirty on Monday morning and her solicitor, Ms Pierce, sounded genuinely excited when she made her early call. Mrs Bishop had allowed Ember access to the phone in her office to carry out the private conversation.

'I could do with some good news. What is it?' Ember brushed the dust from the leaves of the ficus on the window-sill. A disconcerting memory of her mother showing her how to clean the leaves, her standing on a chair to reach, bubbled up in her mind. She had forgotten how much her mum had liked plants; she used to tend them with almost suffocating concern. Mum would've said that Mrs Bishop needed some tips in the management of house plants.

'I've just got home from a weekend away and found that the lab got back to us at last. One of the forensic scientists isn't convinced the knife found in the bedroom is the same one as that used in the attack. The other is disputing the findings, but that sliver of doubt is enough for our purposes.'

Ember already knew that the knife wasn't the murder weapon. While she was blurry about the events running up to that moment, she had a clear recollection of Devlin, who had turned up for the breakfast meeting with Mick only to find Ember in shock by the dead body. He had been quick to turn the situation to his advantage. He had pointed out the white-handled knife in her father's chest when he gave her the choice whether Max or she took the fall for the murder. She had recognized it as the one coming from the block in the annexe kitchen, identical to the set in the main house, apart from the colour of the handle. Devlin had known she'd protect her twin at all costs and he loathed Ember, so was delighted to tamper with the evidence to frame her.

'How do they know that about the knife?' asked Ember.

'Something to do with a small discrepancy in the post-mortem measurements. The blade of the knife at the widest part is slightly larger than the wound. Comparing it to the angle and depth of penetration, this means there is now a whisper of doubt that they've got the murder weapon.'

Ember felt a ray of hope. Devlin couldn't blame her because it was he who had made the mistake of assuming the knives were interchangeable. He had fetched the knife from the kitchen, wiped off any prints, and then made her clutch it before dropping it in the pool of blood by the body. She had been shaking so hard she could barely grip it. He had taken the white-handled knife away then called the police anonymously, reporting a 'disturbance' at their address. He must've left the front door wide open because the police had just walked in on her. She had been crying so hard, sobbing, she hadn't even heard them, only felt them when one took her by the arm. She had been incoherent, desperate to find Max, so resisted arrest. By the time she pulled herself together she was in a police cell in restraints. 'Does this mean they're going to drop charges?'

'Unfortunately not. The police are convinced they have the right suspect and have asked for a second opinion. And the fact remains that the blade was found in the bedroom covered in your father's blood with no other prints but yours. Clearly, it is involved in the crime in some way, even if not the implement that delivered the killing blow. Can you cast any light on this for me? Something I can use to argue that they've got the wrong person in custody?'

'Sorry, no.' She hadn't lied to Ms Pierce about not being able to remember clearly what had happened when she went into the bedroom, before Devlin had arrived. She remembered waking up, remembered staggering around the house looking for Max and being in a panic, but then, when confronted with the bloody scene, the shock had set in and all her reasoning processes froze. Fragments loomed large, like the knives, but didn't make much coherent sense. Had Devlin already been there or had he followed her in? She didn't even know that. As Mick's second, he was given preferential treatment and had a key for the house and annexe. He could've arrived at any time.

He could've killed Mick himself.

Everything inside Ember went completely still—she couldn't move, couldn't breathe, for the new idea that was sweeping through her. How could she have been so brainless? She had been so quick to protect Max she hadn't considered any alternatives. It had looked so damning for her brother that she had rushed to condemn herself.

Ms Pierce was waiting for her to elaborate. 'Nothing at all?'

'I didn't kill my father.'

'You know that? Before you've always said you didn't remember.'

Ember took a snap decision. She wasn't going to go down without some attempt to reach the life raft the forensics had sent her way. 'Ms Pierce, I didn't like my father, but I didn't want him dead. I didn't kill him.' It was liberating to say it.

'What did you want, Ember?'

'To be left alone to live my life.'

'That sounds a perfectly healthy thought for a teenager.' Ms Pierce's tone was bracing. 'No one can blame you for that. It's time we thought about building a counter case, challeng-

107

ing this trial by media that's been going on since your arrest—a couple of unflattering photos of you and they decide you're guilty. They should be better than that. They've made terrible mistakes in the past for similar reasons, jumping to conclusions because it sells papers. Do you know anyone who would speak up for you?'

'You can't involve my brother—or Nanny Roe.'

'Understood. But any friends, or people who have seen the real Ember?'

Were there? Her friendship with Joe was too fledgling. She didn't want to tip it out of the nest before it could fly. 'I'm sorry, Ms Pierce, I've not been very good at making friends. My father didn't exactly encourage it.' That was understatement of the year.

'Well then, never mind. We'll fight with what we have. "Beyond reasonable doubt" is what the prosecution has to prove and I'd say there are some very reasonable doubts in this case. To that end I want you to tell me everything about your relationship with your father. Put your thoughts in order and when I next come we'll go over your account.'

Most of it would sound like motive for murder. 'I'll give it some thought.'

'Good. You know, Ember, this really is exactly the breakthrough we needed. I won't let it slip through our fingers.'

Ember put the phone down feeling a strange warmth in her chest. Ms Pierce, a stranger, did genuinely sound like she was weighing in on Ember's side. Doubtless it would be good for her career to be the lawyer who cleared an infamous prisoner of the charge of murder—that didn't worry Ember, it just made Ms Pierce's motives more trustworthy, just like with Joe and his drama college applications. Having been isolated in her home for so many years, surrounded by her father's cronies, Ember was discovering that the world beyond wasn't as bad as she had assumed. There were people on whom you could rely, who would think the best of you rather than the worst, as long as it suited their interests to do so.

At the next rehearsal that came more than halfway through the week, Joe didn't know what to make of Ember's behaviour. She was actually pleasant to him from the outset, thanking him again for the snowdrops, telling him how nice they looked in her room, and then went on to make a joke about Henry's bold choice of waistcoat (gold fans on blue silk). It was like she had been spinning in the microwave on defrost since he had first met her. He had thought her still frozen but when prodded by the simplest of hellos today her response proved her to be well on the way to warming up all the way through. He almost wished he wasn't making such progress so he didn't have to press on with his mission. He would much prefer just to stop here, trying to be a genuine friend to her with no ulterior motive.

'The flowers?' Joe gave her his best smile, feeling all the while more like a bag of popcorn about to reach the point where the kernels were beginning to pop. After a dressing-down by Isaac for getting caught out by the bugging devices in Ember's room, Joe had been ordered to make his move on Ember immediately before someone tipped her off that she was being investigated, not befriended. As Joe anticipated, Isaac had rejected the idea of appealing to her conscience about the dirty bomb as too risky, nor, fortunately, had he wanted to use the brother, not until there was no choice. So charm and deception it was. 'I'm glad you like them. I'll bring more next time. Though I could go wild and get some daffodils.'

'Yeah, push the boat out, why don't you!' She chuckled, a totally new sound from her.

'Or maybe I'll branch out into cuddly toys. I've a really gross gorilla I won at a fair you could have.'

She smiled and shook her head. 'No thanks. Don't like stuffed animals. I find them creepy—dolls too.'

He pretended to be distracted by unpacking his script, hoping his question would seem less interested. 'So you've never had one?'

She shrugged. 'Probably when I was a baby.'

'Really? Not even a much loved bear tucked away somewhere? I thought everyone had one of those.'

'Not me. The only one I've allowed in my room since I had a say over these things was a gift from my brother.'

Result. Max had been the source of the bugged toy. 'You must really love your brother if you took on a creepy doll for his sake.' Joe tapped the pages of the play straight and flicked through to find a scene they shared.

Ember smoothed her copy out on the table, unfolding a bent corner. He had noticed she liked keeping everything straight. 'It wasn't a doll but a tiger. He got it at a fair too. He's surprisingly accurate at those duck shooting games, the one skill our father bothered to teach him.' Her expression darkened.

Joe knew when it was time to back away, though that comment was tempting to follow up with more questions about guns and shooting. That would be way too obvious. 'Cool. A tiger. Much better than a gorilla. So daffodils it is then.'

'You needn't bring me presents,' she said shyly.

'If you can't go outside, then the outside has to come to you.'

She thanked him and turned the conversation to ask him about his plans for drama college. This could've been a disaster but, fortunately, Joe always went into his undercover situations fully prepared for questions, so was able to make some convincing sounds about audition pieces and the claims of Central School over RADA. All the while, though, he really had his mind on the strategy he should use. It was like knowing when to lay down your cards: too soon you lose the game; too late and the best moment might have passed.

'What do you want to rehearse today?' he asked her, buying himself some time before he worked his way round to the subject of sharing her secrets.

'I think we both know our lines. Let's do the dance,' she said. 'I feel as though I've been sitting around and doing nothing for too long.'

'OK. I'm pleased to report that Henry thought our choice of track was promising and wants to see what we'll do with it.' After much searching through the back catalogue of favourite bands, they had picked a recent track that had gothic elements about a doomed wedding that fitted with the marriage-in-Vegas theme of Henry's adaptation of *A Midsummer Night's Dream*. A dream gone sour. 'I think we should do this as a kind of street version of a paso doble. Start with one couple—Titania and Oberon—then have all the others join in.' He had worked out the routine with some help from YouTube instruction videos.

Her eyes sparkled. 'That's like "Roxanne" in *Moulin Rouge*. It's done as a tango but it builds in the same way, one couple to a group number. Ewan McGregor is brilliant in that, singing the counterpoint.'

Joe had seen that film a long time ago but remembered the scene, one of the best in the whole musical. 'Yeah, exactly. Like the tango, the paso has the right kind of harnessed violence that fits the Titania and Oberon relationship.'

'Sounds intriguing. Where do you get your ideas from?' she teased. 'Don't tell me you're a *Moulin Rouge* fan too?'

Joe shook his head. 'I'm more nightclub than ballroom

for dancing, but as an aspiring actor I know my movies. Baz Luhrmann is an interesting director. Did you see his *Romeo + Juliet?'*

'Yes, it's brilliant.'

'He uses dance in that too. Shows how Shakespeare can be transformed with some neat moves.' And didn't that sound cheesy? He suddenly felt hot under the collar. Playing a super confident drama student enjoying putting on a show was close to being a parody of himself. He thought he sounded a jerk.

Fortunately, Ember chose to be more impressed than annoyed by him. 'OK, show us your neat moves then, Oberon.'

The next half hour proved to be more fun than Joe had had on any job. Ember paid attention and caught on quickly, never losing sight of the character she was supposed to portray: the queen of the Vegas underworld, haughty but a mistress of her craft, which in this case meant dancing.

'Are you sure you haven't had lessons since you were a kid?' he asked as she did a flawless travelling spin.

'Just lots of practice dancing in my bedroom,' she said with a shy smile. He got the impression she rarely got any praise and this thought was then followed by the less welcome one that he should use that to reel her in.

'Any other talents you want to share?' He let his tone drop to an intimate one, keeping her in hold longer than necessary. God, was he really doing this?

'I can sing a little. I'm not trained or anything but Max says I sound good.' She smiled self-mockingly. 'Then again, he isn't the most demanding audience.'

'My Titania can dance and sing. I'm one lucky Oberon.' Joe lined up again for the *chassé* step beginning with arms held ready like a street fighter rather than the traditional matador stance, Ember mirroring him, her role in the dance to be the notional cloak. It summed up the inequality in the fairy king and queen marriage, the wife being a trophy to the arrogant Oberon. That was all very well for the demands of the play but the thought entered Joe's head that he wished it could be like when Kieran and Raven had learnt to dance together; their rehearsals had been an important part of their relationship, when they worked out without words how well they went together. By contrast, this time he was betraying his partner, lying with his body as well as what he said, a sour parody of something good.

He finished the dance with a dipping clinch, his face hovering above hers. He could tell he was getting to her, luring her in with his all-too-smooth moves. Problem was she was getting to him too. Just then the mission was the last thing on his mind.

Caught up in the spell of the music, Ember raised her hand and tentatively stroked his cheek. 'I think we should kiss.'

Joe thought that was a terrible idea, though he had been thinking the same. Holding her in his arms, seeing her being so shy with him and sweet, was a temptation. 'You sure?'

'To show that they—we—really are reconciled.'

She was opening the door wide for him. For the mission, for the sake of his promise to see this through, he had to do it even though it would make things far worse for his conscience. He closed the gap and kissed her, using all the tenderness he could find within himself. He could at least make this good for her even if he was betraying her. Her lips were as soft as they looked, slightly parted as they relaxed to accept the light pressure of his mouth. He lifted his head. 'Like that?'

She smiled dreamily. 'Yes, like that.'

He guided her to stand straight. He felt a complete snake. 'You've got that now? All the dance steps?'

'Yes, I think so. You're a very good teacher.'

He took her hand and raised it to his lips to kiss the knuckles. He wanted to honour her, look after her, not lie to her with his charm. Yet what he wanted wasn't what mattered here. 'And you are an exceptional student. Look, Ember, you remember what I said about being able to talk to me the other day?'

She nodded. 'Yes, that was really kind of you, to offer I mean.'

'I want you to take me up on it. I think I could help you.'

'Help me how?'

'Since we met, I've been reading up about you—about your situation, how bad it seems, the way the press are being vile about you.'

'It's horrible, isn't it? I'm surprised you want to talk to me.'

'But I know you're not like that at all. If you tell me you're innocent, I'll believe you. Will you tell me your side of the story? I'd like to be able to put people right when they bad-mouth you to me.'

Looking sweetly touched by his offer, she brushed a hand over his chest. 'You and my lawyer think alike. She says I need to win the trial by press as well as the one in court.'

'And I was thinking . . . if you have something the authorities want, some information, then maybe you could use it to get some concessions?' He ran his finger gently along her jaw. Her skin was incredibly silky.

She stiffened in his arms, instinct for self-preservation tripped. 'Like what?'

Joe knew he couldn't sound too clued-in or she would rumble him. 'Oh, I don't know. In the US where I come from people plea bargain all the time. Don't they do that here?'

'Funnily enough, I'm not the expert, having never been charged with murder before.'

She was getting all snarky again; he was overplaying his hand. 'Sorry, that was tactless of me. I was thinking of how

114

you could get to see more of your brother, get moved nearer or something. I don't suppose you know anything anyway so it was a stupid idea.'

She looked down at the mention of Max. 'Maybe I do have some things I can use to bargain with. You don't live in my father's house without getting an idea of what's going on. I'll mention it to my lawyer. I'd like to be nearer Max.'

'What was going on?'

She arched a brow. 'Researching your next role, Joe?'

He tried to laugh it off. 'Geez, I sound nosey, don't I? Guess it's the actor in me always wanting to understand the lives of others. You never know when it will come in handy.'

She moved away, effectively swimming out of the deeper waters of the conversation by putting physical distance between them. 'I think it's the Oberon effect making you believe you have command over my life. I suppose I should count my lucky stars that you're not a method actor, assuming fairy king privileges all the time.'

'You know about method acting?'

'I like the theatre. I've read up about it—and gone to see plays when I could.' She smiled suddenly as a thought struck her. 'Did you know that Daniel Day Lewis demanded he be wheeled around like his disabled character in *My Left Foot* all during the filming so he didn't break role?'

'And he learnt to build a canoe so he could play the last of the Mohicans.'

'That's awesome! I didn't know that one. Did it float?'

'No idea. But he keeps winning Oscars so he's doing something right. And he's not alone. Brad Dourif, the guy who played Wormtongue in *The Lord of the Rings*—you know, the smarmy adviser to Theoden?' She nodded. Good, she'd watched his favourite films too, more common ground. 'He insisted on using a British accent all during the hundred or more days of production, on and off set, so when he finished and went back to his American accent everyone thought that was fake.'

She laughed. 'Even better. So, Joe,' she poked his shirt, 'are you faking it too? Do you really have a cut-glass English accent, or a German one, or Irish? I'd like Irish. I'm part Irish, so I'm programmed to think the accent is very attractive.'

It was hard to join in the joke when he wanted to shout that, *yes, I am a fake*, and that she shouldn't trust him. 'I can be Irish if you like.' He adopted his best imitation of an Irish accent.

She bit her lip to stop another laugh. 'That's not too shabby. But I wouldn't use it for your RADA audition.'

'OK, I won't. So, do we show Henry our dance now? From the looks he is sending us from the other end of the room, he's ready for us.'

'Let's do it.' She linked her arm with his. 'Lead on, my lord.'

Chapter 8

'How close would you say she is to confiding in you, Joe?'
asked Isaac on that evening's video conference between the
mission centre in the sixth-form block and the YDA headquarters in London. 'Our week is almost up.'

Joe wanted to say Ember was miles away but after today's
rehearsal that wouldn't be the truth. 'Very close. She's well
on the way to trusting me. I'll ask a direct question tomorrow about the shipments. I can say I came across mention of
it on an online news site. She doesn't have access to the web
outside class so won't be able to question how I came by the
information.'

'Excellent. I'll use that to hold off the spooks for another
few days. They're not happy with the speed of our progress so
they're champing at the bit to take over.'

'Thanks, Isaac.'

He waved that away. 'I'll divert them on to tracing the bugging devices you found. Have you given the implications of
that more thought? It's possible someone was still listening,
and seeing you doing a search will certainly have shaken them
up. They'll want to know who you are. The best case scenario
is that it'll make them tip their hand. Worst case is that they
tell Lord and she withdraws all cooperation.'

The boys exchanged grim looks. 'Yeah, we know and we're
sorry,' repeated Joe.

'And I expect you guys to be perfect.' Isaac's tone was wry. 'But my money's on the father being behind the devices in the bedroom. He was a suspicious individual so I can believe he kept his daughter under surveillance even if she were just down the corridor. As he's gone, it will probably turn out to be another dead-end.'

'There've been quite a few of those on this job,' admitted Joe.

'You can't succeed in every mission—that's part of what I have to teach you. But time's against us. We'll have to pull you out if you don't get anything from Lord by the deadline I've agreed with the spooks.'

'What about the play?' asked Nathan.

Isaac looked taken aback. 'The play? What's that got to do with anything?'

'We're due to perform next week for an invited audience including government inspectors who monitor what goes on at Lockwood.'

Joe nodded. 'Henry won't be able to go on with it if he loses half his key actors in one fell swoop, and we'll let the training centre authorities down after they've given us their full cooperation.'

Isaac muttered something damning under his breath. 'You're right. Henry'll never forgive Jan, and by extension she'll never forgive me, if I take you all out before then. Joe, you'd better get results so I can justify keeping the team there.'

'Raven and Kate wouldn't mind staying for a final week if it helps,' said Kieran. 'They're committed to this.'

'They'll stay in prison for the sake of a play?' marvelled Isaac.

'Yeah, you know: the show must go on and all that,' said Nathan, exchanging a grin with Kieran. They were having more fun than Joe as they got to explore the subplot of mixed-up lovers.

'It was a good result you got about that tiger,' said Isaac, returning them to the main topic. 'So it was from the brother. Do you think there's more going on with him than meets the eye? Rose and Damien are convinced he's the innocent he seems.'

'So why put a listening device on his sister?' asked Nathan.

'He could be worried about her, anxious she'll leave him. My sister used to want to know where I was every moment of the day,' suggested Kieran.

Joe was touched Kieran was sharing something so personal about his sister, who had had Downs syndrome and died tragically early of a connected heart condition. Max didn't have anything like that but he clearly relied on his sister for so much. 'That's a good thought, man. Yeah, he could have separation anxiety.'

'But the camera over the wardrobe? That's way more sophisticated,' said Nathan.

'If it's the same person who planted both then they could've just put it in the tiger, as it was there on the bed. It could have nothing to do with Max at all,' argued Joe.

'*If* it's the same person,' repeated Kieran. 'I would say the pattern isn't consistent. The technology behind the camera would've suggested they'd use a similarly advanced listening device. You can buy the one we found on the high street. Very much a do-it-yourself bug.'

'What do you think Lord would say if she found out about the devices?' asked Isaac.

'Why tell her?' Joe countered quickly. 'Does she need to know?' It would hurt badly to find her most private moments had been spied upon, particularly if Max had been involved. If Joe understood one thing about the enigmatic Ember Lord, it was that she loved her brother.

Isaac fixed Joe with one of his laser blue stares. 'The more ammunition we have, the quicker we might be able to break her from her existing loyalties. We want her to turn to us and away from her old associates. You know that, Joe, so I'm a little worried you're thinking of Lord's feelings rather than the job.'

The pause that followed was more than slightly awkward for everyone sitting with Joe. He felt he had to defend himself and, by extension, Ember. 'Isaac, she isn't what we thought.'

'People usually aren't.'

'She's . . . nicer. I think she's vulnerable.'

'I'm pleased to hear it. A nicer, more vulnerable person will want to stop a dirty bomb being exploded in a European capital. But we don't have time to find that out. We have to get her talking to us straight away.'

'Yes, but—'

'And she admitted to you that she learnt a thing or two living under her father's roof.'

'Yeah, yeah she did.'

'I'm not saying she's personally responsible for the shipment of nuclear material but she's likely to know the key players involved, the usual routes, the people bribed to turn a blind eye.'

Joe knew all this and felt embarrassed that Isaac felt obliged to remind him. 'Sorry, Isaac.'

'It's OK, Joe, we all know we're pushing you to do something out of character. If I thought another method would work as well I'd be on it like a shot. You're right to keep challenging me on it: just because she's a suspected murderer doesn't mean she doesn't deserve as much careful handling as we can give her. She's only seventeen after all. That's what I've been telling MI5.' His gaze flicked to his phone. 'Hold a moment: there's a call coming in from Damien.' He switched to the mobile, expression turning grim. 'Yes? What? In hospital? How bad?'

'Has something happened to Damien?' asked Joe. 'Rose?'

Isaac shook his head, intent on whatever it was that Damien was telling him. 'Yes, I'll pass the information on. You stick with him for now.' He ended the call. 'Max Lord was set upon by a gang a few minutes ago while he was out walking his dog. Fortunately, Damien and Rose were waiting in the park to meet him so were able to intervene and run the guys off. Damien is in the ambulance taking Max to A&E, and the boy's likely to be admitted as the paramedics suspect concussion and possible fractures to his wrist and ribs. Rose has stayed behind to look for the damn dog, which ran off on the first sign of trouble. Bloody useless excuse of a guard dog if you ask me.'

'Random?' asked Joe, fearing he knew the answer. He'd been half-expecting something to happen after they had been caught by the cameras, he just hadn't anticipated the backlash going in Max's direction. None of them had.

'What are the odds of that? I'm fairly certain that being Mick Lord's son will factor into the equation somewhere. I think your night time excursion has driven our spy to take action. They've tipped their hand. Whoever was monitoring that room feels the need to ramp up the pressure on the Lords. If they hit the boy, they hurt the sister.'

Joe swore. That made it his fault. Who would gain from this? Mick's successor? Seamus Devlin? And what did it mean if Devlin had been the one monitoring Ember? Had he just taken over monitoring the devices after the death of Mick or had he been the one to plant the bug in the first place as a way of neutralising his rival? Joe thought the first option was most likely. While Mick, well-known to be careful about his personal security, would not allow his second-in-command freedom to plant the bugs without his say-so, that didn't mean that if Devlin had done it on the father's order, he hadn't exploited his knowledge that the CCTV feed existed. Eliminating

Ember from the running before she became an adult left him in uncontested control of Mick's organization. As Joe tried to puzzle that one out, Isaac continued:

'Damien mentioned that Max is extremely distressed. He wants to see his sister and Damien—whatever happened to my steely Cobra?—thinks we should see if we can swing a visit to comfort him.'

What had happened to hard man Damien? Rose had happened, thought Joe, recalling how his friend was no longer afraid to show his softer side since he fell in love with the cute genius who had lived next door to Joe's family in Manhattan.

'Are you going to do it? Arrange a visit, I mean?' asked Nathan.

'I think that would be a good idea. For the mission, of course.' Isaac smiled.

'Yeah, for the mission,' echoed Joe. And not because Isaac had his compassionate side too, naturally. 'And if we were the ones to upset the balance, then I think we owe them both, don't you?'

Ember felt like she'd stepped on ice and plunged through into water.

'What do you mean "Max is in hospital"?' Standing with her back to the window she couldn't make sense of the sympathetic expressions of Mrs Bishop and her colleague, Miss Kearney.

'I'm sorry, Ember dear, but it's true. He was set upon by some thugs and has ended up in Mile End hospital. Now don't panic—he's going to be fine—but he wants to see you and we have agreed to escort you over there now.'

'Not Max. Why would anyone harm Max?' Arms crossed, she clawed at her elbows, nails digging in against the gnawing panic threatening to take over.

Mrs Bishop exchanged a worried look with her colleague, neither of whom had ever seen Ember so distraught. 'The good news is some friends came to his rescue. One of them is with him right now.'

'Who?'

'A boy called Damien. Apparently his girlfriend has found Max's dog and is looking after it.'

Ember tried to shake off her frozen state. It was horribly like how she had reacted when she found her father. Why wasn't she better at dealing with shock? God, she was so pathetic.

'I can see from his letters he likes that dog, so he'll be pleased, won't he?' Mrs Bishop gestured to the pictures Ember had recently pinned to her cork board.

'Yes, he will.'

'The injuries aren't life-threatening so he'll bounce back, you'll see. So get your coat then. It's cold.'

It finally penetrated Ember's consciousness that she was being taken to Max. She sprang into action, grabbing her jacket.

'I'm afraid you'll have to be handcuffed to Miss Kearney here,' Mrs Bishop continued.

Ember didn't care as long as it got her to Max as quickly as possible. She thrust out her right hand and didn't even flinch when the handcuff snapped around her wrist.

'Good girl. We'll be there in an hour and a half driving at this time of night. Follow me.'

They drove to Mile End in a police car, Ember's cuff locked to a restraint loop attached to the seat belt for the journey. There wasn't much conversation so she had plenty of time to worry about Max. She remembered the last time she'd rushed to get to the hospital on the occasion of her mother's overdose. In the last few weeks of her life, Mum had lost interest in everything, including her children, almost as if she were no longer there. Then one night, after a terrible row with Mick, she had taken her sleeping pills and never woken up. To this day, Ember blamed her father for driving her mother to that extreme, grinding her down with his constant belittling and bullying. He'd told her repeatedly she was worthless, laughed at the idea of divorce, saying no one would let her see her children, and one day, in a weak moment, she had believed him, and taken what she thought was the only way out for her. That's what it was like to get dragged into the black hole of Mick Lord's crushing gravity, and why Ember had struggled so hard to make sure she and Max escaped.

The car turned off the motorway and slowed for the city roads. The windscreen wipers battled with the drizzle. Ember leant her head against the back of the seat, incredibly weary. Was that how her mother had felt at the end, out of all resources? No, no, Ember reminded herself, she'd always thought that taking an overdose had seemed out of character. She could imagine her mother drifting in a tranquillized haze, but not giving up entirely. Ember had sometimes wondered if their father had been responsible, or at least manoeuvred Anne-Marie into doing it. He hadn't grieved even for one second when she passed, not even bothering to attend the funeral.

It was a dire comment on her family, thought Ember, that she preferred to think her father capable of murder than her mother of suicide.

The car turned into the Mile End Hospital car park and drew up at the entrance. A policeman came out and opened the rear door. Miss Kearney unsnapped the cuff from the restraint and put it on her left wrist.

'Ready, Ember?'

Ember slid out and followed her escort into the building.

'Where is he?'

'He's in a single room in the Head Injuries Unit,' said the

policeman. 'We thought it prudent to put a guard on his door.'

'A guard? Why?' But she knew.

'Indications suggest this wasn't a random attack, Miss. Your family has its enemies.'

A policewoman stood in the corridor outside the little room given to Max. She opened the door for them on seeing her colleague return.

'The doctor said it was fine for him to have visitors.'

Ember looked down at her wrist. That would distress Max. 'Please, do I have to . . . ?' She held up her right hand.

The two members of staff from Lockwood exchanged looks.

'I suppose there are police officers on the door, and we're on the fifth floor,' said Mrs Bishop.

'I give you my word I won't take advantage of it.'

Mrs Bishop suddenly smiled. 'No, I don't think you will.' She gave a nod to her junior colleague to undo the cuff.

'Thank you,' Ember said softly.

'You've been no trouble until now, so I prefer to trust my evaluation of your character rather than your reputation,' explained Mrs Bishop.

'I . . . thank you.' Ember felt incredibly moved by the woman's faith in her on so little evidence.

'You're a changed girl since you started joining in—we've all noticed. Go on, go see your brother. Poor lamb.'

They were letting her go in alone. Ember stepped inside. The curtain was drawn a little so she couldn't see his head but his left arm was lying by his side in plaster.

'Max?'

A blond-haired boy emerged from behind the curtain, putting down a magazine on the bedcover.

'Ember? I'm Damien,' he said quietly. 'Max has just drifted off. I'm due to wake him in twenty minutes to check on him.'

Ember returned the introduction with an awkward shrug. She didn't want anyone else here but she couldn't ignore the boy who'd saved her brother. 'Is he OK?'

'Yeah, or will be now you're here. He's been asking for you and Patch in that order since he was admitted.'

She tried to smile but it didn't come right. 'I'm glad I rate above the dog.'

'Only just.' Damien smiled back. 'Patch is with my girl-friend so you needn't worry about that.'

Ember went round to the other side of the bed and could now see Max lying, eyes closed, head propped up on pillows.

'Did he say who attacked him?'

'No, but there's footage. The police are looking at it.'

'That's lucky.'

'Taken by a passer-by. On a mobile.'

'I hope that means they catch them.' She brushed a lock of hair off Max's forehead noticing the bruising to his face. He was going to have a terrible black eye by morning.

'Ember?' Max must have heard her. He shifted on the pillow and opened his eyes, familiar smile warming her chilled heart. 'You came.'

'You know me: wild horses wouldn't keep me away.'

'I was attacked.'

'I know, love.'

'But I'm OK.'

'I can see.'

'My friends saved me.'

'Yes.' Ember wished she'd been there herself. Swallowing, she turned to Damien. 'Thank you.'

'It was nothing,' he said, dropping his gaze to the floor.

Max struggled to sit up. 'It wasn't nothing. He was like a ninja turtle, launching himself on the people who attacked

126

me even though there were more of them. And Rose—she whipped them with her dog lead.'

Damien smiled at that. 'Yeah, she did. Been taking lessons from a friend.'

'In what?' asked Max.

'Using a whip. It's a party trick thing. Circus skill.'

Odd. Joe had said that Kieran was a fiend with a bull whip. How had it become so popular among her age group without her noticing? Or was it just a weird coincidence?

'So Ember, are you going to stay with me now?' asked Max in his usual direct manner.

Ember sat on the edge of the bed and caressed his fingers where they poked out of the caste. 'You know I can't.'

'But I need you.'

'I'm trying to fix things so I can be with you soon. I promise.' *Please don't argue about that*, she thought. *Not now. I couldn't bear it.*

Damien grabbed his jacket. 'Look, you don't want me hanging around. I'll go down and get something to eat at the canteen. Can I fetch you anything?'

'No, I'm good, thanks.'

'I'd like a muffin,' said Max quickly.

Damien nodded. 'Sure thing, partner. Chocolate if they've got it?' It was disconcerting to find a stranger knowing so much about her brother.

'Yes please.' Max's eyes were shining. 'The hospital food is terrible.'

'I'll grab a couple in case your sister changes her mind. See you in half an hour.'

'Oh, you don't need to stay,' said Ember quickly.

Damien looked serious. 'I wouldn't if you were able to do so, but I guess they're going to take you back tonight?'

She gave a reluctant nod.

'Then I think it best Max has a friendly face with him, don't you? His foster parents have their own children to look after and Nanny Roe is too distressed to be an asset. They had to sedate her and send her home earlier. She won't be back until tomorrow. It's me or no one.'

Yet another thing to thank him for. And Nanny Roe? She'd had one shock after another; she couldn't cope at her age. Ember would have to get a message to her. 'That's . . . very kind of you. I'm grateful.'

He gave her a wink. 'Just making sure I play the Good Samaritan all the way to the end of the story.' He looked down at his phone as it vibrated. 'And another piece of good news for you, Max: Rose is outside with Patch. She's walking him on the grass verge and if you . . . yes, there she is.' Damien pulled up the blind. Sitting up, Max had a good view of a red-haired girl walking the boxer up and down the sorry strip of green outside in the floodlit car park, her coat collar turned up against the rain.

'Patch!' Max stretched his fingers towards the window. 'He's OK.'

'Of course he's OK. I told you he was. Right, muffins it is. I'll tell Rose you've seen him so she can take him home.'

'You're my best friend, Damien,' Max declared stoutly.

A strange expression flickered across the boy's face.

Please don't hurt my brother's feelings, pleaded Ember privately.

'I'm honoured to be your mate, Max. And mates bring muffins to people with bumps on their heads so I won't be long.'

Thank you, breathed Ember, glad the boy had dealt with Max's outpouring of gratitude so diplomatically.

'Isn't he so cool!' Max was grinning now. She had expected to find him downcast but now he had both Ember and Damien there he seemed in good spirits.

'How are you feeling?' she asked. 'Tell me the truth now.'

'My arm hurts, and my head. My chest too. The doctor said it was mostly bruising and that I'd live. I could've told him that I would live. It isn't too bad. Father hit harder than those wimps.'

'Wimps?'

'Damien said they ran off like scaredy cats when he unleashed Rose on them. He called her his secret weapon.'

Ember added another reason to be grateful to Damien to the long list, he had managed to turn a terrifying incident into something amusingly heroic for Max. It didn't solve the problem, though, of how to protect her brother in future. If there were policemen on the door, they were expecting more trouble. 'I'm sorry it happened, Max.'

'Don't worry, Ember, I'll be better very soon. I don't even have to stay in hospital after tonight if there are no . . . oh, I forgot what he said . . .'

'Complications?'

'Yes, them.'

'I'm glad. And I'm glad Damien and Rose were there.'

Max reached out and pulled her head down to his shoulder for a hug. It was devastating to have her back patted by her lovely brother. He was the one who was hurt, not her. 'You don't need to worry about me, Ember. Worry about yourself for once.'

With the long drive back, Ember didn't return to her room at Lockwood until the early hours of the morning. After dismissing Miss Kearney for the night, Mrs Bishop hovered outside for a moment.

'You'll be all right now? I've asked the hospital to give me regular updates but it's likely your brother will be discharged tomorrow.'

'I'll be fine, Mrs Bishop. Thank you for taking me.'

Mrs Bishop gave her a nod and walked away. Ember's first impression of her had been right: she really was a kind woman.

Ember opened her door and felt along the wall for the light. She was ready to fall face down on her bed with exhaustion. Even half a muffin at ten o'clock wasn't giving her a big enough sugar rush to continue any longer. Hanging her jacket on the back of the desk chair, she saw someone had left an envelope on the bed. Flipping it over she discovered that there was nothing written on it. Strange. Debating whether it was worth checking before turning in, she slid her finger under the sealed flap and pulled out the contents to have a quick read through. Perhaps Henry had sent her a script revision?

But it was nothing like that. The top sheet was a white piece of A4 with a chilling message: *Tonight was a warning. Next time we won't stop at a kicking. Say* _nothing_ *to anyone. You are under surveillance.*

A lump formed in Ember's throat. As she feared from the moment she had heard about it, the attack on her brother hadn't been bad luck; he'd been targeted. Devlin—who else?— had hit out at her brother to remind her that her only use to him was her silence. He'd warned her and now he'd delivered on his threat. But why now? She'd been keeping her side of the bargain, hadn't she?

She dropped the message on the bed and leafed quickly through the rest of the contents. At first it took a moment for her to work out what she was seeing. Her bedroom. Two shadowy figures conducting a search. The torch light fell on the face of one of them, revealing a profile very like that of Damien. No, it couldn't be. She took the photos over to the bedside light for a better look. Yes, it was Damien, wearing a black hat pulled over his fair hair, and the other one . . . The photos fell from her nerveless fingers when she came across

130

the last picture in the file. It was of Joe looking straight into the camera, three other boys behind him. Damien she had already identified, and the other two looked like his fellow actors, Kieran and Nathan.

Was it a clever hoax? Had Devlin mocked this up in Photoshop to unnerve her? But who would link a boy who had befriended her brother in London with three drama students near Milton Keynes? And another thing: how had the envelope got on her bed? Whom had Devlin bribed? Was she being watched even now?

Stop, Ember. Think. She collapsed to her knees, head on the duvet. She had to sort out the truth from the lies if she wanted to survive. But how could she think when she felt like she'd just been pushed down a flight of stairs in the dark, and was lying broken at the bottom? How many more hurts could she take?

You take one more, Ember. That's what life had taught her. She could always take another hit because she had to; there was no ducking option when she was blindsided like this by the blow.

What did she know? That Joe had shown unusual interest in her case, tried to make friends from the outset. She had found excuses for him, but what if he were just doing it because he was paid to do so? Who could be behind that? A newspaper? And as for Damien, he had been conveniently on hand to stop the attack on Max, as well as not hesitating to drive her brother all the way from London to Lockwood on the pretext of dog-walking. That wasn't normal. She should've been more suspicious. Was he also being paid to get the inside scoop? Throw in Nathan and Kieran and you had a full-blown conspiracy. Who else knew? Henry? Mrs Bishop? How far did this go?

Ember screamed into the duvet. It had all been a set-up.

Nothing had been real. No one had liked her, or wanted to be her friend. The boys had broken into the house, causing Devlin to strike out at Max. Worse still, her lovely innocent brother who treated the whole world as his friend, had been betrayed and would be crushed when she broke the news. She had to tell him though, else he'd think his new mate was looking out for him. He'd be unbearably hurt. She could strangle Damien for that betrayal alone.

I can't stand this. She ground her head into the duvet but that wasn't enough. She wanted to smash something, storm, rail, and weep, but there was nothing big enough that she could do, no gesture that would relieve the pressure inside her.

You've been here before, a small voice in her brain told her. *When Father broke Max's tooth, when he slapped you so hard you blacked out. You're Mick Lord's children. People hurt you. It's what they do. You shouldn't be surprised.*

Yet she would've preferred Mick's blatant violence to this disguised attack on her trust; at least then her hatred had felt healthy, clean-cut, not this horribly twisted emotion. She had been aware of something emerging in her over the last week, like a moth from a chrysalis, a frail hope that she could begin to fly free. These photos swatted that dead.

Exhausted by the torrent of emotions, Ember turned to sit on the floor, head resting on her knees. An odd memory came to her. She'd found an old moth in the spout of a watering can in November. It had crawled in there to overwinter but died before spring came and ended up blocking the nozzle. The only way to clear it was to poke it free with a stick, and it immediately crumbled into dust. That was what this felt like. Everything crumbling.

Habits of a lifetime came to her rescue. *Come on, Ember. You know what to do. Tough as nails. Mean as a snake. Chip off the old block. You can handle this.* She might cringe to remember how she had trusted enough to suggest that Joe kissed her—God, what an idiot she'd been—but there was no shame in that. She had been honest in wanting to kiss him even if he hadn't.

Fury bloomed again, red and bitter-tasting. Enough of making herself vulnerable. No more cooperation. No joining in. To give Devlin no excuse to hurt Max, she wasn't going to say anything to anyone, and if that meant she was found guilty then she'd take her sentence too. She couldn't, wouldn't risk her brother.

And as for Joe? The two-faced jerk would soon learn that Ember Lord was no one's fool.

Chapter 9

Armed with daffodils and a fresh supply of chocolate bars, Joe breezed into the education centre determined that this was the day when he would get some usable intelligence out of Ember. After the dance and the kiss, surely she would be ready to listen to him? He couldn't stop thinking about her, how she was shifting in his mind like an image put through a photo filter, turning harsh colours soft. She appeared to like him too and would be ready, he guessed, for some sympathy after last night's events. And he wanted to be the one to comfort her, Joe realized. She had ceased to be just a target and had become Ember, his complex, mercurial Ember Lord.

About time too, said his conscience, kicking him in the notional butt.

The room was busy, as set-building had begun, but Joe couldn't see his quarry. In one corner, Kate wielded a paint brush while Kieran rigged some lights over the casino sign. Nathan was using his artistic skills to do the fancy lettering. Raven was closest, perched on a table as she tacked the hem on a navy blue evening gown. When she saw him, she signalled for him to join her.

'Where's Ember?' Joe asked her.

Raven quickly checked that no one was close enough to overhear.

'Bad news. We've not seen her. She's not left her room.' She snipped off the thread.

'What? But I thought the visit to see her brother would reassure her?'

'I don't know about that, but she refused breakfast.' Raven wrinkled her nose in thought. 'When I say refused, I mean she just blanked all requests to come and eat. She's sitting at her desk writing and not saying anything to anyone.'

'But why?'

'I'm not sure but something's definitely changed. Kate and I called in to ask her to come over to rehearsal and she just looked at us as if we were nothing.' Raven shook her head. 'No, that's not right. She looked at us as if *she* were nothing, not even there. It's like we're back to square one.'

'Damn, we can't have that now, not when we're so close. I don't want the spooks to take over, do you? They'll chew her up and spit her out.'

'No, but I don't want that shipment to reach its destination. She's got to tell us what she knows one way or another.'

'It must be something to do with her brother.' It wasn't the first time Ember had been difficult but it was really inconvenient that she'd chosen today of all days. What could Joe do about it? 'Look, I can't go over there without an escort. Will you take her these and say her Oberon requests her presence, or something charming? Hopefully that will cheer her up.'

Raven took the daffodils. 'I don't know, Joe. I think the situation's gone past charm.'

'Please?'

Against her better judgement, Raven put aside her sewing and hopped off the table. 'Here goes nothing.'

Joe prowled the room, not settling to any of the hundred jobs that had to be done to get the production ready. Kieran and Nathan kept meeting his eyes but what could he say? For some reason, Ember was cutting up difficult this morning, and Damien had said she was very pleasant to him at the hospital just a few hours ago. What had gone wrong?

Raven came back with a handful of bent daffodils. 'Here, I suppose you could call that some kind of response.' She thrust them back at Joe. 'I think it's safe to say that your Titania is in a royal snit.'

Joe's gut was telling him this was more than a snit. Ember could be moody but she wasn't petty. 'Tell me what you saw in her room.'

'Nothing. I mean there's nothing personal on display. There never was very much.'

'I gave her some snowdrops. She said she put them on the windowsill.'

'No, that's bare. She did have some things on her cork board last time I called in, some cute pictures of a dog, her brother's handiwork, but they've gone.'

Joe kicked the table leg. 'Dammit.'

'What are you thinking?' Raven picked up her gown again and pretended to sew.

'Isaac mentioned a worst-case scenario—someone tells her about us and she stops cooperating. I think we've gone one beyond that: Ember's been silenced.'

'The attack on her brother?'

'Yes. But I guess she no longer trusts me.' He held out the daffodils. They flopped pathetically in his fist. 'If it were just Max, she wouldn't have done that.'

'She did look really angry when I gave her your message.'

'Did she say anything?'

'No, just snapped the stems and threw them out into the corridor. I took that as my cue to leave. I got the impression she wasn't going to talk to anyone, and certainly not me. I think she thinks I'm stupid.'

'Don't be so sure of that. She defended you when she thought I'd said you shouldn't get together with Kieran.'

'What?'

'Yeah, she noticed you were more than friends and took my expression as disapproval. I was just going to tell Kieran to take care not to tip anyone off that you already knew each other.'

'I see. Oh, OK, I think I like her more now, even if she is being a difficult cow.' Raven grinned. 'I have it from reliable sources that I have my obstreperous heifer days too.'

'Don't we all. Any suggestions how we handle this?'

'I don't think either Kate or I will get through to her. You're clearly not flavour of the month.' Raven threaded a needle to begin alterations on another costume. 'How about seeing if Henry can coax her out? You saw what she was like when he praised her the other day: it was like he'd presented her with a precious gift.'

'You're right. Let's see if Henry can bring her out of herself.' Joe sought out the director and spotted him draping fabric over one of the actors. The waistcoat alone—candy stripes—might be enough to conjure a smile from Ember.

'I doubt he can get her to spill the beans about the shipment,' said Raven.

'One step at a time: let's get her over here first and go from there.'

Ember ignored the brisk tap. She had lost count of the number of people who had knocked on her door but so far her refusal to respond had worked. She didn't lock it, as that would only spark an emergency use of the pass key, but neither did she engage when someone came in. Apart from the flare of anger when Joe sent his fricking flowers, she had managed to pass the morning in a numbed state where nothing much mattered.

She had experienced this numerous times before in her up-bringing, knew it could last for days. In the past it had worried her, made her think of her mother's decline; today, however, she welcomed it like a friend. It could be a muffling blanket between her and the world.

Underlining the title of the poem she had just written, she had wondered idly if she had a case for prosecuting Joe, Damien, and the rest. They hadn't exactly hacked her voice-mail, but they'd presented themselves to her under false pretences. Was that illegal? Who would care what a murder suspect thought anyway? She was too exhausted to put any energy into pursuing it. Apart from a few smiles and a kiss, they hadn't got much out of her to feed the tabloids. She'd keep that as her victory.

The door opened and Henry Rawlings came in, Mrs Bishop at his shoulder.

'Do you think I could have a word in private with Ember?' he asked the manager politely.

The woman nodded. 'I'll stand out in the corridor with the door open, if that's all right with you. Child protection poli-cies and so on.'

'Quite right, quite right.' Out of the corner of her eye, Ember saw Henry sit on the bed, keeping his distance. His waistcoat was the only colourful thing in the room; it stuck out like a robin's breast in the snow.

A few minutes passed and still he said nothing. So he was playing some psychological game with her, was he? That made her feel angry again. She put down her pen. No, she wasn't going to react, that was what he was waiting for.

Finally, his silence pushed her to breaking point.

'If you've not got anything to say, then why are you here?' she snapped, furious with herself that she had been the first to blink.

'I'm sorry, my dear, I was just resting. I've had a hellish week, driven from pillar to post by conflicting demands. I found your silence soothing.'

She turned and saw that he was indeed leaning with his head against the wall, eyes closed.

He was an actor, or at least a director of actors, he was probably bluffing.

'Do you want to know what's upsetting me?' Henry continued.

She bit her lip.

'I'm going to tell you anyway. You see, Ember, after a horrendous month, I had begun to enjoy myself here, believing that I had something to give. Ideas had flown from me like sparks from a blacksmith's anvil. I'd begun to glow and people noticed.'

In Ember's opinion, he had always shone with creativity. This didn't sound like him. Was he speaking for her?

'Then I got scared. Something happened to someone I love and I retreated to my safe place.'

Oh God, he *was* talking about her. Ember's throat closed up as she struggled against tears.

'The problem is my safe place is very lonely. I have to live there like Robinson Crusoe on his island without even a Man Friday to keep me company. I manage by wrapping myself in fog, letting it take over and blank out everything that's too painful. I tell myself if I don't move, don't speak, then I can't be held responsible for anything that happens. I won't be to blame.

'There's a hitch though. Life doesn't stop just because I pretend it does. Bad things still happen. I can't protect the one I love so I'll eventually have to trust someone else to do the job. If I say nothing, then I won't be able to shape that outcome. Ride the horse or be trampled by it: these are the only two options life gives us.'

Ember rubbed at her throat, doubting that her voice would emerge even if she wanted to say something. 'Did you know?' she croaked.

'Know what, Ember?'

'Did you know that your students are investigating me? Are the papers paying you too?'

'The papers? Whatever put that idea in your head?'

Ember took the last photo out of her desk and handed it to him.

He dug his glasses out of his breast pocket and took a closer look. 'Intriguing.'

'Intriguing?'

'Quite good lighting, considering. Gives the sense of danger, doesn't it?'

'It's not a still from a film, Henry. It's real. It's Joe and the others breaking into my bedroom.'

'And you think it's the papers that put them up to it? Some cheap journalistic ploy?'

'Who else could it be?'

'You're a clever girl: work it out.' He sat in silence, photo on his knee.

Her sense of betrayal deepened. 'My God, you did know!'

'With five young detectives on my team, I'm either stupid or devious if I appear not to notice. I prefer devious.'

'Five?'

Henry grimaced. 'Perhaps I shouldn't have said that. I'm not cut out for this secret-keeping malarkey.'

How far did this thing spread? Who else had distinguished themselves as trying to make friends with her. 'Kate? Raven? Simone?'

'Not Simone.'

She gave a mirthless laugh. 'You'll have me questioning baby Johnny's motives next. I hope you asked for money up

140

front as you're not getting anything else from me, nothing to feed the piranha press. Go away, Henry.'

He closed his eyes, head back as before. 'I'm offended you think I'd have anything to do with a paper of that species. They've gnawed on my bones often enough; I'm hardly going to feed them someone else. I've better things to do. And you haven't answered the real question yet.'

'What question?'

'Who brought us here, and why I'm able to sit in your very Spartan room with the full cooperation of Mrs Bishop outside?'

Ember's eyes flicked to the open door. 'This is official?'

'Oh, I'm not really part of it, just a means to an end.' His shrewd gaze returned to her face. 'My interest is in putting on the best play I can next week and making a difference to the lives of the cast members who've been brave enough to get involved. Don't you forget that. But yes, you've got the authorities very worried. You've got me worried, as I love London too.'

'Me? What've I done?'

'That's what you need to find out. I think it's time you had a frank talk with the team, don't you? You might find it very therapeutic. Have a good shout at Joe: the boy can take it and it would make him feel better. He's hated taking this approach with you from the beginning. He's fighting the fact he's sweet on you.' Henry got up. 'Now, Ember, I know once I leave you'll be tempted to go back to your silent act but consider this: these young people are the good guys, even if you've been hurt by their methods. Ask yourself if you're such a saint that you haven't made mistakes with other people too? They didn't beat up your brother but stopped the ones trying to do so. If you are going to rely on anyone, who are you going to pick?' He checked his watch. 'The cast is on a break until twelve. I'll expect you back for then.'

'Henry, I hate you.'

He beamed like she'd just given a good answer in a test. 'That's encouraging. Most actors end up hating me at one time or another during the production. It means I'm getting through to them. And don't forget, there is a law here even greater than the ones our friends are interested in.'

'What law?'

'That the show must go on.' He shut the door behind him, proving he also knew how to judge his exits.

Ember glared at the door. If she hadn't stripped her room of all personal touches, she might've still had a mug of flowers to throw at him. What right did he have to waltz in here and tell her she had to cooperate? She didn't care about the bloody show! None of them understood what the real stakes were if she spoke to them. Could they keep Max safe? They hadn't last night.

But you're being manipulated by Devlin and you hate him far more than you hate Henry, Joe, and the others.

It didn't help that she knew that voice in her head was right. She'd been backed into this corner and the more she struggled the more her room for manoeuvre shrank.

Devlin might've been the one to kill your father. You could be suffering all this to protect entirely the wrong person.

That was a depressing thought. Had she got this whole situation upside down from the beginning? She'd been like a row boat adrift in a storm, chucked one way then another. All her life she had wanted to be the powerboat cutting through the waves, making others sorry they got in her way. Ember Lord had decided early she wouldn't be weak and here she was moping, allowing others to trick her without any comeback?

She got up so quickly the chair clattered to the floor. Quarter to twelve. Right: she was going to have this out here and now. Stuff Henry, stuff the play, and most especially stuff fricking deceitful Oberon. Titania was going to give him a piece of her mind.

The double doors to the rehearsal space banged open. Joe looked up to find Ember standing in their centre, fury emanating from her like a force field.

'Get out—everyone but those five.' She pointed an accusing finger at Raven, Kieran, Nathan, Kate, and Joe. The two staff members jumped up but Henry waved them back.

'It's fine. I asked her to do this. It's an improvisation,' said the director. 'They're perfectly safe.'

From Ember's expression, Joe wasn't so sure about that.

'Rest of you, out!' demanded Ember.

'What the—!' said the big guy playing Cobweb. 'You can't order us about.' He took up a belligerent stance, chin thrust forward.

Henry, however, moved swiftly between the two most feisty members of his cast. 'I think our play queen has something she needs to get off her chest. Come now, Raymond, I'll take your fairy enforcers to the performance space and we can go through your fight scene.'

Cobweb-Raymond dropped his chin. 'We have a fight scene?'

'You do now.'

'Cool. OK then. Leave Queen Tit here to fly through fricking flood and fire to have her tantrum.'

'Excellent, Raymond. That's exactly what I've been telling you: use your words not your fists to lay the other low.' Henry patted the big guy on the back. Shakespeare had done wonders for the boy's vocabulary as he delivered his 'Over hill, over dale' speech as a rap.

'Fine, don't want to stay in here with her anyway.' Giving Ember a rude gesture, Cobweb led the rest of the actors out.

After a whispered conference with the staff, Henry withdrew, leaving Ember alone with the YDA students.

'The game's up.' She threw a pile of photographs on the floor. From the ones that fell face upwards, Joe quickly gathered what the rest showed. 'I'll have you charged with breaking and entering.'

Joe swept them up. Wouldn't do for the other cast members to see that. 'It would be wasting your time, Ember. We had police permission to search the crime scene.'

'Of course you did. Who the hell are you?'

'Why don't you sit down?' Raven pulled out a chair.

'No, I don't want to sit down. I want answers.'

'Then we're after the same thing,' said Joe.

'Hah! I doubt that very much. What are you doing here? You don't look more than my age but Henry says you're detectives. What did he mean?'

So Henry had finished the job that the photographs had begun: well and truly blowing their cover. Joe had to make a snap decision: carry on lying to her or see what the truth would do? Henry hadn't really left them much of an option. 'We're students of a college that trains young people for roles in law enforcement. On occasion we take on undercover assignments like this when an older operative can't do it.'

'And you're all here to . . . what?' Her gaze lingered on each in turn, expression cold. 'Spy on me? Get something out of me?'

'Yes.'

'So the play, the pretending to be my friend, "Oh Ember have some flowers", was all a set-up?'

'Yes.'

She turned away in disgust. 'At least you're honest now. I suppose I have to thank you.'

'For what?'

144

'For reminding me of what I already knew. Trust no one.'

'Ember—' She couldn't be more disgusted with him than he was with himself. He had said all along the damage would be serious when she finally worked out she'd been a target in their operation.

'You can tell the ones who sent you that you're wasting your time. Go back to wherever it is you come from. You're not getting anything out of me.'

Joe could see any chance of cooperation from her sailing out of sight unless he did something to change her mind quickly. Five against one wasn't helping. 'Guys, could I have a moment, please?' he asked his friends.

'Sure. We'll see how the other fight is coming along.' As Raven passed Ember, she draped the gown over a chair next to her. 'I finished your hem. It's going to look great on you.'

'You just don't give up,' said Ember, folding her arms.

'No, we don't.' Raven ushered the others out, Kieran and Nathan sending him commiserating looks.

Joe got out his last pretty feeble weapon: his selection of chocolate bars. He began juggling them. 'Which one do you want?'

'Are you making fun of me?' Ember sounded hurt as well as aggrieved.

'Nope. Raven said you'd not had any breakfast. Same as last time?' He flipped one of the bars towards her but she let it fall at her feet.

'I suppose that girl, Rose, was in on it too?'

'Why do you say that?'

'The whip thing. And she's Damien's partner. Anyone else spying on me?'

'We weren't spying on you, not like that anyway.' He jerked his head at the photos and changed direction with his juggling. 'We found a camera over the wardrobe and a listening device hidden in the tiger on your bed. We didn't put them there. Someone who had access to your bedroom must've done it.'

'I don't want to know.'

'I think you do. You need our help even if you don't want it. You've got too many enemies and precious few friends.'

'Will you stop that?'

'Your wish is my command.' He gathered in the bars and took one for himself.

She paced, her sleek fall of dark hair shining in the watery light of the January day coming through the window. She was so vibrant, so alive: total shame all that energy was directed in hostility towards him. 'You obviously want to talk to me alone for some reason. So, get on with it.'

He snapped off a piece of chocolate wafer and held it out to her. 'I'm sorry.'

'You're not.'

'I really am. I didn't like how we were going about things. We wanted to do it gently, wanted you to make friends with Kate and Raven, but when that failed, I was plan B.'

She took the chocolate but didn't eat it, putting it down on the desk next to the dress. 'Plan B, huh?'

That sounded cold. No wonder she wasn't warming to his explanation. 'But if it helps, I had begun really to like you, for yourself, not because of the job.'

If her glares were arrows he would be bristling with them like Boromir in his death scene. Ember hugged her arms to herself. 'I don't understand: what is it you want from me? Are you . . . are you trying to mess with my trial?'

'It's not about your father's death.'

'Then I really don't get it.'

'It's about a shipment of nuclear materials heading for the UK.'

'A what?' Her surprise read as genuine.

146

'Your father's organization is known to run guns illegally into the UK. This time we think the cargo includes some radioactive waste that can be used to make a dirty bomb. Let that off and you kill many with the fall-out and make an area a no-go zone for centuries.'

She pressed a hand to her temples. 'And you think I know about this?'

'Do you?'

'No comment.'

'Ember, this isn't something to use because you're upset with us. It's much bigger than that.'

She dug her hands in her pockets. 'You think that because I'm accused of murder, I'd sit by and let radioactive material get used in a terrorist attack?'

'Ember—'

'Don't. For all your trying to befriend me, you didn't get to know me, did you, Joe?' She walked out.

So that told him. She was magnificent in her put-down. 'Crash and Burn', one of the songs by his favourite band, Gifted, played in his head mockingly. He'd ruined the operation, messed up at the Lord mansion, and now handled her badly. This wasn't a training exercise: this was real life and would have real consequences. The team would be sent home, Ember be left to MI5 to pick apart, and the shipment might still possibly get through. Just as at Westron, he'd let his friends, let Isaac and Mrs Hardy, down. Joe put his head in his hands. Personal doubts at his fitness for the career he had chosen had flourished like weeds since last summer's brainwashing debacle. He was obviously just not good at his job. He couldn't see any other response than his resignation. Time he went back to America and left detecting to other people.

Ember took refuge in the library, still fuming with the rush of adrenaline arguing with Joe had given her. She felt so bloody used! She had woken up from her dream of friendship to find she'd kissed the ass, not the lover she had imagined. Shakespeare had got it wrong. Titania should've slapped Oberon for doing that to her, giving her a dream, making her a laughing stock, then ripping it from her; no woman should go off dancing with the one who betrayed her with a smile and a simper. Had the queen no pride?

She sat folded up on a sofa by the magazine section, knees hugged to her chest. The grinning faces of the celebrities on the covers swam before her eyes. God, it was her pride speaking, wasn't it? She was reacting like this because she'd begun to value herself, think she was worth something to someone else, and then lashed out when she found that she hadn't mattered, that they were after a much bigger prize. She forced herself to recall Joe's words. They weren't out for their own gain but to fend off disaster. Nuclear material had got into the arms shipment. She knew about these shipments in a hazy fashion, had heard her father talking to his fixers on his private phone in coded terms while he was alive, but as far as she was aware he had always kept to conventional weapons. While that didn't make it OK, she had always resigned herself to this part of the business—what, after all, could she have done to stop him? She had told herself that he had had some standards. He did not deal with terrorists on the grounds that they would turn and bite the hand that fed them.

So what had changed?

Obviously his death. That meant Devlin could expand the business in the ways he had always been pushing, taking them into darker areas of the world. Had that been the real reason her father had had to die?

Her mind played over the implications of what might happen if the shipment got through—a truly nightmarish scenario.

Despite her hurt feelings, she couldn't completely exonerate herself. Her family had set this up, dug the channel that Devlin was now using, probably via Kamal in Turkey and Szabó in Hungary. Neither man had any detectable conscience, happy to traffic people, drugs, and guns so why would a canister of nuclear waste be any different? Mick would've killed Devlin for doing this. With him gone, Ember was the only Lord left to right the wrong.

These people were slippery and she did not trust the British authorities to make the right calls. Her father had always boasted that he had his shadows, people in his pay in both the police and intelligence. He had told her that anyone could be bought for the right price. What if one of them gave the smugglers a tip-off and the material was diverted and ended up in equally bad hands elsewhere? Better for it to come out of the pipeline and for her to control who met it. She couldn't arrange that stuck in prison. She could only do that if she were Ember Ann Lord, Mick Lord's daughter and protégée again. She'd made one stupid deal and ended up here. It was time she made a good one and finally took control of her own destiny.

Chapter 10

That night in the boys' rented house, Joe pondered the draft of his resignation email on the laptop screen. The cursor beat like a little pulse, measuring out the last moments of his time at the YDA. He'd tried to sound grateful to Isaac but firm in his decision. He knew his friends would try to change his mind but they didn't see inside him. He was done. If he left now, he could finish the year in high school and think about college. If he stayed any longer he'd get swept along into a career to which experience had shown he was unsuited. Better to cut his losses before he got to that point.

He put his name on the bottom. His parents would be glad to have him back and not blame him for his failure. His dad's motto was, it was better to have tried and failed than never to have tried at all. And it had been a good idea once, appealing to Joe's deep sense of justice. Ever since he was little, he'd wanted to save the world; growing up he had found all the superhero slots were taken by fictitious characters and mere mortals like him had to make do with the more modest goal of becoming a good detective. He'd imagined joining the FBI in the fullness of time, or maybe the police service as an undercover officer, but it seemed his nature just wasn't flexible enough. He couldn't stomach the damage he had to do in order to do good. He made the wrong calls. He wasn't mentally strong enough to take what was thrown at him.

'You OK, man?' asked Nathan, putting a cup of coffee next to Joe.

'Thanks. I'm fine.' He took a breath. Now or never. 'How do you think this reads?' He turned the screen so his friend could see the draft.

Nathan's eyes scanned the first few lines. 'What the hell do you think you're doing? Kieran, get in here!' He grabbed the laptop. 'You are not sending that.'

Joe sat back, trying to maintain his calm. 'I am. It doesn't mean we can't still be friends, Nat. You'll be welcome to visit me in New York any time.'

'Stuff that.'

Kieran raced in straight from the shower, towel knotted at his waist. 'What's up?'

'It's Joe. He's gone crazy. He's trying to resign.'

Kieran read the email. 'No.' His statement was final. 'I'm blocking your email account. You can't send this tonight.'

Joe got out his phone.

'And I'll take the YDA network down too if you try to text Isaac. You are going to sleep on this.'

Nathan made a quick dive and snatched the handset out of Joe's hands. 'Key, you know Isaac hates it when you do that. We'd better just keep Joe away from all electronic devices.'

Joe sighed. 'Look, guys, I appreciate you trying to save me from making a knee-jerk decision, but it's been coming up on me for some time now. I know what I'm doing.'

They took seats on the sofa opposite him, Nathan clutching the phone on his lap, and Kieran the laptop to his bare chest. It would almost be funny, thought Joe, if they weren't so distressed by his decision.

'Why didn't you say something?' asked Kieran. 'I'm your best mate. I talk to you, tell you when I mess up or need advice. You could tell me if you had doubts.'

151

Joe shrugged, though he was far from feeling careless. 'It was too difficult, Key, because it was you I let down. It was why I took time off in the autumn. I tried to resign then but Isaac persuaded me to give it another go. Westron messed me up. Killed my confidence.'

'But we thought helping Damien save Rose, the time back in Manhattan and the rescue mission at the container port, sorted that out?' said Nathan.

'I thought so too or I wouldn't have volunteered for this assignment. I was wrong.'

Nathan looked furious. 'It's that girl, isn't it? She's the one who's done this to you.'

'Don't blame Ember. I didn't handle her correctly.'

'No one could. She's impossible.'

'That's not fair. She's just fighting the only way she knows how. I picked the worst method of getting to her. She'll never trust me now. I should've been straight with her from the start.'

'You think she would've listened?' asked Kieran.

'Maybe.'

Kieran wiped a few beads of water off the top of the computer. On hearing Nathan's shout, he hadn't even had time to towel off his hair. 'I was going to tell you: there's been an update in her case file. The forensic evidence is beginning to look shaky.'

'Meaning?'

'The knife on the scene is possibly not the one that killed Mick Lord.'

'The one with Ember's prints on it wasn't used for the attack?'

'Yes.'

'So where is the murder weapon?'

'The knife Nathan mentioned, the one from the annexe,

was never logged into evidence. The police made another search when I tipped them off that they'd missed this, but even a fingertip examination of the garden has turned up nothing. Someone removed it from the scene.'

'Ah.' A new picture took shape in Joe's mind. He'd been getting bits and pieces and now they were falling into place. 'You think she was set up?'

'It's possible, but that doesn't explain why she's not been trying to defend herself properly. I'd expect even a guilty person to make more noise than she has.'

'Your conclusion?'

'I think she's protecting the person who did it.'

What a horrendous tangle Ember was in. They all knew for whom she would go to prison. Joe's heart broke for her but what could he do? He'd decided he was off the case. 'You should no longer tell me this, Key. I've resigned.'

'Your resignation hasn't been sent yet.' Kieran had a mulish expression on his face. Joe seriously doubted that any of his internet services would be working for some time to come.

'And if Ember is banged up in jail because she's protecting her brother, don't you think you owe it to her to try and help her? It makes her an innocent victim,' added Nathan.

'One whom we've betrayed. Yeah, she'd really love us to help her, I'm sure,' said Joe sourly.

Nathan's phone buzzed in his pocket. 'It's Kate.' With the mission unravelling, the girls had smuggled a mobile back to their unit after rehearsal in case they needed a quick extraction. 'News just in. Ember wants a deal.'

'What kind of deal?' Kieran asked eagerly.

'Not what we expected. She says she'll finish the play and keep our cover intact if we promise a guard on Max twenty-four-seven until the threat to him is eliminated. Doesn't she know we'd've done that anyway?'

'She talked to Kate?' asked Joe.

'And Raven. Yeah, they said she was very business-like about it, didn't seem to hold their subterfuge against them.'

'That's not enough to stop the spooks moving in on her.'

'No, but it's something. At least she's talking to us again.'

But not to Joe. Going to the girls was a clear signal of that.

'We can help her, Joe. With us on site, MI5 can't do anything too drastic,' said Kieran. 'She's got a public performance. There are other stakeholders involved in her case than intelligence services—social workers, lawyers, the Lockwood staff. The more people surrounding her the safer she'll be. Even her public notoriety helps. She can't just disappear to some interrogation centre.'

'I'm sure she'll be delighted to hear that her crucifixion in the tabloids serves some purpose.'

'Joe, please.' Nathan handed back the phone, a sign of his trust that Joe wouldn't do anything rash. 'You're angry at how this has turned out but we need you. If Ember is going to continue with the play for the sake of the other trainees, then so should you. We've been focusing on her but there are others with their own problems in that prison. If we pull out, we'll be another set of people who've let them down.'

Joe rested his head against the back of his chair, thinking of Simone, so thrilled to be playing Peaseblossom. They'd even kitted out her son Johnny with his own costume and given him a walk-on part—or carry-on part, more accurately. Graham, the market stall boy, had doubled up in two roles, both of which he delivered with idiosyncratic style. The courtier Philostrate's role as play promoter he spoke with a gusto that would've delighted Shakespeare, even if he sometimes missed out chunks and improvized others. As Puck, he travelled the stage with quicksilver energy. Raymond, aka Cobweb, had proved to be the hidden diamond in the rough, taking to acting like a duck to water, pulling off his gangster role with a huge sense of professionalism. He'd been discussing with Henry trying out for parts once he got out of prison. He'd been assured that his background would only lend him street credibility with casting agents as long as he didn't reoffend.

'OK, I'll stay for the play. But then I'm out.'

Nathan and Kieran nodded at each other. He knew what they were thinking. He'd given them a stay of execution which they intended to use to change his decision. Too late. His mind was made up and it would take a miracle to alter it.

'Now can I have my laptop back?'

'So the gang's all here then.' Henry beamed at the cast gathered for the dress rehearsal. 'I can't say that we've had a bump-free run at preparing for this but I believe you're ready for tomorrow night. You've worked hard and now it is all about enjoying yourselves. We're going to do a technical run-through first so my friends on sound and lighting know what to expect.' Henry gestured to some volunteers who had come from the stage crew at the Globe. They were sitting in the booth at the back of the sports hall, which was doubling as the performance space. 'You'll say your first line and any cues, walk through your blocking, and I'll stop you if there's anything I want to highlight for the team.'

Joe's gaze went to Ember standing alone on the other side of the room, arms folded. No surprise to see her keeping herself aloof again.

'I anticipate that we'll need to run the dance in full as we've not had all the pieces in place—music, lighting, the full stage. Then we break for lunch. This afternoon we'll do a complete run-through in costumes and make-up. Everyone clear?'

'Yes, Henry,' echoed from the young people lounging on the floor in front of him.

'And finally I'd like to introduce you to the last member of our cast to join us.' Henry gave a wicked smile and pulled something out of a basket beside him: long ears, doleful eyes, and grinning teeth like Donkey out of Shrek, a much better prop than the party-shop ears and nose they'd been using. 'Bottom's ass's head. On loan from the Globe props department so please treat it gently.'

The cast hooted with laughter. Jamie, the actor who would have to wear it, got up to try it on. He held it out to Ember. 'Hey, Queen Titania, what do you think of your boyfriend? Fancy a snog?'

She didn't storm off as most expected on his teasing. She merely gave him a cool look. 'I'd prefer kissing that to what I've had to kiss during rehearsal.'

This provoked another round of laughter at Jamie's expense but Joe knew from the look darted in his direction that she had had another target in mind.

Henry clapped his hands to gain their attention. 'Excellent. Now, it's going to be a long day but the job not started takes longest to finish. Places for Act I please.'

Joe and Ember weren't required for the opening scenes so they retired with the rest of the fairy court to the back corner of the hall. Joe waited to see where Ember sat then settled down beside her, long legs stretched out in front. Hers were curled protectively beside her. She had a book open on her lap.

'What are you reading?' he asked.

She lifted it up to show him.

'Emily Dickinson again? She's one of my favourite American poets. She understands darkness, doesn't she? On that note, I have something to brighten things up a little.' Joe got out the bunch of sunflowers he had bought from a supermarket on his way over and put those and a bar of Swiss chocolate on the floor beside her.

Her fingertip grazed a yellow petal, tempted against her better judgement by the glorious burst of colour. 'You don't need to get me presents any more, Joe. Remember, I know.'

'I know you know. These aren't presents. They are an apology,' he pointed to the sunflowers, 'and this is a peace offering,' he gestured to the chocolate.

She sighed. 'I'm not angry any longer. Not really.'

'No?'

'I understand why you all did it. You're serving the country, though in your case I'm not sure what that means, seeing how you're American.'

'My interest is in protecting innocent people everywhere, regardless of nationality.'

'Fine. I get it. You're driven by altruism.'

'But I didn't want to drive over you in the process. It just . . . happened.'

'Then I accept your apology and your peace offering. But we're not friends. You're not my best pal. You're not my anything.'

She thought she wasn't angry? That little bitter speech gave away how deeply she still smarted from the injuries he had inflicted.

'If it makes you feel any better, I'm giving all this up.'

'What do you mean by "this"?'

'I'm leaving the training programme for young detectives and going back to the US.'

'Why would that make me feel better?'

'When things go wrong, people want a sacrificial victim, don't they? Football manager, head of a bank, politician, you name it, there are always calls for resignation.'

'I'm not people, Joe.'

He turned to meet her eyes, noticing properly for the first time how they were the colour of the dark chocolate he'd just

157

given her. He'd not looked at her enough, not cherished her; he'd sold her short, as so many others had. 'No, you're not people. You're Ember Ann Lord and I hurt you. I wish I hadn't and you deserved better than that from me. I'll keep on telling you I'm sorry until you really believe it. And talking about sacrifices, why the hell are you sitting in here taking the rap for a crime you didn't commit?'

Her eyes widened in shock.

'Right, fairies, you're on,' called Henry.

'What did you say?' Ember clutched her throat.

Joe got up and held out a hand to pull her up. Her reaction told him Kieran's theory was correct. Why hadn't they asked this question earlier? Everything shifted in his mind, what had happened, the implications of what she had done. 'You heard me. You're throwing away your future to protect your brother.'

'Leave Max out of this!' Her expression turned fierce. 'He didn't do anything!'

'Oberon, Titania, leave the argument for the stage!' ordered Henry.

'Good. So you'll start fighting to clear your name, then?' pressed Joe.

'Joe, Ember, you're holding us all up!' Henry was losing patience. The director had given his prickly Titania many chances already; she'd missed the full run-through last rehearsal, and he wasn't in the mood to allow her any more slack.

Joe turned. 'Sorry, Henry. Come on, Em.'

'I'm not called Em,' she hissed, stomping after him.

Joe smiled, pleased to see a glimpse of the old Ember. It gave him hope that she would bounce back after the knock to her confidence he'd given her.

The technical rehearsal reached the dance. Joe anticipated it with a mixture of excitement and dread. He wanted to hold her again, use touch to convey his regret and care for her, but the kiss was going to be a challenge. Ember took her position next to him, glaring at him fiercely from under her dark brows.

'I don't think we should do the kiss,' she said as they waited for the music cue.

'It was your idea,' he reminded her.

'When I was . . . before I . . .' She swallowed and looked away.

'When you liked me, before you knew,' Joe completed the sentence for her. 'But Ember, it wasn't all a lie. I was trying to be your friend even while working on another agenda. I just didn't understand you, thought you were on the wrong side. Trust me, I genuinely wanted to kiss you. I loved kissing you. And the play needs it.'

'I'm not kissing you back then.'

Joe smiled. His partner was bristling like a black cat shown a cold bath. 'Fine. I'll have to put twice the effort into it.'

Her annoyance still snapping away at him in her expressive eyes, they went through their moves without a mistake. Joe was only half aware of the point where the other members of the fairy court joined them, attention fixed on Ember. She met his gaze, whether because she was staying in character or because she felt the pull between them too, he didn't know. Maybe it didn't matter? He spun and dipped her down for the final kiss. Departing from what they'd practised before, he brushed his thumb across her lips.

'Smile,' he whispered. 'You deserve to smile again.' He closed the distance and softly pressed his mouth to hers. After the merest hesitation, she returned the kiss. Despite the image she projected to the world, she was so sweet, so ready for a little tenderness in her life. Of course, she wouldn't be able to resist it when he offered it to her. Joe felt the privilege of being one of the few to know this about her. This time he was doing it for her own sake, not to exploit her.

Henry cleared his throat. 'Guys, that's probably enough for now. Save the full fireworks for the performance, OK?'

Joe stood up and helped Ember regain her balance. He didn't miss the knowing smiles on his friends' faces. 'Sorry, Henry.'

'No problem. That was great—no need to run that again. Act V people, positions please.'

Ember took her plate of sandwiches over to an empty corner of the hall. She could kick herself. She'd completely succumbed to Joe's kiss after having said she'd not return it.

The lady doth protest too much, methinks, she thought grimly. Betrayal had not killed off this awkward attraction she felt to her acting partner.

Her solitude didn't last long. First Kate and Raven, then Nathan and Kieran joined her. Joe, she saw, was talking to Henry and the lighting guys about some problem to do with the spotlight. At least she was spared his 'I told you so' smirk.

'Ember, we need to talk to you,' said Raven.

'It looks like I don't have much choice. I can't get rid of you even when I didn't invite you to join me.' She unscrewed the cap on her bottled water.

'It's about Joe,' said Kate.

'What about Joe?'

'He's resigned.'

'I know. He told me.' She shrugged. She was hardly responsible for the future of the guy sent to spy on her.

'He did?' Nathan frowned. 'And what did you say?'

'That he didn't need to do that because of anything that happened here. I'm not going to file a complaint. I mean, who'd care if I did?'

'You'd be surprised. We aren't rogue agents. We do have people we answer to and question our methods.'

160

'And did you fail to carry out your orders?'

'No, but some people might think our methods were dubious. Joe certainly did.'

'Yes. Henry told me. Joe sounds like a natural boy scout.'

Raven smiled at that description. 'Rose says he's more like Captain America, the straight-down-the-line warrior when we're the rest of the Avengers, a bunch of misfits. He tries so hard to do the right thing—and that's the problem. He is tougher on himself than anyone else and doesn't forgive when he gets it wrong.'

'I'm sorry, but what has this to do with me?'

'We think you can change his mind, persuade him not to give up.'

Ember did sympathize with Joe, as she was always holding herself up to an impossible standard too. She had long since got used to the fact that she took on too much responsibility; in her world there was no choice, as there was no one else stepping forward to protect her and Max. Maybe she could help Joe, just so long as it didn't stop her seeing through her bigger plan? 'How exactly can I do that?'

Raven quickly checked Joe was still busy. 'Can you keep a secret?'

Ember choked on her mouthful of sandwich.

'Yes, of course you can. It's about what happened last summer when I met this bunch.' Raven smiled affectionately at Kieran.

Kieran took her hand and covered it where it rested on his thigh. 'We were undercover at Raven's school. Bad stuff was going down there—a form of brainwashing to bend students into being the people their parents wanted them to be. Joe was given the full treatment and it began to work on him, wiping out parts of his memory.'

'They used drugs,' Raven explained.

161

'And a form of sensory torture,' said Kieran. 'Seriously perverted. They had us for days. Anyway, Joe shook it off and helped us round up the bad guys but he hasn't forgiven himself for what he sees as his weakness.'

Ember no longer felt like eating her sandwich. Living in the Lord household had taught her what it was like to be continually browbeaten to be a certain kind of child. Her father had used fists and insults but never drugs on her. A small mercy. If he'd known about it, he would've tried.

'And now Joe feels he's failed again. It's been made worse because he hated manipulating you in ways he compared to what he'd experienced, making you believe a lie.'

'From what you describe, I doubt what he did is anywhere on the same scale—a few gifts and kind words. I never lost control of myself. I just wanted to believe I had a friend. More fool me.'

Kate edged closer and nudged Ember with her elbow. 'I know how that feels. I spent a year on the run, betrayed by a boyfriend, not knowing whom I could trust until I got caught by these guys.'

'You?' Ember wondered if this was another lie.

Kate showed her wrist tattoo. 'Do you know what this is?'

'Yes. It's a gang tat. Aren't the Scorpions based out in Indonesia?' Her father had had dealings with them. 'I did wonder about that.'

'Yes, they were. We kinda took them down a few months ago.' Kate smiled at Nathan who had shuffled closer to put his arm around her, a comforting gesture that Ember envied.

Her respect for the people around her went up several notches. 'That's remarkable. They were thought to be untouchable.'

'It's funny what a jar of these little guys will do to even the toughest gangster.' Kate rubbed her tattoo, thoughts clearly elsewhere. 'I'll tell you the full story some other time. Joe's coming, guys.'

'But you'll try?' asked Raven.

'I really don't know what you expect me to achieve,' murmured Ember.

'Help him regain his confidence. Please.'

It was a novel idea that she could be a positive influence on someone outside her immediate family. 'I doubt I have the power, but I'll see what I can do.'

'Thanks. Oh, and we've an update from Damien. Max says hello.'

Joe joined them with his lunch. 'Max?'

'Yes, Damien told him this morning how he and Rose were two super spies sent by Ember to protect him from bad guys. He took the news well.'

Ember had to laugh. Of course he would. Presented like that, Max would see it as a huge adventure and love Damien and Rose all the more. 'You lot better make sure he comes out of this OK.'

'We will, Em, and you as well. We'll fight in your corner, get you out of here,' said Joe, much to the surprise of his team mates. 'You didn't know? She's innocent. Didn't kill her father.'

'Then who did?' asked Kate.

Joe met Ember's anxious gaze. 'I don't know. But it wasn't her.'

Ember lingered after the dress rehearsal to get a chance to speak to Joe alone. Observing him, she saw that he had begun to hold himself separate from his friends, a position made all the easier by the fact that they were two couples. He was beginning to learn what she knew: that life was essentially a lesson in managing the fact that you were alone. The poet, John Donne, had got it wrong. Every man was an island. You could hide it in the temporary warmth of a relationship but in the end it was always going to be down to you.

That's not true. It doesn't have to be temporary, a voice whispered in her head. It reminded her of all the love poetry she had read, the stories of devoted couples, the kind of perfect relationships of love-and-marriage plots.

But they are fiction, she countered, hanging up her blue gown on the girls' wardrobe rail. *Life is messier. People more selfish. And they change, usually for the worse.*

'Ember, are you almost done?' asked Joe.

'Yes.'

'I've got your flowers. I put them in water earlier so they're OK.'

'Thanks. I hadn't thought to do that.'

He came around the barrier of the clothes rail and handed them over. 'So, tomorrow's our last day.'

'You'll all leave afterwards?'

'Raven and Kate will get transferred to another prison in the morning as far as the other trainees are concerned, but yes, it's back to ordinary life for us.'

'And you're still going to resign?'

Joe smiled knowingly. 'My friends have put you up to saying something, haven't they?'

'They're your friends. Of course they have. For what it's worth, I think you'll make an excellent detective. You care about right and wrong. I think that's more important in the long run than whether or not you always make the right calls.'

'Ember—'

'No, please, just let me finish what I want to say. I know what it's like to do wrong things for the right reasons. That's what my life was like before prison. You all took down a criminal gang, Kate told me. Well, I didn't. I lived in one. I'm not as clever or resourceful as you, and I just did what I could to survive and protect my brother. So, yes, I know what it feels like to be a failure, but I was the best failure I could be. I don't honestly know if I had another choice but I didn't go looking for it, did I?'

Joe looked down at his toecaps. 'I'm humbled you're telling me this. And I don't judge you, Ember. You were trapped.'

She still was, Ember thought. 'But what I really want to tell you is that if you want to make up for what you think you did to me, then do so by becoming a better detective. Don't give up now. You've nearly finished your two years. See it out and then decide.'

'Careers advice from Ember Lord?' Joe smiled at her, tenderness in his eyes.

'For what it's worth, which is probably nothing.'

He moved in closer, taking the sunflowers from her and placing them on a nearby chair. They were screened from the others in the room by the row of costumes. 'Thank you.' He framed her face in his hands. 'Now this is just for you: not for any other reason than I'd like to be your friend, your something. I want you to know you are worth everything. Don't dismiss yourself so lightly.' He bent down and kissed her, a light press of his lips to hers.

Ember knew this was likely to be the last time they kissed outside the performance—considering what she was planning and the risk involved, it might well be the last time anyone kissed her. She wanted more than a gentle kiss. Going up on tiptoes, she put her arms around his neck and deepened the contact. He immediately responded by putting his arms around her waist and pulling her closer to him so their bodies touched, chest to thigh.

'Em, what are you doing to me?' he whispered. He resumed kissing her, caressing her, pressing her spine with his big warm palm so there was barely space between them for either to breathe.

A thrill shot through her. It had been real. His attraction to her was making him shake off his Captain America politeness and give in to the passion that had always run between them like their own form of electricity; he was entering a place where he was a little bit out of control. As that was how she felt too, she was glad he was passing through the fire with her. He kissed her like he couldn't get enough of her, like he wanted to fold her inside him and carry her away from this place. She wished he could. But that was a dream she couldn't have, not yet, not here.

Reluctantly, she broke off the kiss. 'Joe.'

'Ember?' He looked intently into her eyes.

She smiled. 'Nothing. I just wanted to say your name. To remember.'

He frowned. 'I suppose it is impossible, that we can't carry this on after tomorrow?'

'If you're in America and I'm in here, yes it is.'

'But you'll be free soon. I'm going to set that in motion whatever else I decide about my future. Our boss has contacts, resources he can mobilize.'

She rubbed at the patch of his T-shirt in front of her nose. 'And if I were free, would you still want to know me? Despite where I've come from?'

'You didn't pick your parents, did you?'

'So . . . so you would?'

'I'd be willing to give it a try. Yes, I would.' He gave a nod, partly to himself as he made his pledge.

But would he still want that after he discovered what she was planning tomorrow? She feared he'd be upset, wouldn't understand her decision to go it alone.

So could she ask him to help her? Could she actually trust him?

'Hey, Joe, the minibus is leaving!' called Nathan from the far side of the room.

Joe flicked his eyes to the ceiling in an expression of frustration. 'Coming! Sorry. Let's talk more tomorrow, OK, sweetheart? After the show?'

The moment passed. She nodded, feeling a little better that she hadn't spoken the lie about there being time afterwards.

'Sweet dreams, fair Titania.' With a twinkle in his eyes, he kissed her hand and joined his friends.

Ember leaned against the clothes rail, wondering quite what had happened in the last few minutes. The fundamentals of her life had shifted and fallen into a new pattern. Someone outside her close family appeared to like, maybe even love, her a little. It felt wonderful.

But what about her plans?

She was taking action for the right reason, to be the best version of herself, rather than the defeated, manipulated Ember of the last few weeks. If she succeeded she would've proved her worth to Joe; if it went wrong, then at least he wouldn't know and get blamed. It was just as well the moment of confiding in him had been interrupted. She'd do this alone and then see where she stood with him. She just had to hope he still wanted her.

Chapter · 11

Lockwood had a completely different atmosphere the day of the performance. Even the trainees who had only taken a very minor part in proceedings got caught up in the anticipation. Ember was amused by the rumours flying at the breakfast table: if they were to be believed, A-list celebrities and casting directors were coming, as was the press. News had got out and the public were fascinated by Henry Rawlings' latest project. The fact that the girl accused of the Lord murder was taking a prominent part in the action had only added further intrigue. Ember's lawyer had advised her to allow a photograph of Titania in costume to be released as part of the publicity, a step in her campaign to rehabilitate her client's reputation. Mrs Bishop had brought in the newspaper articles for them to read so Ember could see the shot of herself in navy evening dress cradling Jamie, wearing his ridiculous ass's head, featured in most articles on the inside pages. It would certainly muddy the water about her being a merciless killer if people began to suspect she had a sense of humour.

And they'd all have something new to write about her tomorrow morning, if things went to plan.

'Feeling OK about tonight?' asked Kate as they stood at the sink to load the dishwasher.

Ember was startled, for a brief second fearing Kate had been able to read her thoughts. 'Oh, the play? Yes, I'm all right. It's good that it doesn't depend on just one actor, not like *Hamlet*, so I don't have to worry if I mess up.' She dumped the spoons in the cutlery basket. 'I can count on the rest of you.'

'You won't mess up. You've always been on top of your part. I'm worried I'm going to get my Lysanders and my Demetriuses mixed up.' Kate scrapped the remains of Johnny's Weetabix into the food bin. 'Geez, this stuff is like glue.'

'If you did, I don't think anyone would notice.'

Kate laughed. 'True. When you get out of here, you should consider drama school. You're good—no, you're better than that, you're great.'

'I thought that was Joe's fake plan, not mine?'

'You should make it a real one for yourself.'

It was sweet: Kate was assuming Ember would get free and clear. Having disliked her peer pal at the beginning, mainly because she'd bought the stupid act, Ember was warming to the young detective. She sensed of all the YDA team, Kate really did understand the dark places in which Ember had dwelled. They might even have become good friends if things had worked out differently.

'How likely is that, do you think? I don't have any qualifications. They wouldn't look at me.'

'I wouldn't be so sure. You're well read, have Henry on your side, you might just be able to persuade them to take a peek. Once they see you in action, they'll give you serious consideration.'

'Thanks, Kate. Even if you've just made that up, it's really nice to hear.'

Kate smiled and shook her head. 'Such a cynic. And I don't blame you. I always thought the worst too. You should hang around with our guys for a time. I found it lifted me out of my darkly cynical stage and now I'm just plain old sarcastic, according to Nathan.'

'You two go together very well.'

'We do. He's like Joe, you see. Those guys are just the positive balance dark-side girls like us need.' She bumped the door of the dishwasher closed with her hip.

'Ember?' Mrs Bishop was at the door. 'I'm sorry to interrupt your morning, but there are two gentlemen to see you.'

Ember shot Kate a questioning glance but the fair-haired girl looked puzzled. Not a YDA delegation then.

'Who are they, Mrs Bishop?' Ember asked.

'I think they're from the government.' The manager pursed her lips. 'I don't approve of them coming here, especially not today of all days, when you should be concentrating on your play, but they have authorization from the Home Secretary.'

Kate turned so her back was to Mrs Bishop. 'Sounds like spooks,' she whispered. 'Demand a lawyer.'

Ember dried her hands slowly. 'OK, Mrs Bishop. I'm happy to see them if I can call my lawyer.'

Mrs Bishop's expression of disapproval intensified. 'Apparently Ms Pierce is unavailable. They've brought her colleague, a Mr Nash.'

'Stitch-up,' muttered Kate. 'Don't go anywhere with them.'

'I've not heard of him. Can I refuse to see them?' asked Ember.

Mrs Bishop beckoned her to follow. 'No, dear, I don't think you can, but you don't have to say anything. Just listen. They explained it was important. I won't let them keep you long.'

Ember met Kate's eyes, seeking advice.

Kate gave a slight nod. 'It'll be OK. I'll tell my boss. He's got a lot of influence.'

'I'm counting on you to rescue me if they try and take me away.'

'We'll think of something.'

And the odd thing was, thought Ember, as she followed

Mrs Bishop down the corridor, passing the caretaker with a floor polisher, she trusted that the YDA team would. If only she had the luxury of a bit more time, she would bring them in on her plans. Right now, her scheme was too risky to involve anyone else, as she'd not had a chance to refine it.

Ember was shown into a sunny office in the administration block, not a building she knew well only having been in it for the arrival search. The room had a benign atmosphere completely at odds with the purposes of the meeting. Three men sat at a table, an older sandy-haired official with the reddened face of someone who had recently spent too long in a hot country, a tall dark man with an olive complexion, and the one she took to be her lawyer, a faded-looking individual in a grey suit. He reminded her of a printout from a cartridge with low ink-levels, compared to the vibrant photo-paper-quality Ms Pierce. He offered her his hand which she shook reluctantly. His palm was clammy to the touch.

'Miss Lord? I'm Jeremy Nash. Ms Pierce is unfortunately engaged in court this morning so sent me to represent you during this meeting.'

Ember murmured something appropriate and took the seat next to him. She didn't have much hope he would defend her but she'd give him a chance. Despite Kate and Mrs Bishop's reassurances, she knew enough about the ways of the intelligence services to feel afraid. They didn't play by the same rules as everyone else.

'This is Mr Bradford,' continued the lawyer. The sandy-haired man nodded. 'And Mr Reubens of the Home Office.'

By which he really meant MI5, thought Ember.

'Shall we get started, gentlemen?' Mr Nash gave Bradford an enquiring look.

'Miss Lord, when is the consignment of nuclear material due to arrive in the UK?' Bradford's question was slapped on the table with no prologue, a clear attempt to wrong-foot her.

Toying with her necklace, Ember took her time, not letting them rush her. 'I don't know anything about it, other than what the other people working on this case have told me,' she replied truthfully, meeting his eyes with a straight look.

'You were deep in your father's organization. Can you not make an educated guess?' Bradford's tone was sneering.

She could, but the stakes were high and she couldn't afford to waste what she had worked out. Either of these strangers, maybe even both, could be one of her father's shadow men, passed on to Devlin now that he had taken over the contacts. Sending a spook to test her loyalty was exactly the kind of underhanded tactic Devlin would use. If she trusted the wrong person, the weapons would simply slip through her fingers. Best to continue with her plan. 'You overestimate my importance. My father's business was not my concern.'

'It should be. Do you want to see thousands of innocent people harmed by his activities?'

'The obvious answer to that question is "no, I don't".'

'And the less obvious answer, Miss Lord?' asked Reubens.

So he was the clever one, was he? The one looking for the subtext. 'I only have one answer and I've given it to you already.'

Nash shifted in his seat. 'Ember, the gentlemen here explained to me before you came in that if you cooperate with them on this matter then they would do all in their power to see that the charges against you are reduced to manslaughter. If we can show a history of mental abuse at the hands of your father, your sentence will be much shorter than the one you are currently facing.'

'Mr Nash, you are missing something,' she said quietly.

'What's that?'

'That I'm not guilty. It should be in my file. Ms Pierce has hopes that my innocence will be made plain at my trial.'

Bradford cleared his throat.

Nash pulled at his tie. 'Well, I wouldn't want you to have your hopes raised on that count. My junior colleague, admirable though she is in many respects, is apt to be too optimistic.'

Snake. 'It's the truth. I didn't kill my father. I have no intention of changing my plea or admitting to something I didn't do on the grounds I'll get an easier ride.'

Bradford sat back and crossed his arms, studying her. 'You like it here, don't you?'

'Are you asking if I like being in prison? What kind of question is that?'

'We've been side-copied on the reports posted on you. After a slow start, the team began to make progress with you and it was thought that you were enjoying the extra-curricular activities we allowed to take place in here.'

Ember picked up the implication that the presence of Henry Rawlings was all on the say-so of the intelligence services.

'You've even become quite close to one of the young men, I believe?'

If that snide remark had been made before yesterday evening, then it would've hurt, pressing on the bruise of betrayal. Since her reconciliation with Joe, though, it felt more like a badge she could wear with pride. 'Yes, I am.'

'There are still months to go before your trial. If you don't cooperate with us, it is very likely you will shortly be transferred to a high-security women's prison. No more Shakespeare, no more attractive young men flirting with you, no more freedom to wear your own clothes. I can imagine the women in that kind of place would make Mick Lord's little princess very welcome.'

So the gloves were off. Ember glanced over at her lawyer.

'Aren't you going to say something, Mr Nash? That was clearly a threat.'

Mr Nash didn't even look shamefaced. 'I'm afraid, Ember, these things do happen. Prisoners get shuttled round the system. Mr Bradford is just helping you think through the consequences of your decisions.'

Any doubts about withholding information from these people got shot down. If she were going to trust anyone, it would be the YDA team, not the spooks.

'I'm sorry you had a wasted journey, Mr Bradford, Mr Reubens. I have nothing to tell you.' She crossed her arms on her chest. 'I think this interview is at an end.'

Ember was still feeling shaky when she got back to the girls' unit. That had been horrible, and a glimpse of what might lie ahead if her plan failed. While she had been good at acting the privileged princess role when called on to do so by her father, inside she no longer felt anywhere near as self-assured. It was no idle threat the spooks had made, that she would be picked apart in a prison with much tougher customers than the small group of her peers in Lockwood.

What's wrong with me? Where's my confidence gone? Ember wondered. *Am I becoming weak just because I've fallen for someone and begun to need people?*

Opening the door to her room, the smell hit her first. Not crossing the threshold, she gazed in horror at the ripped bedding, scattered sunflowers, the confetti of her brother's letters, the torn up library books and, worst of all, the excrement smeared on the walls spelling the word 'Bitch'. Gagging, she stepped back. Here was proof that the authorities could not be trusted. Someone had got to her here, reached out and smashed the little haven she had made for herself. She remembered the photos left on her bed the other night. She hadn't raised with the YDA how they had come into her possession, hadn't thought much about it as she concentrated on the betrayal they contained.

Trembling, she banged on Raven's door as it was the nearest to hers. No answer.

'Oh, come on!' she whispered. Feeling tearful but refusing to cry, she went to Kate's room.

'Yes?' called Kate in answer to her tap.

Ember opened the door, relieved to find Raven there too. 'Could you guys come, please?'

'Ember, what's the matter?' asked Raven, jumping up from the floor cushion. 'You're so pale!'

'Did your visitors upset you?' Kate pulled out a phone from under her pillow. 'I can call Isaac, head off whatever it is they threatened you with.'

Ember mutely shook her head. 'Please.'

'OK, show us.' Raven let Ember tow her down the corridor to her bedroom. 'Oh my God, that's so gross! How can this happen here?'

Kate gave a shocked intake of breath when she saw the damage. 'I'll call the staff member on duty.'

Ember grabbed her sleeve. 'No, call Mrs Bishop. I don't trust some of the staff.'

Kate nodded and went to the wall phone that trainees were allowed to use in emergencies and asked to be put through to the senior manager.

'You think one of them did this?' Raven asked quietly.

Ember gulped. 'The photographs.'

Raven didn't need any more hints. 'Of course, they had to come from outside. This isn't about some grudge from a prisoner here, but someone reaching in to scare you. But who? Your old associates?'

'Or the spooks,' said Kate grimly, replacing the handset.

'It can't be a coincidence they were here this morning. Mrs Bishop is coming and told us to stay out of the room.'

'I don't think any of us will want to go in there by choice,' said Ember.

Raven surveyed the vandalism more closely. 'Oh, Ember, your brother's letters!'

'It's OK, he can always draw me more.' Ember rubbed her arms, really wishing Joe was here to give her a hug.

'It's not OK. We must find out who did this and make sure they're punished.' Raven looked quite militant on her behalf.

Their voices in the corridor began to attract others out of their room.

'What is that smell?' Simone arrived carrying Johnny on her hip.

'You'd better keep him away from here,' said Ember quickly. No child should be exposed to that.

'Someone vandalized Ember's room. Put shit on the walls,' said Kate bluntly.

'Oh God, oh, God, that's so horrible.' Simone backed away. 'Ember, come into my room. No, even better, let's go into the kitchen, right away from here. You shouldn't have to stand here looking at this.'

By the time Mrs Bishop arrived, accompanied by two members of staff and a team of caretakers, all the girls in the unit had shepherded Ember into the kitchen and insisted on making her a cup of tea. Johnny had been put on her lap to comfort her, and they had made a start on lunch, making her favourite cheese toast. Rona, the girl with the pony tail who had asked her if she was a murderer that first morning, put on an upbeat playlist, insisting that they drive out the bad vibes with some seriously good music. Ember wanted to cry for real now. Their kindness and indignation on her behalf was something she'd never experienced before. They might not be her friends like Kate and Raven, but they were her mates in the sense that they stood together if any one of their number was hurt. She was more convinced than ever it hadn't been one of them who had done the damage.

Kate came into the kitchen, having volunteered for the task of keeping an eye on what the Lockwood staff were doing for Ember. She sat down next to her, stealing a tomato off the side of Ember's plate.

'Need something to take the bad taste away,' Kate explained. 'They're photographing the damage and then they're clearing the room. Anything that can be salvaged will be washed and given back to you. You're moving to another bedroom, of course.'

'Do they know who did it?' asked Simone, touching Johnny's head protectively. 'I mean who would want to do such a mean thing?'

Ember handed the baby back to his anxious mother. 'You needn't worry, Simone. This isn't about here; I think it's caused by the mess in my life outside. Someone was probably paid to do it by my enemies.'

Simone gave the smiling baby a hug. 'Thanks, Ember. But still, it's really terrible. How can we feel safe if people will do that kind of thing for money?'

Kate grimaced. 'I heard them talking and apparently the CCTV in the corridor was conveniently off during the window of opportunity—that's from when Ember finished clearing up breakfast with me to when she came back from her interview, about an hour. Did anyone see anything?'

Rona put the sandwich in front of Ember. 'That's when the staff do their rounds. I saw several of them. Mrs Gardener came into my room with Mr Forest to do a quick toss and search.'

'I saw the caretaker and two cleaning staff in here,' added

another inmate. 'We had a chat when I got myself some water. Nothing odd going on, just the usual floor mopping and sink cleaning.'

'Do you suspect anyone, Ember?' asked Raven.

Ember didn't like Mr Forest but dislike wasn't enough to make an accusation. Anyone could have been tempted by the money or scared into doing it. Perhaps the authorities had even colluded to drive home the threats made by the spooks? An alarming thought came to her. Was she absolutely sure Kate and Raven hadn't been involved? She scanned their faces for any sign they were hiding something. 'I don't know who could be behind it.'

'You should demand an enquiry,' said Kate. 'You don't have to put up with treatment like this. They have a duty of care to you.'

Raven and Kate seemed genuine in their concern. Ember decided that at some point she had to put her faith in others. It was exhausting suspecting everyone all the time. 'Yes, I'll do so.' She lowered her voice so only the two detectives could hear. 'They should be able to work out who was on duty the two times someone got in.'

'I'll put Kieran on to it. He can check the staff roster,' said Raven.

'I can lend you some clothes while yours are being washed,' offered Rona.

'I would too,' said Simone, 'but I'm about twice your size.'

'You mustn't let it put you off your performance.' Rona poured another round of tea. 'I'm looking forward to seeing it all the way through.'

'Yeah, you're the leading lady from the girls' unit tonight. Prove to those boys we have the best performers.' Simone batted Johnny's hands together in applause. 'And the Oscar goes to . . .'

Ember smiled despite her vicious tangle of emotions. 'I'll do my best.'

'That's good. Put it behind you.' Raven nudged her. 'I won't say it but you know what I'm thinking.'

'If it involves the words "show", "must", and "go on" then you're wise to keep quiet.' Ember took a bite of sandwich, finding her appetite returning thanks to the support she was receiving.

'Then it'll have to be "break a leg, Ember".' Raven grinned.

She gave an ironic nod of thanks. 'You know, in my world that has quite another meaning, a very literal one.'

'But you're not in that world any more, are you? That's behind you. You're free of it.'

Ember hoped that would be true for her eventually, but it couldn't be, not just yet.

Chapter 12

Joe grabbed Ember as soon as she arrived in the class that had been transformed into the green room for one night only. He towed her to a quiet corner through the excited crowd of actors applying make-up and doing their hair in front of the bank of mirrors. They looked good in their sharp suits and evening gowns, a little like a crowd of students off to prom, though in this case the idea was they were heading to Vegas.

'I'm so sorry to hear about what happened, sweetheart. Kieran's working on it. He's narrowed the list of suspects to three and is seeing if he can cut that down further.' Joe was so angry on her behalf that he wanted to smash through the prison walls till he located the culprit.

Ember pulled a face. 'It was my fault.'

Putting his anger aside—she didn't need that from him—he smoothed away her frown with a brush of his thumb. 'How can it possibly be your fault?'

She smiled bleakly at his tender gesture. 'I knew someone had got in to leave the photos. I should've suspected they'd step up the attacks. It's a classic intimidation technique.'

'And what could you have done to stop it?'

She shrugged. 'Not kept anything personal lying around. The flowers, the letters, they hurt. The rest was just bedding, a few library books.'

Joe had a sudden insight into why her bedroom at her

home had been so Spartan, the only indulgence her collection of novels, music, and framed photos, all of which could be replaced with a little effort or printed off again. 'Oh Em, you shouldn't have to live like this.'

'Like what?'

He wanted to say 'in fear' but that wouldn't go down well. She was actually one of the bravest people he had ever met. 'Like you're under siege.' He straightened the chain of her necklace that had got tangled with the sequinned collar of her gown, making sure the puma lay flat.

She put her hand over his, holding it to her heart for a brief moment before letting go. 'Is there another way of living?' She gave him an ironic look, showing she knew full well her existence was peculiar.

'When you're cleared of this accusation, when you're out of this place, I promise you I'll help you find somewhere— somewhere you can decorate the walls to your taste without worrying that it'll be torn up or defaced.'

'It's a lovely dream. A midsummer one, perhaps?'

'No, it'll be a reality. I've let you down once, I know, but this is a promise which I'm going to deliver. I'll even put up shelves for you.'

She smiled. 'Greater love have no man than he put up shelves for his friend?'

'That's right. I'm darn good at that kind of thing thanks to training under a practical parent.'

'I have something new to look forward to: you in one of those handyman belts brandishing your power tools.'

They both laughed at the ridiculous image she painted. She was amazing. She humbled him by her ability to withstand all that had been thrown at her and still have a sense of humour.

'Oh Ember, you are so going to get that dream for once, cordless drill and all.'

'I will refrain from any cheap innuendo about cordless drills.' She adopted a cute butter-wouldn't-melt-in-her-mouth expression.

'Now you've put it out there, you can't call it back.' He kissed her, a friendly buss on the lips. 'And to think I once thought you weren't clever.'

'I thought the same of Raven and Kate. Shows you how wrong you can be, doesn't it?'

Henry entered and leapt on a chair to call the cast to attention.

'Now, peeps, we are at the midnight hour: the performance! This is what you've been working for. I want you all to relax and have fun. Respect your fellow actors, help them if they get into difficulties, try to remember your own lines,' he gave improviser Graham a pointed look, 'but most of all enjoy this wonderful play you've been given by the greatest writer of all time. Shakespeare would've completely understood each and every one of you. There was no human experience beyond him. So after this, when you feel you've been misunderstood or let down by the system, remember that you have the writings of a friend to turn to. And me too, of course. I at least have an email I check.' He gave them an amused look.

Cobweb-Raymond put up a hand. 'Is it true, Henry, that there are casting directors out there?'

Henry gave his star-find a mysterious smile. 'Maybe, but I don't want your performance to be affected by that, Raymond. You are performing for the entire audience, not just a favoured few. Do it exactly as rehearsed, don't change anything or improvise to impress. That will only trip you up.'

'*Speak the speech, I pray you, as I pronounc'd it to you, trippingly on the tongue,*' murmured Ember for Joe's benefit.

Of course his clever girl would be thinking of Hamlet's advice to the players. Joe wasn't as ready with an apposite quote as her so went for a famous line from another part of the same play. '*The play's the thing . . .*'

'*Wherein I'll catch the conscience of the king,*' she finished. 'I knew there was a reason I liked you, Joe. I've never had anyone I could trade quotations with before.'

Joe smiled brashly, while making a resolution to get hold of a book of Shakespeare quotes so he stood a chance of matching her. He didn't think she would be impressed by his stock of Tolkien and *Game of Thrones* quips.

A member of staff dressed in the all-black uniform of the front-of-house team came to the door to give Henry the nod.

'Right, that's our signal. The audience are in their places and I'm going out to join them. I'll see you all in two hours.' Henry shook hands with Raymond, patted Graham on the back, then made a detour to Ember. 'My dear, prove them wrong about you,' he said fiercely, before kissing her on the cheek and hurrying out.

Joe watched the emotions play across Ember's face. She was struggling to keep her composure. 'He's amazing, isn't he?' he said.

'Normally I wouldn't want to meet my heroes, but Henry hasn't disappointed. He's a genius at saying the right thing to each person, isn't he?'

'He rates you, you know?'

'Then I'll try not to disappoint.'

Their first entrance came from opposite sides of the stage. Joe waited behind the black curtain that had been rigged up to make wings for the rostra platform. He could see Ember on the far side, her arms folded defensively across her middle. It was frustrating, this separation. Not the physical one imposed by the stage, but the walls of the prison. He wasn't able to spend as much time with her as he needed. There was so much he was still missing or failing to understand about her. She was keeping secrets from him, he knew enough to be sure about that. He had told Isaac that he suspected she did have more information on her father's operation and that with just a little more time together she would tell him of her own free will, as she wouldn't want London exposed to radioactive material either. He had seen something in her expression, questions in her eyes, but they were always being interrupted or hurried on to the next thing. He had asked Isaac to persuade MI5 to back off. At the moment the spooks were pressing the Home Secretary to transfer Ember, claiming that throwing her into a less comfortable situation would make her more likely to trade what she knew for a deal. They were wrong. Ember would clam up if they did that to her—and he wouldn't blame her. It was in the best interests of both the country and Ember herself if the YDA was allowed to finish its mission with her.

One last job for me, thought Joe. At least then he could resign knowing he'd gone out on a high note. *That's if I'm still going to resign.* If he went back to New York, where would that leave his relationship with Ember? She believed in him, had tried to persuade him to stay at the YDA even though she was the one he had hurt with his deception. That had showed her true nature and her resilience. Maybe people weren't as break-able as he feared? Maybe he should reconsider?

Raymond got a spontaneous round of applause for his rapped 'Over hill, over dale' speech. Joe readied himself for his entrance. As the sound effect of the casino jackpot siren echoed in the hall, he swept in with his bodyguard of fairy heavies. Ember glided in with her entourage.

'Ill met by moonlight, proud Titania,' he declared.

'What, jealous Oberon? Fairies, skip hence,

I have foresworn his bed and company,' Ember snapped back, dark eyes flashing with haughty insult.

Thoughts of his mission vanished and Joe got sucked into

the drama, the complex verbal sparring with his frustrating, alluring spouse.

'*Tarry, rash wanton, am I not thy lord?*'

'*Then I must be thy lady.*'

The dialogue zipped between them like a tennis rally with both players close to the net. He could feel the attraction sizzling, the furious argument that only those who felt so strongly about each other would have.

'*I do but beg a little changeling boy,*

To be my henchman,' he reasoned. The words were received by the audience with a ripple of pleasure as the appropriateness to the gangland theme put the exchange in new focus. Henry's reinterpretation was working.

'*Not for thy fairy kingdom. Fairies, away!*

We shall chide downright, if I longer stay,' declared Ember.

Joe had to wait before delivering his next line as her magnificent exit earned its own applause.

Meeting backstage, Ember all but jumped into his arms.

'It's going well, isn't it?' Her eyes were shining.

'We're not the RSC but we're not half bad,' agreed Joe. 'The audience seem pleased at least. And you were awesome.'

With a delighted laugh, she whirled away, ready for her next entrance.

By the time they reached the reconciliation dance, Joe told himself he could relax. They were nearing the last act and there had been no disaster. They performed the paso with spiky passion that was nothing short of exhilarating and earned whoops and whistles from the onlookers. Surely nothing could top that?

Maybe it could. Joe was looking forward to Henry's final coup de théâtre. The director had broken with tradition and divided Puck's famous epilogue between the three key members of the cast drawn from Lockwood inmates. With its talk of fault and mending and appeal for forgiveness, Henry declared he was breaking down the fourth wall between the real people behind the roles and the public who sat in judgement on them for their crimes. They'd rehearsed it, but now, in the presence of the press, invited guests, and government inspectors, how would it play?

Ember, Graham, and Raymond stepped forward into the spotlight as the other members of the cast disappeared into the dark.

'If we shadows have offended

Think but this, and all is mended,' said Raymond with gangster charm.

'That you have but slumb'red here,

While these visions did appear.' He stepped off the stage and slapped Henry's cheeks as if waking him. The director hammed up someone startled from sleep. The audience laughed.

Graham moved into his place.

'And this weak and idle theme

No more yielding than a dream,' declared Graham with a cheeky twinkle in his eye, holding up a sign with a spoof returns and refund policy.

'Gentles, do not reprehend.

If you pardon, we will mend.'

'And as he is an honest Puck,' Ember said wryly, indicating the opposite, *'If we have unearned luck*

Now to 'scape the serpent's tongue,' she shot a fulminating look at the press core,

'We will make amends ere long.'

Graham popped up again, fists raised in a 'put-em-up' gesture. *'Else Puck a liar call,'* he announced.

Ember pushed him aside with regal disregard. *'So good night unto you all*

Give me your hands, if we be friends.'

Hesitating a second, she then departed from what they had rehearsed and turned not to the audience but to Joe. She held out her palm, a plea for support. Coming to stand proudly beside her, Joe took her hand and raised it to his lips. He held out his palm to Graham who seized it, realizing where this was going. One by one the cast emerged from the shadows, prisoners and student volunteers mixed so no one could tell who was who. They held hands in a line, coming to the front of the stage.

With tears glittering in her eyes, Ember gave her line again:

'Give me your hands, if we be friends.' She nodded to all who stood with her.

'And we all shall restore amends,' concluded the cast in unison.

The applause was instantaneous. First to her feet was Mrs Bishop, who appeared to have forgiven Henry for turning a play about fairies into a gritty drama about gang leaders and drug abuse. She was joined by the row of inspectors, as well as the family and friends who had been invited to see their problem children in a new light. Having vetted the guest list, Joe knew the faces. He was particularly pleased to see the critic from *The Guardian* getting to her feet, then pulling up her colleague from *The Times*, who gave in with a smile. *The Daily Mail* was less eager, but eventually gave in after a few pokes from those around him. Henry jumped up on to the stage to join his cast. The applause continued for a few more minutes before he held up his hand.

'Thank you, ladies and gentlemen, thank you.'

The noise died down.

'You have indeed been our friends by offering our poor play such a warm reception. This may not have been the most perfectly acted version of the *Dream* that you'll ever see, but it was the most honest, the most important to many of those standing around me, and that in my book makes it the best production in which I have been involved. As our young Puck, Titania, and Cobweb have said, we all need pardon so we can mend. I hope you remember that next time you think or write about the young people society has sentenced, sometimes even before a formal trial.' He took Ember's hand and squeezed it. 'So on behalf of the cast, I'd like to thank you once more for coming. Good night.'

The girls' dressing room was buzzing as the actors enjoyed their post-performance high.

'Did you see Mrs Bishop?' Simone addressed Ember's reflection in the mirror as she unzipped her gown for her. 'She was so impressed! You were awesome; the passion between you and Joe made the hairs stand up on the back of my neck!' Johnny, asleep in his cot in the corner, began to stir. Simone rolled her eyes. 'His lord and master awakes.' She hurried over to pat his stomach, a tactic to make him go back to sleep. 'I'd better take this little monster back to the nursery.'

Waving a goodnight to mother and child, Ember hung her dress on the rail. Now the moment when she was about to take action had arrived, she was plagued by second thoughts. Would she spoil the positive coverage Henry had earned for everyone by what she was doing? Was she being selfish?

No, she told herself, this wasn't about Lockwood. This was about saving the country from a much worse fate. If it meant being crucified in the press for taking advantage of what journalists were bound to call 'naive do-gooders', then so be it.

Raven came to find her as the dressing room emptied. Kate had already rushed off to join Nathan at the party in the hall. 'You're very quiet. Not that you're exactly a chatterbox at the best of times. Are you OK?'

Ember nodded. 'I'm fine.' She swiped off her heavy make-up with a cottonwool pad, taking as long as she could over it.

'Are you coming to the cast party? Henry wants us to meet with the reviewers and I think he has plans to introduce you and Raymond to talent scouts.'

'I'm not sure I'm ready for that. He's assuming rather too much.'

'Like you'll be free and not serving a long sentence?' Raven's brown eyes were full of compassion. 'You've got to believe it, Ember. We're not going to let you go down for a crime you didn't commit, particularly not when you're the victim here. And we'll make sure your brother is OK too, no matter what.'

Even if he'd committed the crime? Raven couldn't promise that. For the moment, Ember was more than half persuaded that the murderer had been Devlin, or someone acting on his order, that made the most sense; but there was still the sliver of doubt that Max might've been involved. It was up to her to sort all this out before the authorities made yet more mistakes. 'I'll be along eventually. Just give me a moment, OK?'

Raven smiled. 'Take as long as you need. But don't forget, Joe's waiting out there too. If you don't want to talk to acting people, at least you'll want to see him.'

'Tell him I'll be with him as soon as I can.' True words that misled.

'OK. Will do.' With a final smile, Raven left, closing the door behind her.

Finally, she was alone. Ember quickly changed from petticoat into jeans and a black sweater. She didn't have much time. She had picked up from eavesdropping on Henry's conversations with the volunteers from the Globe that they were heading back directly after the performance, striking the set as soon as the applause ended as the equipment was wanted for

189

another show the following day. They'd be loading their van even now.

Passing the props table, she saw that the ass's head had been put back in its basket. There was her excuse. Tucking her jacket inside, she picked it up and carried it out into the car park. No one spared her a second glance as they were too busy sorting out the spaghetti tangle of cabling and dismantling lighting towers. Taking a quick look around her, she was grateful to see that the car park was deserted. She walked into the open back of the van and put the basket towards the far end. Was it really going to be this simple? Making herself a cocoon in the black material that had been used to drape the sides of the stage, she hunkered down to wait, wedged in so no one could see her unless they decided to unpack and start again.

The technicians soon filled up the space in front of her with a variety of poles and lighting rigs. Each barrier made her feel a little less exposed. They worked remarkably quickly, showing all the signs of a well-oiled machine.

'Is that it?' asked one of the men.

'Yep. We'd better get our skates on if we're to get this back before midnight. We've got to set up tomorrow at ten and I could do with some sleep myself before then.'

'I'll just tell Henry we're off. He did a good job here, didn't he?'

'Can't believe how he drew so much out of those kids. He's a miracle worker.' The driver slammed the door shut.

The next thing Ember heard was the engine starting and the vehicle beginning to move. Remembering how poorly she had travelled on the journey here, she shuffled round to face the direction in which they were heading, bracing her back against the basket. There was still one all-important test to pass. She was banking on the party still being in full swing and the night-time roll call being held later than normal. If not, and her absence had been noticed, she was stuffed.

The van slowed. The front door slammed and footsteps walked round the van. They were going to look inside. Burrowing down so no betraying pale skin showed, she held her breath. Cooler air flowed in from open doors and a torch beam danced over the contents.

'I hope, mate, you don't want me to unpack the lot?' asked the driver cheerfully.

'No, that's fine. Amazing how much you can get into a transit van.'

'Comes with practice.'

'Off you go then. Thanks for volunteering your time.'

'Well worth it.'

'So I've been told. I was the poor sod who got stuck on gate duty.'

'They were filming it. You should take a look.' The rear doors slammed shut and Ember could breathe again.

'Goodnight!' With a friendly tap on the side of the vehicle, the guard let them through the gate.

Ember gulped. She'd done it. She'd managed to break out of prison. Now she just had to make it worthwhile.

Chapter 13

'Have you seen Ember, Raven?' asked Joe. He was tired of making small talk with people he'd never see again. He just wanted to be with her.

Raven looked up from her perch on Kieran's knee. 'I left her in the dressing room a while ago. She seemed a little down and didn't want to talk to the casting people Henry lured here.' She nodded to where Raymond stood with the director talking to two women, who were eyeing the young man with professional interest. Joe could almost read their excitement in having found a face so suited for gritty drama, an actor far more authentic than the well-brought-up middle-class kids who tended to fill acting schools. 'Maybe she decided to cut the party? The press are here and they've been so foul to her, making her into some horrible daughter of King Lear, out to kill off Dad and take over his kingdom.'

Joe didn't like the sound of that, even if Ember would've appreciated Raven's Shakespearian comparison. If Ember was upset then she should be with him, not alone in her room. 'Could you just check for me?'

Raven gave a put-upon sigh, quite happy where she was. 'You know, Joe, I'm going to be so relieved when she's somewhere you can go look for her yourself. I feel like Noah's messenger bird, flapping between the two of you.'

'You make such a lovely go-between,' said Kieran, squeezing her waist, then boosting her up.

'Thanks, Raven,' added Joe.

Kieran watched his girlfriend leave the hall. 'You know, she's got in deep with Ember, too deep, maybe?'

'What do you mean?'

'She's been telling Ember that we'll clear her name.'

Joe rubbed his throat, remembering he'd promised the same thing. 'Can't we?'

'We can't interfere with the courts. There's a fragment of doubt about the knife but still no better suspect.'

'What? Do you think she did it then?' Joe had to clamp down on the wild impulse to punch his friend.

Kieran turned to look at him. 'Joe, I'm not your enemy here. I'm convinced she didn't. That doesn't mean she'll win her case, especially if someone is doing a good job of framing her for it.'

'Then we'll do a better job of breaking the frame.'

'Joe . . . ?' Kieran stopped and shook his head as if reconsidering.

'What? You don't have to pull your punches with me.'

'I'm just worried I'm going to be on the end of one of yours.'

Joe sat down, trying to relax. 'Sorry, I'm just on edge tonight.'

'OK, look, you remember you told Ember that being in a play could cast a glamour over short-term relationships—you know, when you were trying to put her off the scent about Raven and me?'

Joe nodded. 'Are you implying that what I feel for her is me getting caught in my own trap?'

'Is it?'

'I hope not, because that would mean I've led her on unforgivably.'

'Or has she led you? She's a survivor. She's had to be. Has she made herself what would appeal to you: clever, vulnerable, innocent? Maybe she's tougher, guiltier than you think? Not of her father's murder, but of other things.'

'I don't think I really want to contemplate what she had to do to stay alive in that vipers' nest of a home.'

'But that's my point. She was raised in the snake pit. If she were one of us, she'd be a Cobra, Joe, not a Cat like you. She's got a ruthlessness to her and I'm just afraid you'll not see it in time to protect yourself.'

Joe couldn't stop his anger billowing up like a summer squall, partly because Kieran was only speaking what a little voice inside his head had been whispering. 'She's not pretended to be a saint. That was me.'

'Yes, but how well do you really know her?'

Raven seemed to be taking a very long time in locating Ember. Joe was forced into a conversation with one of the reviewers from *The Daily Mail.* After the brief bonhomie of the performance, the journalist had returned to type and was fishing for gossip on Ember, what it had been like to kiss her, dance with her, how she had treated Joe and the other cast during rehearsals. As the tabloids had been the ones to give Ember the hardest time, Joe was disinclined to answer but reminded himself he could do her a service by stressing how cooperative she had been, how she had revealed herself as a thoughtful and gifted actress. He enjoyed making his answers as dull as possible.

'We were all a little scared of her of course,' he said, laying out some bait.

The journalist's eyes glittered. 'Oh yes? Why was that?' He was clearly imagining her turning into some kind of crazed Wolverine, blades flashing from knuckles.

'Because she's so intelligent. She knew her part, and ours,

well before we did, so could give us a prompt when we dried up,' replied Joe, pretending he didn't notice the disappointment in the man's eyes.

He felt a tug on his elbow. Great, Raven was back. Finally. 'Excuse me.' He let her direct him away from the journalist. 'She's not coming?'

Raven looked more serious than he'd seen her for a long time. 'Joe, I can't find her.'

'What?'

'She's not in the dressing room, not gone back to the girls' unit. She's vanished.'

'They were moving her to another room, weren't they?'

'Yes, next to mine. I checked that. No Ember. There's no trace of her anywhere. What do we do? I don't think Mrs Bishop knows yet.'

'What are you getting at?'

'I think she's run. The attack on her here must've made her feel unsafe, maybe even desperate?'

Joe didn't want even to entertain the possibility. 'She hid that well.'

'That's what she does: hides what's upsetting her.'

'But what's the point? She knew we were going to help her. Going on the run is the absolute worst thing she could do.' He tried not to think of it as a betrayal of what they had between them.

'But what choice did she think she had? We said we'd look after her brother but we didn't stop him being beaten up in the park. We said we'd help her and MI5 came calling and then her room was trashed. Our promises must look very thin.'

Joe swore. 'Get the team together, tell Mrs Bishop you and Kate are leaving right now, don't worry about maintaining cover. We've got to find Ember, work out where she's gone.'

Raven nodded, her gaze already going to Kieran, who instantly broke off his conversation and came to her side.

'Trouble?' he asked.

'Yes, Ember's just dumped us all in an episode of *Prison Break*,' said Raven.

'You're kidding me?'

'I'm not. Titania's done a bunk, but she can't have gone far.'

Joe shook his head. 'Don't kid yourself. She doesn't do anything without thinking it through. She'd've had a plan—and a damn good one at that.'

'What do you think she's doing?'

'No idea. As Key reminded me a few minutes ago, maybe we don't know her very well at all.'

Kieran was tapping on his phone.

'What are you doing?' asked Joe.

'Taking a look at the CCTV coverage. If she didn't walk out, she went in a vehicle. She could've stowed away in the back of one if the driver wasn't paying attention. She might still be here if she chose the wrong one and the owner's taking their time.'

Joe didn't wait to hear any more but rushed out into the car park. A cold light rain was just starting, cutting short the cheery goodnights. The visitors hurried to their vehicles, heads down. None checked the seats behind them as they started the engine. She could be anywhere. He could hardly throw himself on the bonnets to prevent them leaving.

Raven caught up with him. 'There's a guard at the gate, remember? They check ID, back seats, and trunk.'

Of course. He'd been through the process himself enough times. He should've thought of that. So what did that leave? 'Where's the equipment van?' Joe spotted the paler patch of tarmac where the Globe vehicle had been parked.

'They had to go early. Looking at the rain spots they left

196

after the shower at ten and before this one started.' Realization dawned on Raven's face.

Kieran joined them. 'The van drove out forty-five minutes ago. That puts them well on their way to London.' The vehicle was searched at the gate but not thoroughly. I'd put my money on her being in the back.'

'Do we tell the police? Get the van pulled over?' asked Raven, looking to Joe for instructions. Even though he had resigned, they still insisted on treating him as mission leader.

At least, Joe thought, he could look after his team even if he made a hash of everything else. He led them to stand under the cover of the porch, out of the rain. He knew what Raven was really asking: how much did they trust Ember's intentions? It would be better for her if they picked her up quietly at her destination without anyone else being involved. They might even be able to smooth it over with the Lockwood authorities if they got her back before morning. Mrs Bishop wouldn't want the bad publicity a prison break would attract to dent the positive coverage of tonight's performance. Such things could be finessed.

Or maybe it was time he went with his head rather than his heart? The right move for the mission was to let Ember do what she felt she must, even if she paid the penalty by facing further charges. He didn't buy that she was running because of intimidation, but he would accept that she had a purpose which went beyond escape. She'd known there was a chance the charges against her might be dropped; running wasn't in her interests; so therefore something else was in play. This was just the breakthrough in the case they had been waiting for: Ember had a plan; logic said that they should first see what she was up to before reeling her back in.

And, amazingly, considering the bumpy progress of their relationship, Joe realized that he trusted her. Sure, he was hurt that she hadn't appealed to him for help with it, but he knew her now. She was trying to do the right thing, even if it was in the wrong way.

'The van's heading for the Globe, correct?'

'Yes. The scenery store around the back,' confirmed Kieran.

'Damien and Rose are at the YDA a hundred metres away. We can arrange for them to watch what Ember does.'

'We can.'

'What shall we tell Mrs Bishop?' asked Raven.

'I think we'll leave Isaac to sort that out. That's what they're paying him the big bucks for.' Joe gave a wry smile. 'I'll contact him while you round up Nathan and Kate. And we'll need a lift from someone.'

'We're going after her?'

'You bet we are.'

Raven nodded, then pressed his arm. 'I'm sorry, Joe, about all this.' She meant that Ember hadn't trusted Joe enough, hadn't cared for him enough to go to him rather than strike out on her own.

'Let's not judge her, OK? We did that once and were way off target. Let's see what she's doing first.' The words felt good, fair to Ember. He wouldn't let this destroy what he believed they were building between them.

Kieran stepped away to explain the situation to Damien on his phone. Joe pressed the contact on his for Isaac. 'You'd better give me room to do this, Raven. I might have to make some nifty moves to get him to allow a prisoner on remand to go AWOL.'

Raven smiled. 'I've every faith in your nifty moves, Joe. I've seen you dance. I'll go find us that lift.'

Ember woke up when the engines stopped. Had she really been asleep? It had been a long day—an interrogation, a trashed room, a performance, an escape—she could be forgiven for being tired, she thought with a sardonic twist of humour.

'What do you want to do with the stuff in the back?' called one of the men as the front doors slammed. From their echo she could tell they were in a building. A garage maybe?

'Leave it. Let's sort it out tomorrow.'

Ember had been thinking that maybe her master plan had a flaw, and now she was about to find out. Her dramatic escape might end ignominiously if she got trapped till morning. She had two options: bang on the side of the van till they let her out or hope the rear doors had a release handle inside. She had to decide quickly before they clocked off for the night. Squirming out of her cubbyhole she wormed her way between the van roof and the stack of the poles and scaffolding, going by touch. Someone was still there: she could hear him whistling the song she had danced to with Joe. Sliding down by the doors, she groped around until she found the catch. Squeezing gently, the lock popped. She could get out without calling for assistance. A second piece of luck going her way.

The whistler departed and a door slammed shut in the distance. Ember cracked the rear of the van open and dropped to the floor. From the emergency lighting over the exits she could see she was in the dimly-lit space of the scenery store. Lights and furniture were neatly stacked along the sides. A second vehicle was parked ahead of her van. Nearby was the Tudor theatre with its empty seats and open-air auditorium waiting for tomorrow's performance, but here everything was modern electrical equipment and concrete. Some of her happiest moments had been spent watching plays in this theatre and that thought made it feel a friendly place. Still, friendly or not, would she be able to get out without tripping an alarm?

She walked quietly to the street door, taking care not to

knock over any of the equipment. The door had a key pad next to it and a light showing the alarm was active. She studied the controls for evidence that some numbers had been touched more often than others. Numbers 1, 5, and 9 were definitely more worn.

Ember smiled. Obviously, they kept to a memorable date and assumed thieves would not know about the life of Shakespeare. She typed into the pad '1599'—the year the Globe was established on the South Bank. The light went from red to green and she pushed the door open. Not wanting to leave her favourite theatre vulnerable, she rearmed the alarm and closed it behind her. There: no one would now get in trouble for leaving the alarm off. The volunteers had been doing Lockwood a good turn; it would've been churlish to repay them by getting them blamed.

Not to mention what would happen when they realized they'd helped a prisoner escape, she thought darkly. Not that she could change that. Zipping up her jacket she headed east, hoping the Underground would still be running.

Henry had been grumbling ever since Raven persuaded him to give the five YDA students a lift to London.

'I can't believe she escaped in our van.'

'I'm afraid so, Henry,' said Joe, sitting upfront and so getting the worst of the complaints. 'Think of it like Falstaff in the buck basket.'

'Very good, Joe.' Henry acknowledged the Shakespearian reference to *The Merry Wives of Windsor*. 'But to take my Oyster card after all the time and attention I gave her!'

'She could've taken your whole wallet, Henry.'

'And you're sure she's innocent, more sinned against than sinning?'

'Absolutely. You know, you really should play this quotation game with her rather than me. She'd give you a run for your money.'

'Or for my travel credit, you mean.'

'We'll make sure you're reimbursed.'

'I'm not worried about a fare on the underground, I'm worried about her! She may think she knows what she's doing, but do I have to remind you she's only seventeen and already framed for a murder you say she didn't commit? That sounds like someone with serious enemies.'

'I know, Henry, and I'm worried too.' Joe looked down to where his phone rested on his thigh. 'Damien confirms she's just left the scenery store and is heading down Clink Street.'

'Do you think she knows she's walking right past the YDA?' asked Nathan, squeezed into the rear seat with Kieran, Kate, and Raven. The guys bookended the girls with their arms stretched across the back but it was an uncomfortable ride for them.

'Why would she? She's got other things on her mind right now, I guess.'

Henry turned onto the M25 orbital. 'Decision time, ladies and gentlemen. Do you want me to head into the centre of town?'

They needed a little more information before they knew where she was going but Henry was correct, he had to know how long to stay on the motorway. 'Turn east, please. If she's going to see her brother or to her old home, she'll head that way.'

Henry indicated and joined the eastbound carriageway. 'I suppose this is rather an exciting end to what has already been an exciting day. One for the memoirs.'

'Henry . . .'

'I know, I know, I'll change your names and so on. But how long do you think it'll be before it's public knowledge I was inadvertently party to a prison break? I might as well make myself sound a hero rather than a fool.'

Damien texted to say that Ember had headed north on the Underground and changed on to an eastbound service on the Central Line. He and Rose were using the cover of the crowds returning from theatres and restaurants on the last train, but he was anticipating close cover would get more difficult as the passengers thinned out. When she passed Mile End without alighting, they concluded that she was heading to her old family home rather than to see her brother.

Joe called up the directions on his phone to guide Henry off the right exit on the motorway. They should be there well before the train, which made stops every few minutes, plenty of time to get into position.

'What do you think she's doing?' asked Henry.

'We don't know. It's not a good place to go if she's trying to avoid recapture. She must guess the police will look for her there,' said Joe.

'She's probably got something stashed in the house that she needs,' guessed Kate. 'A passport in a false name? Cash?'

'I don't think she's running. It's something else. Park over there, Henry.' He gestured for their driver to pull over in the golf club car park. 'We'll make our way on foot from here. Thanks for all your help.'

'My boy, you can't bring me all this way then not let me stay for the final act.'

'Henry, this could be dangerous.'

'I'm a grown man. You lot are all seventeen and eighteen. I should be sending you home to bed. Where are the police for heaven's sake? If there's danger, then they should be here, not putting you in harm's way.'

Joe didn't actually think Ember posed any threat to them, but it wouldn't be helpful having an amateur stumbling about in what was already a messy mission. 'Please, be reasonable.'

'No, my mind's made up. I refuse to write in my diaries that I scarpered just when things got interesting. Besides you need me if she takes off again.'

Joe shook his head in exasperation. He didn't think the director's stubbornness had anything to do with Henry's memoirs but the fact that he genuinely cared for Ember. For that reason alone, he would let him stay. 'OK, but for this performance I'm the director and you do what I say. No improvisation. No ad-libbing. Understood?'

'Yes, sir.' Henry's smile was both triumphant and amused. Joe wished he could add a little fear too to make him suitably cautious.

'If there are other people here, then you must keep back. These people ship guns as well as nuclear material. They'll not think twice about shooting you.'

'Joe, you can trust me. Early in my career, I directed more police dramas for television than you've had hot dinners.'

'That is not reassuring. This is life, not a Sunday night serial.'

'We're wasting our advantage,' muttered Nathan. 'Damien says they're two stops away.'

Joe dismissed from his mind the problem of Henry. He had no manpower to make sure Henry stayed back and, as the director said, he was a grown man brought into this by Isaac and Jan Hardy, not by Joe.

'Let's go.' Joe led the way jogging across the golf course, using the fairways to cut down the chance of tripping in the dark. 'When we get there, Nathan and Kate check the annexe. The nanny should be in residence by now so there's a chance Ember is heading to see her.'

'But you don't think so?' asked Nathan.

'No, my gut tells me her business is in the main house. See

all's quiet there and stay on hand in case I'm wrong. Kieran and Raven, I want you to monitor the front of the house. If anyone else comes in that way, I want you to use your discretion whether to let them. Henry, you get the summer house to keep watch on the back. I've added your number to our messaging group so you'll see what's going on. Make sure your own cell phone is on silent, not vibrate.'

Henry snorted as if to say such a reminder was unnecessary.

'Only use it for text updates on your position.'

'I'm hardly going to be updating my Twitter feed, Joe.'

That was why a civilian didn't belong in a serious operation. 'This isn't a joke. If this goes wrong, lives could be lost.'

'Sorry, yes, I do understand. I was born with an incurable disposition to levity that gets worse with nerves.'

At least he was now nervous. 'Control it or you go back to the car. Everyone to check in each fifteen minutes on the hour and so on, so we can tell if there's trouble.'

They reached the back wall of Ember's garden.

'And where are you going to be, Joe?' asked Kieran.

'Inside. I'll keep a line open to you, Key, so you can hear what I hear. You inform the rest if there's anything significant. Call in reinforcements if you judge it necessary. Isaac's got the people on standby. They'll move in closer once Ember's inside but won't make themselves visible until we call them in.'

Using Henry's car rug, the five YDA students and one award-winning theatre director climbed over the wall and dropped down into the bushes.

'Everyone clear what they're to do?' asked Joe.

His friends nodded and melted into the shadows.

'Henry, I'll take you to the summer house. I need to know you're going to follow orders.'

'Are you stashing me there because it's out of the way?'

'That's part of it but not the whole. I really do need to

know if anyone else comes the way we have. I don't want to be taken by surprise. Can I rely on you?'

'Yes, Joe, you can.'

Satisfied with that, Joe left Henry on watch inside Max's favourite hideaway and hurried to the back door. There was no one to watch him beat Nathan's record for picking the locks. Slipping inside he chose his vantage point and settled down to wait.

Chapter 14

Ember let herself in the front door using the key she'd retrieved from the gardener's shed. Acting against her father's orders, she had hidden it many months ago, taped inside a big metal watering can. Max was often forgetful and she hadn't wanted him to be stranded if she was out for any reason. It had been their secret, one which they both, she was pleased to see, had kept from the police.

She allowed the sensation of being inside settle on her, with its familiar heavy drape of despair. Despite its luxurious furnishings, the mansion always sucked everything out of her, like the Dementor on the train in that Harry Potter film. J K Rowling had an acute understanding of what it was like to feel hopeless, Ember thought. The house itself was cold, with many signs of neglect. A drift of junk mail lay in the porch. Had Nanny Roe not been allowed back in? She almost bent down to collect it but then thought better of it. It would be better not to leave a trace that she had visited. Stepping over the envelopes, she went further, making a quick tour of the ground floor to check she was alone. There was no reason why anyone else should be there—Nanny Roe was likely to be tucked up in bed in the annexe at this hour of the night— but Ember didn't want to take any chances. She estimated she had very little time before the authorities were on her trail and it wouldn't be hard to follow once they twigged she'd stolen Henry's travel card. She meant this to be a very quick visit.

Ember paused at the bottom of the stairs. She had two things to do and was momentarily undecided as to the order in which to do them. That wasn't like her: she normally had no problem taking decisions. Something wasn't right about the house but she couldn't quite put her finger on it. Probably just her mind playing tricks on her. *Come on, Ember, don't dither. Up first.* She needed to check there in any case so that made more sense. Running up the stairs, she walked surefooted down the bedroom corridor, coming to a halt outside her father's door. This wasn't so much from choice but because her feet just wouldn't move. She pushed the door open but didn't enter.

Oh God. She could still smell his aftershave. It was like he had never been murdered but was waiting somewhere to surprise her.

Get a hold on yourself, Ember. Seeing the stained, stripped mattress rammed home that he really was dead. Prison had dulled that fact, made it possible to avoid it for large stretches of time. Mick Lord had been stabbed to death and then been buried. Her father, a man who had always seemed too vibrant, too sure of himself to be beaten down by anyone or anything, had been killed while she slept down the corridor. Memories of her father surged back like the successive waves of a tsunami. Mick trying to get Max into football and then cuffing his son for being more interested in comics and dogs. *You little cretin!* Mick singing Irish ballads to her when he came home drunk after a night out with his mates, her leaning over the bannister, him singing down in the hall. *Ember is me darlin'.* Mick using his belt on Max for breaking a window and then on her when she tried to stop him. *You're mine to do with what I want. No one gets between me and my family!* Mick presenting her with a white ball gown for a New Year's party held by a

Russian friend of his, insisting she come with him. *You're the only hope for this generation, Ember. Don't let me down.* Mick teaching her how to shoot when they went on one of his weekends with his associates, showing off his girl's prowess with a range of weapons. *She's a natural.*

A natural what? Ember wondered. *A natural killer?* Was that what he'd seen in her?

She'd never understood her father, what drove him, why he had no real love for either of his children, only a sense of possession and entitlement. He'd not said much about his own childhood but Nanny Roe had told her once that his parents had been neglectful, leaving his upbringing to her. He had been lucky to see them once a week as they were busy with their lives, her grandmother as a nightclub owner in the East End, her grandfather as an upmarket dealer in stolen goods. Perhaps that had killed off his own parenting instinct? She had decided long ago that he would never really love her, only what she could be for him. It had been a hopeless reality that she had carried with her like a marathon runner wearing concrete boots.

Staring at the stain, she made a mental effort to step out of the boots now. She couldn't carry them with her any longer. Mick Lord had been damaged in ways she would never fathom. Bad parent begetting bad parent like a hellish row of Russian dolls, opening up to repeat the same pattern again and again. She wanted to be different, break that mould. She had Max and maybe she had Joe too. That was going to be enough.

Determinedly shaking off her mood, she walked on to her bedroom and efficiently packed a bag of clothes. The tiger had disappeared, she noticed, and a wire dug out of the wall over the wardrobe. It was nauseating to imagine being watched, her unguarded moments on show. Just as well, really, that she had never allowed herself the liberty to make her inner rebellion an external one. They hadn't had a camera inside her head, had they? She made herself study the angle that the device had covered and was relieved to discover that it wouldn't have captured the doorway to the bathroom where she usually changed. But it was still an outrage—a violation. There was so much that should have remained private, like walking in a bath towel to the wardrobe, or maybe even humming or singing. She must, on occasion, have revealed too much of her real self, that was more truly exposing than being caught half-naked. Hopefully, she would never have to come in here again.

Her last stop was in the basement. Easing open the door to the cellar, she switched on the light. Her father's wine collection stretched before her, rows of circular glass in wooden squared nests like some modern art installation. It was her least favourite place in the house. She'd been shut down here for twelve hours without a light as a punishment for some misdemeanour when she was six, and never forgotten the terror of being trapped in the cold darkness. At least she could reach the light switch these days, and no one had removed the bulb. From the disturbed dust on the shelving she could tell the police had already made a sweep of the area. She had to hope they'd not found the secret cache or her escape would've been for nothing.

By-passing the bottles, she went to the far end where the original inhabitant of the house, the vicar for the church next door, had dug a tunnel from the house to the church vestry, possibly so he could avoid annoying parishioners and keep them on their toes by popping up in church unannounced. Or maybe he'd just wanted to keep his vestments dry in a shower? The tunnel had long since been filled in, as such Victorian whimsies were no longer in fashion and the Church had sold off the vicarage to developers, but the beginning of the passage remained, protected by a metal grill. This wasn't locked and, again, there were signs the search team had poked around here too. Opening the grill she studied the dusty brickwork beyond. Good. As far as she could tell, they didn't go any further, thinking it a dead-end.

Ember knelt down and removed the false mortar between the lowest row of bricks, then levered out two of them. She then took off her necklace. Fumbling for a second, she slid the stretching front legs of the puma into a tiny custom-built key-hole. A narrow door swung open and she pulled out the safety deposit box stowed inside, what Mick called their last resort. This opened with a combination, set to Ember and Max's birthday in reverse. Not having time to sort out the contents, she tipped them into her bag and then replaced everything so no one would know that she had ever been down here.

Brushing off her knees, she stood up.

'That's very devious. I'm not surprised it wasn't found.'

'Joe!' Ember whirled round to find him leaning against a wine rack just behind her. 'I didn't hear you come in!' This was a disaster. She hadn't had enough time. He was going to spoil everything!

'Do credit me with having some skills. I've not made a great showing on this mission but I know how to keep out of sight when I want. I think you should've gone with the red sweater, not the blue by the way. The blue makes you look depressed.'

He'd been following her up in her bedroom too and she hadn't even noticed.

'Returning to the scene of your crime?' he asked, drawing an E in the dust on one bottle of red wine.

That hurt. 'I thought you believed that I was innocent?'

'Yeah, I decided to trust you, but it's now swinging between fifty-fifty and seventy-thirty in my mind, seeing how you've gone straight to a stash you could've told us about at any time. That's not the action of an innocent girl wanting to clear her name. What was in there, by the way? Cash? Diamonds? Contact book for Europe's most wanted?'

He wasn't far wrong. 'You don't understand.'

'Try me.'

'I have a plan.'

'I'm all ears.'

'I'm going to resurrect my father.'

'That's a hell of a plan, honey. Now can you tell me your real one or do I get the police to come tidy this up?'

He was angry with her, and she hadn't really expected anything else. 'I'm not explaining this very well.' She hugged the bag to her chest.

'You're not explaining *this* at all.'

'Can we get out of here?' She took a step towards the stairs but he blocked her way.

'Uh-uh, not until you tell me what's going on.'

'I hate it down here.'

'I'm not too chipper about being here myself, but while we're in the cellar I've no signal so there's no one listening in to my phone. I'm giving you a chance to tell me the truth and we can decide what to do with it.'

He was giving her the benefit of the doubt, even hinting that if she'd made some criminal mistakes then he'd help her arrange the facts to the best advantage. That thought warmed her as nothing else could.

'Oh, Joe.'

'Please, don't.' He held up a hand to keep her back, looking annoyed with himself. She guessed he feared she was going to betray him and it would be his softer feelings that allowed her to do so. 'Just tell me the truth now. If you care anything for me, for us, that's what you'll do. One hint of a lie then I'm done. I won't be your fool again, Ember.'

'You were never that.'

'Quit stalling. If I don't check in with my team in four minutes, they're going to be joining us.'

'OK, OK. Look, I've got my father's personal mobile in this bag.' She held it open so he could inspect the jumbled contents.

Joe looked disappointed. 'No, we've got that in evidence.'

Ember shook her head. 'You don't. He ordered me to put it down here on the night before . . .' She swallowed, not wanting to revisit that scene in her mind. 'Anyway, that was one of the things I did for him, stashed his valuables when he wasn't expecting to make any deals for a few days. I was the only one he trusted with the key as it was part of our bargain.' She touched the necklace. 'He wanted someone in the family to be in on the secret, but just one, so he would know who betrayed him if it came out.'

'Go on.'

'He was famous for guarding this phone like a dragon on his hoard. No one touched it but him. It was part of his way of doing things. I was going to send a message to . . . to the people I suspect are behind the shipment of nuclear material, pretending to be him.'

'So you do know who they are?'

'Suspect,' she reiterated, realizing that had been a false step. 'I'm not sure.'

'You should've told us.' He appeared ready to give up on her, moving away from the rack.

'And have the secret services mess up the rest of the plan? You were going to share the intelligence with them, weren't you?'

'That's their job.'

'I don't trust them to do it. They're compromised—get too close to the arms dealers like they do and some it rubs off on you. My father bought people like that, called them his

212

shadows. They're still out there. My contact would know I was lying before I had a chance to lure him to the UK. Someone in MI5 or 6 would trade that information for their own purposes.'

'You don't have much faith in the people paid to protect us, do you?'

'No, because there are others who can pay them more than the government ever can. But I do trust you.' He stilled, really listening now. She only had words to persuade him or he would hand her over to MI5 and everything would head into disaster territory. She hurried through the rest of the explanation. 'I was going to pretend to be my father and say that I'd faked my own death with Devlin's agreement as the police had got too interested in me. My daughter had been in on it too and I was arranging for the charges against her to be dropped by messing with the forensics against her.'

'Would anyone believe that?'

'In my world, yes. Putting me in prison would be regarded as necessary training and proof of my absolute loyalty. I know several gang leaders who have disappeared and come back with new faces, new identities a few months later. And the people I'm contacting haven't been following the case blow by blow; they're foreigners. All they'll know is that Mick Lord supposedly died.'

'And when you've persuaded them he hasn't?'

'I was going to say that Devlin's got too grand for his own good, trying to take over during my break from the limelight. I'm taking back this operation and changing the delivery details to keep the power in my own hands.'

'And then?'

'And then I was going to tell you what we'd agreed and hope, with you taking the lead, the authorities don't mess up the containment and capture of all those involved.'

'Really?'

Her heart sank: he didn't believe her. 'Yes, really.'

'You could've told me all this back in Lockwood.'

'I thought about it.'

'And decided against it.'

'I decided that I didn't have time to know what was best so I went with what I've always done.'

'And that is?'

'Do it on my own.'

Joe gazed at her for a few moments, looking as if he was trying to burrow inside her head and root out her secret thoughts. There was nothing more she could do. He didn't know that she had been completely honest. But what use was the truth? No one apart from Max had ever thought the best of her, always assuming the worst. How Joe reacted now would decide whether their relationship had a future, but she had no right to ask him anything as she'd not shown any faith in him when she had the chance. She'd failed that test as she had so many others.

Then, miraculously, wonderfully, he opened his arms. 'Come here.'

'Oh, Joe.' She went straight into his embrace. It was the most amazing moment of her life, feeling loved and accepted even with her glaring faults. 'I'm so sorry. I'm just trying to make this right.'

'I know, honey. Give me a moment to hold you and let me think. We've been working against the clock the whole time we've been together, haven't we?'

She nodded against his chest. 'They're bad people, Joe. I don't really want you anywhere near them.'

'You've got to stop protecting everyone at your own expense, that's how you ended up in jail, remember?' He rubbed his hand up and down her spine, soothing her with his firm touch. 'That's why we work in a team at the YDA, so no one is ever left on their own having to carry the weight of the world. Speaking of which . . .'

Ember held her breath. She could hear a creak on the stairs as several people approached but as Joe didn't react she made herself relax.

'I see you've got everything in hand, Joe,' said Damien. He sounded amused.

'Ember and I were just having a little discussion about team work.'

'I'll tell Kate that's what it's called now,' said Nathan.

'You didn't call in.' Kieran had joined them.

'No signal down here. Let's take this away from here. Ember's got a plan and I think it's a good one. I'll need to run it by Isaac.' He picked up her bag, whether to stop her running again or because he was being a gentleman, Ember wasn't sure. 'I'll fill you in when we're back in the car.'

'We won't all fit,' warned Nathan.

'You can take one from our garage,' offered Ember. 'There's a Lexus and a Porsche.'

Damien's eyes gleamed with delight. 'Tough decision.'

'You're taking the Lexus, Damien. More room for passengers.' Joe took Ember's hand and gave it a reassuring squeeze. 'Let's get out of here. I don't think this place is good for you.'

Joe couldn't get out of his mind how Ember had looked at him when he'd offered her a hug. She had the expression of a person braced for a slap being offered a kiss instead. She had expected him to be cruel in his anger, not realizing that he was angry mainly because she had felt she had to do all this alone, that he had not succeeded in convincing her that he was there for her. He hadn't really been angry with her at all.

Rome wasn't built in a day. One of his mother's favourite

mottos came into his head. Carol Masters was a nurturing soul but she also understood from her volunteer work with the young homeless in New York how a damaged person needed time. She would've told him that Ember needed far more experience of his reliability before she was ready to drop her shields. Blame her upbringing, not the girl, she would've said.

Well, Mom, you've been proved right. Again. Joe grinned as Ember nestled up to him in the rear seat of the Lexus. Shields were lowering nicely right now.

'Are you sure it's OK for me to come to the YDA?' she whispered so that Damien and Rose couldn't hear.

'Of course it's OK. We can't have you on the loose else the police will scoop you up, or a well-meaning member of the public report a sighting of a notorious fugitive from justice.'

She shivered. 'I guess. They've probably put a bounty on my head already.'

'Sweetheart, they only do that in Westerns, not Central London.'

'They do that where I come from. Devlin will not want me out of his control. He'll have put the word out that he'd be grateful to anyone who removes me from the picture.'

She was right. He should've thought of that himself. 'We'll protect you. They won't know where you are.'

'Just don't underestimate them. It won't be like in the films where the villains spend all that time explaining what a horrible end they've got planned for the hero, giving him a chance to escape; they'll just send a sniper and that'll be that.'

The very thought chilled him to the bone. 'That will not be that. You will not go near windows street-facing and will wear body armour when we go out.'

'I can't go back to prison yet—not till this is over. Promise me that. The next step after trashing the room is to hurt the person. I don't think I'd last a night in there.'

'We've narrowed down the list of suspects to Tom Forest. He's being questioned right now and will be charged with carrying messages from the outside and vandalizing your room to intimidate you.'

She shrugged. 'Even if he gets the sack or a prison sentence for that, there's always someone else ready to step up for the right price or pressure. That's one of my father's favourite sayings.'

The difference between their family mottos was not lost on Joe. 'Then we'll just have to make sure you don't go back, won't we?'

Rose turned round in her seat. 'Hey, we've not really met yet, have we?'

'Only from a distance,' said Ember. 'Thanks for being so nice to my brother.'

'I like him. He's not just a job, you know. Did you realize he's really good at sketching? He showed me some of his work.'

'Yes, I know.' Ember admitted this with fierce pride. 'Everyone always underestimates him but he's quite brilliant.'

'You never have.'

'No.'

'And you didn't kill your father.'

'No.'

Rose smiled. 'What I meant was that you really didn't, on the strength of the evidence. I don't have to take your word on that. Kieran showed me the forensic reports and I ran an analysis of them on some software I've developed. I think I can help your case. I've added a new imaging function which will assist the jury in visualising the attack in 3D and that will prove the knife with your prints on is not the murder weapon.'

'What did happen to the real knife?' asked Joe, realizing no one had actually stopped to ask Ember what she knew.

'Devlin took it.' Ember placed her hand over his heart as if unconsciously protecting him from assault. He put his hand over hers.

'So he was the attacker?'

'I don't know. Possibly. Probably. But he came in after I found my father as far as I can remember. My memory isn't proving very reliable.'

'Why is that? You don't strike me as being forgetful.'

'I . . . I don't know. I slept heavily and woke up in a panic that I'd be late. First I couldn't find Max, then I found my father—it's all a horrible blur.'

'The police said you were disorientated and frantic when they found you.'

She nodded.

'That doesn't ring true either.'

'I guess it must've been the shock? I don't know. I've never stood over my father's dead body before.' He could feel her shudder.

Rose was still listening in. 'Did anyone screen your blood for the presence of drugs, Ember?'

She stiffened. 'I don't take drugs.'

'That's not what I meant. I'm not talking about drugs you took willingly.'

'Oh. Then no, I don't think they did. In fact, they administered a tranquilliser when they couldn't calm me.'

Joe could join the dots as quickly as anyone and he really didn't like what Rose was suggesting: not only had Ember been spied upon in her own home, she also might've been drugged. Unfortunately it fitted the pattern.

'Shame there's no evidence left so long after the event,' mused Rose.

'You should get your lawyer to talk to the doctor who treated you. See what notes they took on your condition,' suggested Joe.

Ember looked bewildered. 'But why would anyone have drugged me? And how, without me knowing it?'

Rose gave her an understanding look. 'I think you know. It would've been in something you ate or drank and it would've been someone with access to the house.'

'But they wouldn't.'

'Ember, you were living in a house where you were watched in your bedroom. First your own father, then, after his death, Devlin monitored your every move,' Joe reminded her. 'Can you really say that it is beyond belief that someone might have knocked you out to allow them a chance to get to your father without disturbing you?'

'But that's so cold!'

'Premeditated murder is cold—another reason why it was never you. Now we just have to work out what it tells us about the one who did this.'

Chapter 15

It had been a long night but Ember knew it was far from over. She still had to persuade the people in charge of Joe's college to let her stay rather than send her back to prison. Joe seemed quite confident all would be well but she wasn't so sure. No one's contacts in law enforcement were that good, surely?

'Trust me, the authorities still owe us for taking down the Scorpions, not to mention Roman Milanescu, a New York gangster, and the guys using the Weston Academy as a recruiting ground for a corrupt network,' he assured her.

'Sounds like you've been busy.' Head on his shoulder, she tugged on a button of his shirt, a little reprimand for his arrogance. 'So preventing a terrorist atrocity is going to be a walk in the park?'

He stilled her fingers. 'No, Ember. Don't think because I'm confident we can help you tonight that I'm overconfident about how this is going to go. But I do know we have a good team behind us. That counts for a lot.'

Henry dropped Raven, Kate, Kieran, and Nathan in the underground car park belonging to the YDA, pulling up next to where Damien had parked the Lexus. The director got out and gave Ember a hug.

'Now, my Titania, you look after yourself. These are good people and they'll help you sort out your situation.'

Not used to a world where friends hugged each other so easily, Ember hesitated a second before returning his embrace. 'Thanks, Henry.'

'When you're clear of all this, come and find me. I'm just down the street at the Globe for a few more months. We'll talk about your future.'

Her throat felt strangely constricted. 'I don't know what to say.'

'Say "I'll be seeing you, Henry".'

She smiled through blurred vision. 'I'll be seeing you, Henry.'

With a final wave, he drove off.

Joe put an arm round her. 'Come on, Fairy Queen, let's take you upstairs. Our boss wants to meet you and he doesn't want any other students to spot you wandering the corridors.'

'Why? Do you think they'd tell someone where I am?' Ember wondered just how much trouble she was getting everyone into at the YDA.

'Nothing like that. They're trustworthy. But it's standard procedure. Need to know. And outside the team around you and our superiors, no one needs to know you're here.'

She nodded, acknowledging the sense of that, and let him steer her towards a lift. 'So what is this place exactly?'

'You know some of it already,' said Raven. 'It's a college for students in sixth form to train for various aspects of detective work, everything from undercover to forensics. We go on from here to a variety of destinations: some join the police force, others the military, but most go on to university to study something which applies to their interests before joining one of the law enforcement agencies.'

Ember shivered, feeling the cold of the early hours of the morning this close to the river. Joe moved in closer to warm

221

her with his body heat. He always seemed to know what she needed before she did. 'I didn't know there was an A level in detective work,' she said.

Kate laughed. 'There isn't. We do normal A levels too but the detective training is why most of us are here. Graduating from here is the qualification, not to mention the reference we get. And the experience helps us decide if a career in that kind of work is for us.'

'And has nothing to do with the fact that you are all thrill-seekers wanting to save the world?'

'It could be that too.' Kate grinned at Nathan. 'See, I told you she was clever. She'd fit in here, no problem.'

The doors opened before Ember had a chance to reply to that surprising statement. Fit in? How would a girl who spent more time on the wrong side of the law than the right find a place here? Unless she was to be the hare and they the grey-hounds to chase her—she could give them more practice at that, she supposed.

Joe took her hand. 'It's going to be all right,' he said in a soft voice.

Ember wondered why he felt moved to say that but realized the reason the moment he opened the door to the conference room on the top floor of the building. A for-midable-looking commander sat at the end of the table, coming to his feet as they entered. A grey-haired older wom-an sat at his right hand, last seen moonlighting as a minibus driver at Lockwood. A man in a smart suit sat beside her, eyes narrowed as he judged Ember. Opposite them was a rock of a soldier in military fatigues, not bothering to hide a yawn, and a woman in a lab coat with her hair bundled up in a messy bun who blinked owlishly at the incomers.

'Ember Lord, welcome to the Young Detective Agency,' the commander began. Tired though she was, Ember suddenly remembered where she had seen him too: he'd been Raven and Kate's visitor a week ago. The net woven around her had been tighter mesh than she realized.

'Thank you for taking me in.'

Joe squeezed her hand approvingly and guided her to a chair at the near end of the table. The team then took places around her, a silent show of their support.

'I'd better quickly run through some introductions. I'm Isaac Hampton, head of the college. Jan Hardy is my deputy and in charge of C stream—that's Joe and Kate's branch. Dr Waterburn is mentor for A, Kieran and Rose's department. Taylor Flint here is the leader of B stream, Damien's section. And last but not least, Jim Rivers, who looks after Nathan and Raven's cohort.'

'Cats, Owls, Cobras, and Wolves,' said Joe, writing out a list on the notepad in front of her to help her keep track. Just as well, as at two in the morning, Ember wasn't sure she'd remember anything anyone told her.

'So Joe tells us you made an effective prison break,' said Taylor Flint.

She wondered where he was going with this. 'It wasn't that effective. The team caught up with me easily enough.'

'I should sincerely hope so, as that is what they're trained to do. No, I'm talking about how you seized your chance and got all the way to your destination without being stopped by conventional police forces. Well done.'

That was unexpected. 'Er, thanks.'

Mr Flint smiled at her confusion. 'You probably think we are odd, but we like to see initiative in young people.'

'But I broke out of jail.'

'And your point is?'

'Shouldn't you be arresting me?'

'I expect we'll get round to that eventually. At the moment

we're far more interested in your plan to intercept the ship-ment.'

The lab-coated lady, Dr Waterburn, cleared her throat. 'Are you sure the phone is unique? I'm concerned that someone might have already cloned it.'

Ember reached into her bag and put it on the table, a sign of her good faith. 'I'm not sure of the technicalities, but I know my father spent a lot on ensuring no one else was able to inter-fere with his orders.'

Dr Waterburn picked up the phone. On the outside it looked perfectly ordinary. 'What do you think, Kieran?'

'There's not time to take it apart and analyse the software,' said Kieran. 'The balance of probabilities suggests that there's no incentive for anyone to mess with it if they think Mick Lord is dead. There was no sign they looked for it.'

'They didn't know where it was kept,' explained Ember. 'Only my father and I knew. They'll assume the police have it.'

'Perhaps you'd best tell us the rest of your plan so we can get to our beds. I take it that nothing need be done before the morning?' asked Isaac.

'That depends on two things. Will news of my escape be in the press? I wanted to make a move before then.'

Isaac brushed his top lip with his forefinger. 'That little piece of information won't be passed on to the public just yet. The Home Secretary has agreed that the Lockwood auth-orities can say you've been transferred for your own safety, along with Kate and Raven, to a new facility. The sabotage of your room works oddly in our favour as an excuse. Paperwork gets lost, delays will creep in, so we have time before we have to issue the report as to where you've gone.'

'Thank you. That makes it much easier. If everyone assumes I'm still in prison, they won't think I'm behind the message.'

'And the other thing?'

'Are you sure the shipment hasn't yet taken place?'

'Last intelligence was that it was sitting in airfreight containers in Albania.'

'So that's, what, about three, four hours flight from the UK?'

'Exactly. So, what else do you need from us?'

Ember sketched out how she planned to take over the delivery, diverting it to an airfield in Essex that her father had used on occasion.

'I'm guessing you'll use the excuse of engine failure?'

She nodded. 'The flight plan will be for Stansted but they'll pretend they have to land early. It will take a while for customs to come and find them, giving us the chance to offload. My father had contacts there who have turned a blind eye in the past.'

'It's a good plan, if it works. My problem with it is that you have one huge loose cannon.'

Ember knew what Isaac was going to say. 'Seamus Devlin? I know he's a threat.'

'What if he gets wind of what's going on and steps in? What if he persuades your contact to go ahead with him?'

'I was hoping my father's reputation would overrule that. He got on well with the gun runners; Devlin was always thought of as being his deputy, the money man. They don't respect him in the same way.' Devlin hadn't been the one chosen to go shooting with Mick Lord on that estate in Suffolk to impress the arms dealers; that had been her.

Joe stirred beside her. 'Isaac, why don't we lure him in as well? Better to have all the rats in one trap.'

'Joe, he won't buy that my father is really alive. He was there.'

'He might well have stuck the knife in himself—yeah, I know. What I meant was that we could tip him off last minute that you're playing a trick. Give him only just enough time to get to the airfield, and then we can arrest him along with the smugglers.'

'But he'll call them while they're in the air. They'll turn round and we'll never find the cargo until it turns up in some terrorist atrocity somewhere else.'

'Not if his phone is experiencing a denial of service. Kieran, can you manage that?'

'In my sleep,' said Kieran.

Dr Waterburn rolled her eyes at her star student's arrogance. 'Miss Lord, we can make sure no one has any chance of getting a message out as long as we know the numbers and where the parties are. We can't take down the entire network in the UK.'

'Well, we could, but they don't like it when I do that,' admitted Kieran. Raven elbowed him in the ribs. 'It was only once—just to see if it were possible,' he added hastily. 'I made sure emergency calls still got through.'

Isaac raised a brow. 'I can see, Kieran, you and I will need another of our little talks. Report to me tomorrow at nine.' He turned back to Ember. 'When will you send the message?'

'I was thinking late tomorrow afternoon. That's the time of day my father usually got down to business.'

'And how long do you think they'll take to respond?'

'Usually immediately.'

'If they give you an option, arrange for the delivery to be made the day after tomorrow. I don't want that stuff washing around Europe any longer than necessary but I also need time to get the special forces and police operation sorted out. We'll need an outer ring of police to control the ground with an inner ring of specialists to do the actual take-down. With so many players who don't know each other's mode of working we'll need at least a day to iron out the wrinkles.'

'Will that give you enough time?'

'It'll have to do. More to the point, will you be ready to do your part?'

'My part?' Ember had rather been thinking that she would step back and let the YDA take it from here.

'They'll need a familiar face in the reception committee to coax them out of the plane. I take it you know these people?'

Ember nodded.

'If you can give me their names before you retire for the night, I'd be grateful.'

She gestured to the phone. 'You'll find them all on there. I'm thinking Peter Szabó is the most likely pilot. My father's contacts are organized into the different networks.'

'How very efficient.'

'He said it helped him keep track.'

'Is it pass-coded?'

'Oh, no. I should've thought of that. It's fingerprint operated.' Ember felt immensely stupid. How could she have not anticipated that hitch?

'No problem,' said Rose, speaking up for the first time. 'Your father's fingerprints are on record and we can create a silicon replica that should work. That's easier than trying to bypass it. I assume it was the right forefinger?'

Ember nodded, side-swiped by a sudden recollection of her father stabbing at his phone and tearing a strip off some person who had let him down. His temper had been volcanic. How could he be gone?

Joe must have picked up on her distress. 'Isaac, can we call it a day? Ember needs to rest.'

'Ah, Joe, so you're still in charge of the mission, are you?' asked Isaac.

'Yes, sir.'

'What was all this about wanting to resign?'

227

'How do you . . . ?' Joe tailed off and scowled at Kieran, who was looking very innocent. 'Key!'

'He might've mentioned, and I quote, that you were being a "pillock" and I shouldn't listen to anything you had to say.'

'He did, did he?'

'Are you going to resign? Because if so, I'd have to put someone else in charge of this case, maybe someone who doesn't understand the ins and outs as well as you.'

'I'm not resigning,' growled Joe.

Isaac got up and grinned. 'Excellent. Somehow I knew you'd say that. Take your young lady to a guest room near yours. Kate, Raven, can you see about a basic disguise for tomorrow so she isn't recognized?'

'Oh great, dress-up time!' Raven sprung to her feet.

'In the morning,' said Joe, repressing her enthusiasm.

The team got up but didn't leave. Ember realized they were waiting for her. She stood. 'Thank you, Mr Hampton.'

Isaac smiled, blue eyes glinting. 'It's Colonel, but everyone just calls me Isaac.'

'Thank you, Isaac, Mrs Hardy, Mr Rivers, Dr Waterburn, Mr Flint.'

They acknowledged her thanks with a nod.

'Get some rest, Ember,' said Mr Flint. 'We've got an operation to plan.' As she went out the door, she heard him say, 'Very promising. Mine, I think?'

Ember woke to see ripples on her ceiling. It took her a moment to remember where she was: in a riverside bedroom on an upper floor of the YDA. The sun must be out as the Thames was reflecting across the white plaster in soothing waves. How long was it since she'd woken in sunshine? Her bedroom at the Lord mansion had always been dark, natural light cut out by the neighbour's wall and a row of evergreens.

In Lockwood she had been on the north side of the building. Perhaps she had never woken with sunbeams playing across her face? She decided it had to be the most delicious feeling in the world, or at least coming a close second to one of Joe's kisses.

But if the sun was up, that meant the morning was far progressed. She turned the bedside clock towards her. Ten thirty. She still had hours before she made the call. It was a huge gamble, with no certainty of success. While she had done a good job selling it to Joe and his team, she was by no means certain that Szabó would take the bait. She'd have to word it very carefully. Fortunately, she'd been present at enough meetings between her father and his business contacts to know the tone to take. With equals he was blustering, with underlings a bully. Szabó, being a younger man just establishing himself as a trusted contact, was treated to a combination of both, with a hint of fatherly patronization. Throwing back the covers, Ember went to the desk, took out the notepad Joe had left for her last night, and began roughing out the text.

A few minutes later, there came a knock on the door but the person didn't wait for an invitation to come in. Max ploughed into her with his usual puppyish enthusiasm. 'Surprise!'

'What are you doing here?' gasped Ember.

'Rose said you were still sleeping but I couldn't wait. The social workers didn't want me to come but Damien said it would be safer. I've been here since nine o'clock and I'm staying. I've got a room on the floor below next to Damien. Patch is here too but Dr Waterburn is walking him with Jellybean. Did you know that the spaniel was hers, not Damien and Rose's at all?' His face was back to its old shape, no longer so swollen with bruises. There was only a hint of discolouration on the jaw and cheekbone. He had his broken wrist in a sling.

'No, I didn't.' Not that this was the most pressing question that needed an answer. Ember sensed they weren't alone. Rose, Raven, and Kate stood in the doorway.

'Sorry, we couldn't hold him back,' said Rose with a rueful smile.

'It's fine. I was already up.'

Raven glanced at the notepad. 'And working. Perhaps, Max, you'd like to join the boys for breakfast? Tell them we'll bring your sister when she's dressed.'

'Remember,' said Rose, putting a quelling hand on his arm, 'you're both here secretly. Don't be surprised if she looks different when you next see her.'

Max grinned, finding it all huge fun. 'That's right. We're hiding from the bad guys.'

And the good guys in her case, thought Ember wryly. 'Can you get me some cereal, Max? You know the kind of thing I like.'

Max bounded off on his mission.

'Now tell me: why is he really here?'

'It's simple: it's the only place where we know we can keep him safe. We didn't want Devlin using him against you.' Rose started unpacking a shoulder bag she was carrying, laying out a change of clothes on the bed. 'Not again.'

'What do you want to be?' asked Raven, opening a white case she had brought with her. 'Blonde like Kate, dark like me, or redhead like Rose?'

'I'm auburn,' Rose said, a little grumpily.

'Why anyone would not rejoice in having hair her colour, I don't know.' Raven laid out a selection of wigs. The two American girls mock-glared at each other until Rose chuckled.

Kate fingered the red enviously. 'Do you think it would suit me?'

'Another time. This is about Ember and getting to breakfast before the guys eat it all.'

Ember picked up the short blonde wig. It reminded her of her mother's hair in the single photo she had of her. 'This one.'

Joe almost choked on his bagel as Ember appeared in the dining room. Most of the students were in class so there wasn't a huge audience to see her entrance as a delectable blonde. Something else had been revealed by the new hairstyle: the face shape and cheek bones so often disguised by her long brown hair. The resemblance to her twin had never been more striking. The alert brown eyes were all her, though.

Max giggled. 'You look so funny, Ember.'

Damien elbowed him. 'Max, remember?'

Max sobered. 'Sorry, Damien.' He lowered his voice. 'But doesn't she look pretty?'

'She always looks pretty,' said Joe, pulling out the chair beside him. 'Did you sleep OK?'

'Better than OK.' With a shy smile, she sat down. 'Max, Coco Pops? Really?'

'You like them—or you used to,' her brother said stubbornly.

She laughed and picked up her spoon. 'I suppose I do.'

'It's Dad who always says they're disgusting.' Max grimaced, remembrance returning. 'I mean "said". He's really gone, hasn't he?'

Ember's humour fled and she put her arm around her brother. 'I'm so sorry, Max.'

He hugged her and began to cry. Joe got up and went over to the only other occupied table.

'Could you take this somewhere else?' he asked.

'Sure, Joe.' The students got up, casting sympathetic glances at the brother and sister who were now weeping in each other's arms. 'Are they OK?' asked one.

'They will be.'

'Are they who I think they are?'

So much for disguises. 'Please, don't think too much. Isaac's orders.'

'Understood. Me? I don't think anything. Completely blank in here.' The girl tapped her forehead and left.

Joe returned to his seat. His friends were letting the siblings have their space. He realized they'd not had a chance to mourn, what with Ember being arrested immediately. They needed this. He could hear her murmuring promises that she'd look after him, that they'd be all right. He was touched to hear Max whispering many of the same vows back. Finally, Max lifted his head from her chest.

'I've made your hair go all wonky.'

Ember patted it back into place. 'There.' She looked around at their audience. 'We're sorry.'

'Please, none of us here think anything of it,' said Joe.

'We can't help loving our parents even if they don't deserve it,' said Rose. Joe knew she was speaking from experience. 'Maybe losing a bad one, with no chance of things ever getting better, is in some ways worse. You have to let the emotion out.'

Damien handed Ember a serviette to mop up her tears. 'Here. Can't have you spoiling that tough girl image with running mascara, can we?'

Smiling through shining eyes, Ember took the offering and dried her cheeks. Max rubbed his with his sleeve.

'So what are you going to do today?' she asked her brother, making a valiant effort to change the subject.

'Rose is going to introduce me to the identifit software.'

'Oh? What's that?'

'You can sketch likenesses from someone's description and then you can run a programme to see if there's a match with the police database,' explained Rose.

232

'That sounds perfect.'

'And you, Ember?' Max's appetite returned and he began tucking into his own bowl of cereal.

'I'm going to make a few calls.' She glanced at Joe, who nodded. They'd set aside a room for her to work in where they could monitor her communications. 'I'll see you next at dinner, Max.'

'Will you be able to come on Patch's afternoon walk?'

'Maybe another day.'

'Ember's got to be careful, Max,' said Joe.

'Oh yes, she broke out of jail.' Max took it all in his stride, clearly thinking that anything his amazing sister did was entirely reasonable. 'We don't want her arrested again.'

'That's right.'

'Maybe tomorrow then?'

'Maybe.'

Ember pushed her empty bowl away.

'Ready?' asked Joe.

'I think so. You know, Coco Pops aren't so bad.'

'Life is full of surprises.' He got up.

'I just wish they were more pleasant ones.' Joe knew Ember was now talking about the outcome of the call.

He led her to the lift. 'It'll be OK. It's a good plan. Mr Flint has started some rumours in the right ears that your father has been seen. There was a sighting in Monaco a few hours ago apparently—and that didn't come from us.'

'How does that work?'

'Once the idea is out there, people start embroidering for their own purposes and become immensely suggestible. Lies take on their own reality after a time.'

'And Devlin?'

'As soon as you press send on your text, his communications will be boxed in. Kieran's rigging it so Devlin, and the other people you identified in his inner circle, won't know that anything's wrong to start with. They'll just think people are either unavailable or taking a time in answering their messages.'

'You're sure this is going to work?'

Joe cupped her cheek, brushing a few strands of pale hair off her skin. 'Sure? No. Hopeful? Yes. And that in the end is all anyone can offer.'

She blinked once and smiled. 'Kate was right.'

'How so?'

'She said that pessimists like us need positive guys like you and Nathan.'

Joe kissed her. 'I think I fell a little in love with you the first time I saw you. Did she mention that?'

Ember's eyes widened in surprise. 'No.'

'Well, it's true. And I spent the next few days fighting myself at every turn, until I just gave up and fell all the way.'

'You shouldn't love me.'

The lift arrived at its destination but Joe didn't move, putting his foot to stop the door closing. 'I get to say what I need in my perfect partner and I've decided it's a cynical girl who's experienced some of the worst sides of life but come through caring and protective, who can escape jail, deliver a speech by Shakespeare with style, and reads nineteenth-century poetry, and looks after her brother.'

Ember bit back a smile. 'Nope, don't know anyone like that.'

Laughing, he pulled her into the corridor. 'Liar. Just accept it: you're it for me. I just hope I can be the same for you.'

She put on the brakes, making him stop by a window looking out on the river scene below. Sunlight glinted off the white dome of St Paul's, seagulls whirled in the air over the slate-grey water. 'I'm not good at emotions, Joe, not so comfortable with them.'

His heart did a little stutter. Had he gone too fast for her? He'd meant to reassure her that he loved her, not spook her. 'Ember—'

'Let me finish, please. I want you to know that I think . . . I suspect that maybe I feel the same.'

With a whoop, Joe picked her up and spun her in a circle, then lowered her gently to the floor. 'You had me worried there.'

'I know.'

'Tease.'

'Someone's got to keep you on your toes. I'm applying for the job.'

'It's yours. Now, let's go sort out the world and then we can look to our own future.'

'Sounds easy.'

'The way I feel right now, it must be.'

In the laboratory on the second floor overlooking the lines of traffic on London Bridge, Ember waited for Kieran to give her the thumbs-up that the phone was unlocked and cleared for her to use. She hoped she hadn't jinxed things by joking that it would be easy.

From the glass-fronted control room, Kieran gave the sign.

Isaac stood next to him, expression focused. His hunting face, Joe had called it. The other mentors stood behind their leader.

'You're cleared to send, Ember,' said Isaac. 'We just have to hope we're in time to catch the plane.'

'OK then.' She sent 'Mick's' text to Szabó as she'd already drafted, asking for the diversion of the shipment.

What she didn't really expect was to get an immediate call back, though Isaac had warned at the briefing that anything was possible as they had no control over Szabó's timing.

'Hey, Mick, glad to hear you're not dead but, man, I'm already in the air. Just taken off from Tirana.' She could hear the drone of the engines behind Szabó. 'What is all this about Devlin trying to steal the deal from under you?'

Ember looked to the people observing her behind the glass. With a brief word to Jan, Isaac took the decision. He pointed to her.

With a gulp, Ember picked up the handset. 'Mr Szabó, it's Ember. Sorry my father can't speak right now. He's just out of surgery.' It was the best she could come up with on the hoof.

'Surgery? Did he really get stabbed then, Lelkem?' Szabó knew her well and had often used this Hungarian pet name for her. It meant something close to sweetie.

'No, no, nothing like that.' Did she sound convincing? *This isn't a moment for self-doubt, Ember.* 'It's for his new identity. He's got the best surgeon over from South Korea to give him a make-over. You know how it is, things were getting too hot with the police so he decided to start again, new face, new name.'

'If I know your father he wants to impress the ladies with a tidy up of those wrinkles of his. Tell him I wish him all the best with that.' She could hear the smirk in Szabó's voice. In his twenties, the problems of mid-life were something for Szabó to mock rather than anticipate for himself. 'So, what does Mick want me to do? I'm heading for that airfield near Ashford. Devlin said to do the drop off there. I wasn't so happy as I've not worked with those people.'

Ember looked to Isaac who gave her the nod that they should continue as planned despite the much shorter time frame. 'The orders have changed. My father wants you to make the delivery as usual to North Weald.'

'The usual place? Good, I trust them. And it's OK as I've filed a flight plan to Stansted. With that revised destination,' she could hear him working it out on his flight app on his computer, 'I should be wheels down at twenty-one hundred hours.'

'Good.' It was far from good: it only gave them a few hours to get a reception committee in place and she needed to reel Szabó in, not let him have second thoughts about trusting her. A bribe was in order. 'My father has just written down here that he'll be very grateful to you for helping him put Devlin in his place. It's worth an extra bonus at least.'

'I look forward to exploring how grateful the old man is. So, Lelkem, you'll be there, I hope, when I land?'

'Of course.'

'Excellent. I've got an idea I want to run by you. I look forward to seeing you both then. Over and out.'

Ember ended the call. There was utter silence for a moment then the people in the lab exploded into action.

Isaac strode into the centre of the room to take control. 'Given the time frame, we have no choice but for the YDA to lead this operation. I'd prefer to work with a team I know and trust than try to put something together at the last moment. Jan, get your contacts moving in Essex police and secure the outer perimeter. No blue lights to scare off the plane or I'll personally roast the person responsible.'

Mrs Hardy nodded and hurried out.

'Taylor, get on to the SAS and tell them what's happened. I doubt they'll be able to scramble a team in time but find out what's possible. They are to report to me if they get there during the operation, not go storming in trying to take over, not with my people in the line of fire. Can you arrange that?'

Mr Flint took out his phone. 'I'll make it very clear what's expected of them, don't worry, Isaac.'

'Jim, get the nuclear people at Aldermaston on standby. Clarice, can you deal with the special delivery if they can't be on site before the plane?'

Dr Waterburn frowned. 'Isaac, I'm not an expert.'

'None of us are, but I prefer our hands to a terrorist's, don't you?'

She gave in, seeing the necessity. 'I have a Geiger counter and a lead-line box that should be suitable for transportation. I'll need Kieran and Rose to assist—they're my best.'

'Fine, you have them. Take every precaution you think necessary. No one steps on board that plane without confirmation that the levels of radioactivity are safe.'

'Unless these smugglers are very stupid, they will have the material well-insulated.'

'Do you think they really care?'

'Point taken. We'll suit up too.'

'Right, get on that. Kieran, don't forget I also want you to block Devlin's communications; that part of our original plan is still operative.'

'Already done, sir, when Ember started speaking to the pilot.' Kieran hurried out in the wake of the doctor to load up the equipment.

'Joe, you take Ember, Sergeant Rivers, and Damien in the lead car. The sergeant can pretend to be Mick, as he's the closest in build. He can appear to have just undergone surgery— inspired thought that, Ember.'

'Yes, sir.' Joe slipped the phone with the silicon fingerprint device into a clear plastic evidence bag.

'Ember, when the pilot lands, see if you can get him away from his plane.'

'My father usually provides refreshments when a deal is completed. He won't think it strange if I take him over to a room where there's drinks and something to eat.'

'What kind of things?'

'Only high class fare for Mick Lord.'

'It would be. Still, the manager at Fortnum and Mason

owes me a favour. Give me a list and I'll have the supplies couriered over.'

Ember sat down to quickly recreate the kind of spread her father would provide.

Isaac sought out the last members of the team not yet given a job. 'Nathan, Kate, and Raven, when Jan gets back, I want you to go in the second car. Girls, your job will be to create a distraction with the rest of the crew once Ember has lured Szabó from the plane. Nathan, Joe, I'm trusting you to assist the girls in taking them down.'

'And leave Ember on her own?' protested Joe.

'Only temporarily. I don't have enough people. We're going to be spread thin.'

'I'll be fine,' Ember rushed to assure him. 'Szabó treats me like a little sister. He's known me for about ten years and won't have any reason to turn on me, not if he's stuffing himself with canapés and caviar.'

'OK, everyone, let's move out. The clock is ticking. This is what you've been trained for and I have every expectation you'll succeed. Don't let me down.' Isaac grabbed Ember's list and walked out the room.

'Well, that was interesting,' said Ember, repressing a shiver. 'Is he always so . . . commanding?'

Joe smiled but his expression was without real amusement. 'Yes, but usually he has more time to ease us into what he wants us to do and I can't remember a time where we've led on such an important assignment. First time for everything. Come on, Em, if we're going to be standing on a cold airfield, we'd better get prepared.'

Chapter · 16

A chill wind blew across the vast expanse of North Weald airfield. A tiny string of lights marked the main road that ran along the fence on the north side but the rest of the airport was in darkness. Flat, featureless, perilous, it was a grim place to wait as the rain lashed down. Ember sat inside the Lexus with her team, Jim Rivers, Joe, and Damien as their driver. They were parked just outside the hangar where a lorry and forklift truck waited to take on the cargo transfer. Rivers was there to give the illusion that Mick was waiting in the car while his daughter was sent into the rain to greet the arrivals. Rivers was about the same height and build as her father had been so it should be enough to convince Szabó if he were expecting to see Mick Lord. Having Sergeant Rivers sitting a metre away, though, was proving a damper on conversation, like having the teacher sit at your lunch table. She was reduced to whispering to Joe as they sat together in the back.

'Do you think they'll come?'

'Relax. Air traffic control still has them on screen.' Joe was following mission updates on his tablet. The soft blue light lit up the curves and hollows of his face, transforming it into an unfamiliar modern art sculpture of himself. She wished they could be somewhere else, preferably with palm trees, white surf, and sand, somewhere they could both be their normal selves and she could be tracing his features with her fingers, kissing warm skin, not shivering in a wind-blasted corner of Essex.

'And the other teams are in place?' She knew the answer but nerves made her go over the same ground.

'Yes, they're still out there. The airport is completely under our control. No one is getting in or out without our say-so. The message was sent to Devlin half an hour ago, and he's heading here from Ashford with six men, according to motorway cameras. We'll run this as we rehearsed. Keep the meeting with Szabó going until Devlin gets on site. We want Seamus Devlin to incriminate himself, not just claim he was out for a spin in the Essex countryside and happened to stumble upon the transaction.'

'I think I've got far worse stage fright than I had as Titania.'

Joe brushed his lips over the crown of her head. '*Speak the speech, I pray you, as I pronounc'd it to you, trippingly on the tongue.*'

She laughed softly, relaxing as he turned back into his normal warm self, not the focused, mission-minded operative. 'Yes, this is all a little like a play to catch the conscience of a king smuggler.'

An alert popped up on the screen. 'That's Kieran. The plane's put in for an emergency landing, just as you said they would. Air traffic is diverting them here.'

She gritted her teeth, searching for that tough Ember who had helped her so often in the past when she was scared. The cues were coming as expected. All too soon, they would see the lights of an aircraft circling to land. Ember didn't feel even half prepared to face this. Then Isaac up in the control tower pressed the switch to illuminate the landing strip. Like lights coming on stage for the arrival of the main attraction, the runway sparkled, inviting the gunrunner into the trap. The small cargo plane lined up for its approach and touched down.

'Ready?' asked Joe.

Ember replied by sliding out of her side of the vehicle. She moved in front of the car, standing in the pool of light cast by the headlamps, umbrella shielding her from the rain. Hood pulled up, Joe came to his position behind her as any good bodyguard would, an earpiece fitted to keep him in communication with mission control. Joe's face was almost invisible, just the intent gleam of his eyes reflecting the lights. Ember swallowed, aware that her throat had gone Sahara dry. Though she knew—and Szabó would expect it as he'd been in the game long enough—that they were both wearing body armour under their winter coats, that Damien and Rivers waited in the car at their backs, and that further out in the darkness were the rest of the team ready to move in on the signal to deal with the dangerous material, she couldn't help but play out in her imagination all the ways this could go wrong. Too often those scenarios ended in Joe lying in a pool of blood.

'I think I'm going to be sick.'

'Courage, Em.'

'I'd only tell you that, not anyone else.'

'Remember, sweetheart, my comm is open. You've just told everyone listening in.'

'Oh.'

'Isaac says he'd be worried if you weren't nervous.'

'Good to know.' She kicked herself for showing weakness.

The plane taxied over to where Ember and Joe were waiting. 'Beginners, places please,' he whispered, raising a ghost of a smile from her.

The door to the cabin opened and a crew member unfolded a ladder. Peter Szabó bounded down the steps, removing his leather gloves. Dark-haired and chisel-jawed, he had a dashing air, like a pirate of old now taken to the skies. Shame he had the morals of a pirate too, otherwise he would've been attractive.

'Ember, my darling! I've been wondering if you'd really be here. I remembered afterwards that I'd heard you were in prison.' His accent was thick Eastern European, guttural like the purr of a Harley Davidson bike engine.

Ember accepted his hearty embrace without flinching, turning her cheek to receive his three kisses, holding the umbrella high to shelter them both. 'Mr Szabó, good to see you. I was in jail awaiting trial but my father arranged for bail yesterday. The charges are going to be dropped soon.'

'I am pleased he did so otherwise I would have missed seeing your pretty face.' He patted her back and upper arms, registering the body armour with a wry smile. 'As suspicious as ever I see. You're truly your father's daughter. But, Lelkem, how many times must I remind you to call me Peter?'

'Peter.'

'How is the old man?'

Ember gestured towards the car. 'He's inside. The doctor told him to stay in bed. He shouldn't really be out at all.'

Szabó nodded as if this was perfectly normal and held up a hand to greet 'Mick Lord'. 'Ah yes, I had a little work done three years ago. It takes time to settle down.' He rubbed the chiselled line of his jaw. 'The stitches can itch like crazy.'

Joe touched her arm discreetly—the signal that radiation readouts were at safe levels. 'Before we get out of this rain, can you show me the cargo? My father is anxious that all is in order.'

'Of course it is. He knows he can trust me, darling.'

This was the tricky part. She needed to get him explicitly to incriminate Devlin without leading him to give the answer. Joe had explained that this would be harder to use as evidence as it would look like she fed Szabó's replies. 'It's not you who's got him worried, Peter. He isn't sure if everyone in his organization is keeping to their orders.'

'You are talking of Devlin, no? He's a slippery customer, working with him is like trying to land a tough old trout. I was surprised when Devlin expanded the order. Mick didn't like transporting that kind of material.' She had to get him to say that Devlin knew it was radioactive waste but Szabó hadn't quite made the connection for her and she was under orders not to feed it to him. She would have to let the conversation run on or he might get suspicious.

He led her up the steps to the cabin and pointed to a red box bolted to the floor in a space usually occupied by a seat. 'Here's the prize. You heard about that, I think? It needs special handling.'

'Yes, my father found out about that. So that's it? Right there?' She had to hope for her own safety as well as Joe's that the Hungarian knew what he was doing.

Szabó nodded. 'I'm holding it separately from the conventional cargo. I will need twice my normal fee for handling it, as well as the bonus you mentioned.'

'It's contained?'

'As specified by the scientist: lead-lined case and a sealed container. I have a radiation counter on board and it is registering near normal levels. Relax, Lelkem, I wouldn't put you at risk. So, what about the money?'

They exited the plane. Ember knew he wouldn't believe her making a decision on this unless she appeared to consult with her father. 'Give me a moment.' She walked to the passenger side window and tapped. Rivers rolled the window down a crack. 'It's here. Nod vigorously please.'

'Not too vigorously,' said Jim with a wolfish smile. 'Wouldn't want to split my stitches. Move to phase two.'

Ember walked back to Szabó. 'My father would like a chat about your commission. He's perfectly happy to consider a raise as well as a bonus, but doubling it? You'll have to explain how you've earned that.' She had to play hard ball as Mick Lord wouldn't just roll over without a negotiation. 'He suggests we meet in the hangar as he can't come out into the rain. He has some refreshments set up in an office there.'

'Ah, Mick's famous single malt.' Szabó smiled broadly at the prospect of a whisky and a haggle over his reward. He probably had not come expecting his million to be magically doubled, but would argue the case over a stiff drink. 'By the way, Lelkem, do you know who your father plans to sell that container to? I wouldn't want it to come back my way.'

'He hasn't told me but I think Budapest is safe.'

'As long as that is understood. Let us leave our men to unload and take this inside. You must be freezing.' Slinging an arm around her shoulder, he began walking towards the hangar, following the path of the car that had driven through the open doors and parked in the shadows.

Ember glanced at Joe who gave her a guarded nod. He'd take care of things out here while she distracted Szabó inside. Damien and Rivers were to unload the goods and secure them before Devlin arrived.

'Ember, allow me to say that you are looking very well,' said Szabó as they approached the hangar entrance. 'Things must be very unpleasant for you even if you are about to be cleared of the charge. What do you say to skipping bail? Get on the plane with me for the return trip? I could show you around my city, take you out to dinner, spoil you a little. You must be ready for that after weeks inside.'

Ember had to think fast. She hadn't realized Szabó had been considering her in that light but it made sense. He was only ten years or so older than her, in the stage where he could consolidate his power by hooking up with an influential man's daughter. Mick Lord had already treated him as a protégé. This was the next logical step.

'That's very sweet of you, but I haven't come prepared to go away.'

He waved that off as of no account. 'I can buy what you need, nicer clothes than these ones you are wearing now.' So much for her own taste. 'Budapest has a very fine selection of designer boutiques set in the heart of an historic city. You will adore shopping there.'

No, she'd prefer to walk over burning coals than down a street of overpriced stores with an air-pirate. 'Peter, that's so kind of you. Let's see what my father says, shall we?' Sometimes having a father with a reputation for keeping her on a tight leash was an asset.

She showed him into the office where a light buffet courtesy of Fortnum and Mason had been laid out on the desk. They had to manage this next stage very carefully as he was bound to be armed—he was a gunrunner after all. They'd purposely made the room extremely warm so that the contrast with the outside was intense.

'Where's your father?' asked Szabó.

'I think he's giving orders to the men in charge of unloading. He's very concerned about the disposal of the special delivery.' Szabó chuckled knowingly. 'He'll be along in a moment. Can I pour you a drink?' She had made sure that the buffet contained all the ingredients her father usually provided: Scotch, caviar, smoked salmon, and a final touch as a gesture to his East End roots, a tray of tiny handmade steak-and-kidney pies.

Szabó helped himself to a caviar-topped square of rye bread. 'Scotch on the rocks.'

'Please, make yourself comfortable. You know my father will take his time.' Ember took off her winter coat, slipped off her body armour, and unwound her scarf, hoping the action would suggest the same to her guest. It was a calculated risk

246

as only then would she be able to assess how many weapons he was carrying.

'I bet he wants a look inside the crates of small arms and ammunition. He's growing suspicious in his old age, but I know better than to double-cross him. Your father is a dangerous man and I respect that. *Ordog*, it's hot in here.'

'Do you want me to hang up your coat?'

He unzipped his flying jacket and passed it over. Ember noted a sidearm in holster under his left armpit and a knife on his belt, no body armour, which followed, as he wasn't expecting trouble from her. 'How was the flight? Was it rough over the alps?'

He shrugged.

'You were cutting it fine on timing when you radioed in your distress call.' She provided the listeners with the key words they'd agreed for the weapon count, 'rough' for one sidearm, 'cutting it fine' for a knife. She passed him the Scotch poured over ice.

'Thank you, darling. Oh, it was a little bumpy but nothing my plane cannot handle. You are sure the customs won't be here too soon?'

'No, that's all in hand as usual. They'll arrive an hour after you land in time to see a nice clean plane. What have you got on your manifest?'

'Nothing, as I filed this as a tourist pickup.'

'Who's the passenger?'

'You, I hope.' He raised his glass to toast her.

'Oh. Well, as I said, that would be lovely.' *Come on, Devlin.* Ember hadn't wanted ever to lay eyes on her father's old ally again but now she just wished this part of the operation was over. Stalling a romantically-minded Szabó wasn't something she had bargained for. 'I'm so sorry for the delay. Do you want me to call and see what's holding him up?'

Szabó pulled out the chair beside him. 'There's no hurry. Pour yourself a drink and tell me all about yourself. How did you get on with all those bad girls in prison?' Dropping his tone to a lower register, he managed to make the question sound suggestive.

Creep. 'If you're sure you'd not rather let me . . . ?'

'Ember, please, I want to talk to you and this might be one of the only occasions I get if your father refuses to let you come with me. Sit down.'

With what she hoped was a flirtatious smile, Ember took the seat he offered. 'Of course, Peter.' She smoothed her hands over the thighs of her jeans to make her palms less clammy. 'So, what do you want to hear first?'

Joe was listening in to the conversation getting increasingly frustrated. Szabó was far more interested in Ember in a personal sense than they had anticipated. By the sounds of it she would soon have to be holding him off with only canapés to defend herself. They had debated drugging the food or drink but had ruled against it in case Szabó grew suspicious and made her consume it first. He hadn't but it was too late to change that decision.

There was no hurrying the operation along, though, as it was time for Kate and Raven to distract the rest of the crew. And here they came, right on cue.

'Ohmigod, ohmigod, it's true! It *is* Kurt Voss's private plane!' Dressed in the overalls of the Fortnum and Mason catering company, Raven bounced up the steps with canapé tray in hand, seemingly oblivious to the co-pilot's move to stop her. 'I can't believe it! Here, Miss Lord sent this out to you.' She thrust the tray at the man, making sure he had his hands full.

Kate was close on her heels, bearing a champagne bottle in one hand and a long roll of paper in the other. 'Do you, like, always fly Gifted around when they're doing concerts and stuff? Are they here?' She handed him the champagne a moment after he had offloaded the canapé tray, and then unrolled a poster of the band which she had brought with her. 'Do you think they'll sign this for me?' She practically blinded the man by shoving it under his nose.

'Miss, you are mistaken. This plane does not belong to a celebrity. It is cargo plane,' said the pilot, pushing the poster away.

She beamed at him as if he had just passed the test. 'And you would so totally have to say that, wouldn't you? Gosh, you're so cute! Don't worry, we won't tell anyone. Can we have a look inside? I'd just die if I could sit in the very seat Kurt sits in!'

Raven hadn't waited for an invitation; she'd already invaded the cabin, forcing the co-pilot to follow her. 'This is it! I can feel him right here. Katie, is that his aftershave?'

Once the co-pilot was out of sight of the men unloading the airfreight from the rear, Joe struck. He enjoyed that part, flipping the co-pilot on his back and cuffing his hands with plastic ties. Nice to do something practical after waiting so long to end this mission. 'Target one down. Nathan, Damien, you're up.'

He didn't need to look outside to know that the last two men in the gunrunning team would now be incapacitated and cuffed. They would then be put in an empty crate and the forklift truck would carry them away. If Devlin thought to check the plane first, they didn't want any sign left that the delivery was well and truly compromised. While he was giving these orders and standing guard, Raven and Kate had gagged, dragged, and locked the co-pilot in the cockpit with terrifying efficiency. From the man's frantic mumbles, he really wasn't happy with this indignity. Joe wondered on whom they had practised. After all this was over, he was looking forward to having a word with Kieran and Nathan as it would probably prove a rich area for teasing.

'Clear for Dr Waterburn,' reported Joe.

The girls left to join Isaac for new orders, giving way in the cramped cabin to the YDA head scientist and her two best students. They immediately began talking their interminable jargon over the casket.

'Can't we hurry this along?' Joe asked.

Dr Waterburn gave him a reproving look. 'Only if you want to cause a major incident. There's a neat little booby trap on the lock to stop anyone but the person with the code opening it.'

Joe glanced towards the building. Szabó had not been playing completely straight with Ember after all, which he supposed was to be expected. It also explained why the co-pilot had been so furious to be gagged. He had probably been left to ensure the material was only released when Szabó was satisfied with his handling fee and now he was worried he was going to be at the centre of a small nuclear detonation. 'Do we need the pilot back in here?'

'It's fine, Joe. Kieran and Rose will crack it.'

Watching two of his best friends crouched over the case, Joe realized that he was entrusting his own life and that of a large part of the population of Essex to them, and oddly he wasn't the least worried. They were both just so damn clever. They'd hooked up a handheld device that looked a little like a barcode scanner and were making tiny adjustments.

'What's that?' asked Joe.

'A little code breaker they've been working on as a side-project,' Dr Waterburn explained, as if this was an entirely normal homework assignment.

'That's it, sweetheart, just give me your secrets,' Kieran crooned to the lock.

Rose was far more straightforward, not sharing Kieran's love for technology. 'First digits are coming through.'

'Come on, baby—I've got the last five, no, six numbers. And, yeah, we're in.' Kieran entered the combination and the box opened. A smooth metal canister lay inside, a little like a torpedo. Rose ran a Geiger counter over the contents.

'Excellent. Dr Waterburn, it's stable. No leakage. I'd say it's safe to move.'

'All right. Move back, Rose.'

Dr Waterburn and Kieran lifted the canister out with the respect such hazardous material deserved and transferred it to the lead-lined box they'd brought with them.

'OK, I'd better take this to the research facility at Aldermaston,' said Dr Waterburn. 'They'll handle it from there.'

Joe felt some of the nervous tension ease seeing the nuclear material finally in the right hands. 'Was it the real thing, doctor?' He had to check they weren't being double-crossed and that the canister was being delivered elsewhere while they chased their tails.

'Yes, Joe. The containment field is good, or I wouldn't have allowed any of us on the plane. You'll be pleased to learn that none of us will need decontamination, and this part of Essex is safe. Even the crew got no more radiation than a week's holiday in Cornwall would give them.'

'Cornwall?'

'Surprisingly radioactive due to the presence of igneous granite, which naturally contains uranium.'

'You're joking?'

'Do I look like I'm joking, Joe? Good luck with the rest of the mission.'

Getting in the front of the YDA van, she drove off, joining up with a police escort at the side gate of the complex. Kieran and Rose returned to Isaac for the next stage in the operation.

Joe's earpiece crackled. 'Devlin approaching,' said Isaac.

'Isaac, we should give Ember some back-up in there.'

'I agree. We hadn't anticipated that the pilot would be romancing her. Get in there and help Ember keep him at arm's length. The video feed shows she's taken her bulletproof jacket off. Make sure you protect her as necessary and see if you can get that jacket back on. I don't want to take chances with any of my people.'

Hurrying to the hangar, Joe passed Damien and Rivers, who were now using the forklift truck to stow the weapons on the back of a lorry. He could hear Isaac ordering his other friends to spread themselves around the hangar. They were to keep out of sight but guard the entrances so that Devlin would be pinned down once he arrived. According to Taylor Flint's latest update, the special forces were reported to be five minutes out and would take over as soon as they could. Joe dug out his shades and put on his best bodyguard scowl. He had to have an excuse for interrupting. Knocking only once, he walked right in.

'Miss Lord, your father wants you to know that everything is in order. He'll be along himself to discuss the little matter of a release combination with Mr Szabó in a few minutes, so wants you to pour him a celebratory drink.'

Ember looked up from the intimate conversation Szabó had pressed upon her. He could read her relief.

'Thank you, Joe. Stand by, will you?'

'Yes, miss.'

Taking his position with his back to the wall, he folded his arms.

'Your bodyguard is very young, Ember,' noted Szabó curiously, not at all pleased to have his tête-à-tête interrupted as she bustled about the drinks tray.

'It's so he can trail me to school and other places without

being noticed. He's actually much older than he looks.'

Szabó nodded, accepting Ember's ingenious explanation. 'Very useful. So, Ember, how did you find the nights inside? Lonely?'

Joe imagined planting his fist in the smirking pilot's face, right on his perfect nose. He would definitely be improved with a flattened bridge and a few missing teeth.

'I could bear it, Peter, because I knew I was fulfilling my father's orders.'

Szabó slithered up to her and framed her face in his hands. 'So loyal. I have always admired that about you. I wonder what it would take to transfer that loyalty to me?'

A miracle. Joe coughed. 'Miss, your security team reports a car approaching.'

Szabó sat back down. 'Not the customs, not yet, surely?'

'No, not them, sir. It's Mr Lord's associates.'

'Yes, my father has invited them along to remind them who's boss.' Ember returned to the bottles with a careless smile at Szabó. 'I'd better pour some more drinks. I hope you gave Devlin a wave as you flew over where he waited for you in Ashford? He is not going to be pleased.'

'And your father? Shouldn't he be here by now? He's taking his time.' Joe could tell that Szabó was beginning to be suspicious.

'I imagine he'll want a few plain words with Devlin, don't you, before they come in here?' Ember refilled the Hungarian's glass. 'He'll want to present a united front before he sees you.'

Szabó's expression cleared. 'True. I can imagine Mick won't take kindly to his man's attempt to go around him, even if Devlin did have the excuse of Mick being laid up after surgery.'

'You know my father: keeps a firm grip on everything.'

Szabó chuckled. 'I doubt even death would make him release his grip on his organization, especially not a faked death.'

Joe noticed the grimace that passed quickly across Ember's face before being suppressed. She was magnificent.

The office door banged open and Seamus Devlin stalked into the room followed by three of his men. That left three outside for the rest of the team to contain.

'You little witch!' Devlin walked over to Ember and slapped her hard.

Before Joe could reach her, Szabó pulled his knife from his belt. He held it to Devlin's throat. 'Touch her again and this will go in right there. Ember and I will be out of the country before your dead body hits the floor.'

Devlin's eyes flashed with fury. 'So, you're in it together? You and your little girlfriend are double-crossing me.'

Ember eased back out of slapping range, hand cradling her cheek. Joe stepped in front of her. He wanted to deck Devlin for that, as well as for so much else.

'Hah!' sneered Szabó, holstering his knife contemptuously. 'That's ironic coming from the man who planned to betray Mick Lord! I thought he would have taken you apart before you came in here but perhaps he wants me to do that?' He gathered the front of Devlin's jacket in his fists, pulling the shorter man to his toes. 'I'd be happy to.'

Devlin prised him off, gesturing to his guards to keep back. 'Mick? What are you going on about, you idiot? Mick's dead and buried.'

'No, he just faked his death, as you well know.'

'Very clever to pretend to be stone cold with a knife sticking in his chest. Ask the girl. She was there.' He pointed at Ember.

Szabó began to reconsider his understanding of the situation, doubt in the glance he sent Ember's way. 'But I got a message from him. He's outside right now.'

'If you think it was Mick who asked you to divert the delivery to this airfield, then you're deluded. I'd look no further than his hellcat of a daughter. This has her fingerprints all over it.'

This was unravelling fast. Joe tensed, wondering whom he should take down first. The team outside would burst in as soon as he gave the code word if they could get past the other men. Surely Szabó and Devlin had both said enough to convict them?

Ember, however, had another idea to pull things back from the brink of disaster. She squeezed Joe's elbow as she moved past him. 'Uncle Seamus, I'm sorry to see you are such a poor loser.' Her haughty ice princess routine was in full flow. She flicked her hair over her shoulder like a cat preening. 'You knew all along that my father intended me to take over his business in the event of his death but you disobeyed his wishes. Surely you can hardly blame me for carrying them out?' She dismissed him with a regal toss of her head then leaned seductively against the Hungarian. 'Peter, I'm sorry to have played this little trick on you, but it was the only way I could think to get you here so I could prove that I was up to the job of heading the organization in my father's absence.'

'Prove yourself?' Szabó blinked down at her. Joe knew first-hand how appealing her fathomless dark eyes could be.

She toyed with the button at the neck of his shirt. 'Well, Uncle Seamus was going to let me rot in prison; I had to do something.'

'Just how did you get out?' snarled Devlin.

'I broke out, of course.' She made it sound so easy. 'Call it another initiative test—one I passed with flying colours. So, Peter darling, you see your offer of travelling to Budapest tonight is very attractive. Now I've taken over my father's empire, we can run it from there. Together. What do you say?'

The pilot caressed her cheek. 'You've access to your father's accounts?'

'Oh yes. I'm the only one who knows the numbers of the ones in Switzerland. Isn't that right, Uncle Seamus?'

From Devlin's poisonous look, they could all see this was true. No wonder, thought Joe, that she had felt relatively safe without body armour. No one would shoot the golden goose. But that didn't meant they wouldn't do a lot of harm to her to get the answers.

Szabó's expression turned from grim to delighted as he adjusted to the new situation: the old man gone, the pretty daughter in control of the money, the guns and nuclear material safely delivered and on her terms. 'Darling, I would like nothing better. I might even waive the bonus if I get you in the bargain. Time for the younger generation to take over, no?'

Chapter· 17

Their accord was interrupted by the sound of gunfire outside. Joe's thoughts immediately went to his friends. The YDA students were not armed, though ex-soldier Jim Rivers did carry a weapon. It sounded like far more people, though, were engaged in a firefight.

'What the hell is going on?' Devlin ran to the door. 'Men, with me!'

From the flurry of communications in Joe's ear he heard that one of Devlin's security team had become suspicious and pulled a gun on Rivers. Unfortunately, with spectacular bad timing, that had coincided with the SAS's arrival, infiltrating the hangar to take over from the YDA. With no time to prepare, they had gone with their training; the special forces had not waited to see if Rivers could defuse the situation, instead providing Damien and the sergeant with covering fire so they could retreat. Isaac was furious, barking orders for the rest of the YDA team to get back now the situation had escalated beyond their capabilities. As Isaac had feared, part of the mission was now out of his control and there had been no time to coordinate with the SAS commander.

With Devlin out of the room for the moment, Joe knew Ember and he had to act fast. She glanced at him, then at Szabó's sidearm, and he understood exactly what she planned. He moved into position.

'Oh, Peter, what's going on?' Ember moved in close to her new protector, playing the unfamiliar role of damsel in distress. Her hand snaked to his side settling on the gun in the holster.

'I don't know, Lelkem. But let Devlin deal with it. I'll keep you safe in here.' He gave her a patronizing pat on the back.

'You're so kind and brave.' She moved back swiftly, sidearm in her grip pointing at his chest.

Szabó's eyes widened in shock. 'Ember, darling, what is this?'

Joe came up from behind and snatched the knife from the man's belt then bent Szabó's arm up behind his back, immobilizing him. When the pilot attempted to break free with a selection of what Joe guessed were choice Hungarian insults, he ended up on his face, Joe kneeling on him.

Ember moved to angle the gun down at him. 'Peter, darling, this is justice. You were prepared to let terrorists get their hands on a dirty bomb. I have no trouble handing you over to the authorities.'

He spat another curse at her. 'If I don't supply it, someone else will.'

The excuse of bad guys everywhere. 'I've restraints in my pocket,' said Joe. 'Will you get them, Em?'

Ember leaned over and took out the plastic ties. 'How very handyman of you.'

He grinned. 'Put them round his ankles and wrists.'

Placing the gun carefully on the buffet table out of reach, she knelt to carry out the instruction.

'It's just as well we don't understand Hungarian,' Joe commented as Szabó continued to curse.

'I know a few words. He is vowing death, revenge, and torture on us, doubting our parentage and suggesting all kinds of unpleasant acts be inflicted on us.'

'You shouldn't have to listen to that, then. Pass the napkin that's wrapped around that bottle in the cooler.'

Joe gagged the pilot with the expensive linen cloth then patted him on the back in a matching patronizing gesture. 'Be thankful it wasn't your sweaty sock in your mouth, as that was my next pick.'

Gunfire was still going off sporadically outside. Isaac was asking impatiently for an update as to how they were.

'We're safe, Isaac. Got the Hungarian secured but we're pinned down in here.'

Isaac's voice crackled on the line. 'I've finally got through to the commander of the special forces. The back-up is moving into position. They'll storm the hangar so keep out of their path.'

'How do we stop Devlin using us as hostages?' Joe asked, mind jumping to the next likely development. 'Even if we barricade ourselves in, he can just stand at the door and threaten to shoot through it. It's not built to withstand semi-automatic gunfire.'

'Take what evasive manoeuvres you can and let's pray he doesn't think of that.'

Ember had already moved over to one side of the door, the safest position if bullets were flying out there. She stood on tiptoe to peer through the glass window set in the middle, Szabó's gun held competently by her side.

'I can see Devlin and two of his men. They've taken position behind the crates just outside. I could take them out from here before they knew it.'

Turn the trap into a flanking manoeuvre? Not bad, but it had one major flaw. Joe joined her. 'No, Ember. You're on remand on the charge of murder. I think killing our prime suspect would be a very bad move at this point.'

'I wasn't going to kill him. Just injure him to put him out of the game.'

'But a gun like Szabó's is military grade. Even a great shot can't guarantee that you won't cause a fatal injury.' He passed her the body armour she'd removed earlier. 'Take this. You've got the right idea but I think I have a better solution. The YDA teaches the use of minimum force. We need to immobilize and distract—that will be enough. I want you to open the door for me, sufficient so I get a clear aim.'

'What are you doing?' She pulled her hair out of the back of the jacket and zipped it up.

'Did I mention about the knife throwing when I told you about the juggling? No? I thought not.' He picked up Szabó's knife, the cheese knife and a pair of scissors used to cut the thread on the patisserie boxes. He weighed them in his hand. 'Not ideal as they're so different but if I'm quick I should be able to give Devlin and his men something else to think about, hopefully put a couple out of commission. The SAS can rush them when I've created the distraction.'

'So what do you want me to do?'

'Your job is to lock and barricade the door as soon as I retreat. Then get back and lie on the floor as near to the wall as you can. Take the gun with you but we only use that as a last resort, agreed?'

She nodded. 'You'd better be as good as you think, otherwise you're just chucking them a weapon that can be turned on us.'

'Honey, you don't know how much I love to rise to a challenge.' He quickly brushed a kiss over her lips then informed Isaac what he had planned. He got the go-ahead to try it. 'Ready?'

She took her position.

'Now!'

Ember opened the door and Joe stepped out into the gap. Scissors went first into the nearest target: the thigh of the man crouching a few metres away. Cheese knife—something of a long shot—hit but bounced off the sleeve of the second man. Joe's prize missile, Szabó's knife, did not fail him. It circled in the air and embedded itself in Devlin's upper arm. Joe jumped back inside, Ember slammed the door and he helped her push the desk across the entrance. They then took cover in the most sheltered spot in the room, ignoring the battering and shouts at the entrance.

'Is Peter vulnerable out there?' asked Ember. By moving the desk they'd left him lying exposed in the middle of the room.

Cursing, Joe scrambled to his feet and dragged the pilot to a safer location.

'You missed one,' Ember said smugly.

He nudged her with his elbow. 'Only one out of three. That's not bad considering it was a blunt knife. Anyway, you shouldn't have been watching. You should've been keeping back.'

'And not see you go all ninja warrior on me? No way.'

He loved how she could tease even though they couldn't predict if they would survive the next few minutes. The noise outside—shouting, screaming, bursts of gunfire—was hard to translate into a clear picture.

'Isaac, update?' He held the earpiece so Ember could hear what he could.

'Damien says they've got five out of the six men. The last is crouched down over Devlin, who appears to be suffering from a knife wound.'

'The guy guarding him is Cheese Knife, I bet. I should've sent a champagne bottle his way instead and knocked him out.'

'What do we do, Isaac?' asked Ember.

'Just sit tight. You've done everything we asked of you. Leave us to mop up now.'

Joe slipped the microphone back in his ear, then put his

261

arm around Ember. 'So, Em, you, me, a gunrunner trussed up like a Christmas turkey, champagne, and caviar: don't say I never take you on romantic dates.'

'Oh, you charmer.' She snuggled against him, keeping the gun levelled at the door. 'Is everyone else safe?'

'Yes. From the reports I can hear that Kieran and Rose are having fun running the technical side in the control room. Nathan, Kate, and Raven are with the crew we took prisoner, moving them out of reach of stray bullets. Damien is with Sergeant Rivers out there somewhere but we'd've heard if they were in trouble. They're probably relishing the chance to see the SAS put through their paces.'

'How will we know when it's safe to come out?'

There came a rat-a-tat-tat knock on the door. 'Yo, Joe, we're good to go!' It was Damien.

'That's how. Come on, beautiful, let's get out of here.' Joe pulled her to her feet and pushed the desk out of the way. 'Damien, glad to see you didn't get yourself shot.'

'Scissors, really?' Damien grinned and hugged Joe. 'Was that the best you could do?'

'I thought the cheese knife was the low point myself,' said Ember. Joe smiled as Damien surprised Ember with a hug.

Damien arched his brows. 'Man, you had to be desperate if you were reduced to cutlery.'

'I thought it creative, myself,' said Joe.

'I'll send someone to take out the rubbish.' Damien nodded to the bound pilot. 'Come on. Isaac wants us for the debrief.' He led the way through the hangar. Splinters of wooden crates lay scattered on the floor, cisterns of water leaking like a rose on a watering can. They passed Devlin who was receiving treatment from an army medic.

'You witch, I'll kill you!' he screamed at Ember, bright spots of colour on his pale cheeks.

Holding her hand, Joe could feel her trembling. 'Like you did my father?' she asked coolly, not giving away any of her inner turmoil.

'Stupid girl! I wish I had killed him—and you too that morning I found you standing over his body. I would've saved myself all this.'

'Keep still, sir. I need to give you an injection,' said the medic.

Devlin was too furious to stop thrashing about. He raised himself on an elbow. 'We both know who did it, don't we, Ember? Do you think you'll be able to save him like you have yourself?'

Joe pulled Ember past. 'Don't listen to him. He's just saying that as he doesn't want to face a murder accusation on top of the trafficking charges.'

But Ember had retreated from him into that distant place inside, where she protected herself from further harm. 'I know him, Joe. I think he meant it.'

He was determined not to let her slip away from him. He rubbed her shoulder vigorously, trying to instil some of his confidence in her. 'Then we'll find out the truth and deal with it. But we'll deal with it together. Anyone who spends even a few minutes with your brother would know he'd never intentionally hurt a fly. It would take more than that vicious man's word to make me believe Max is a murderer.'

Despite the resounding success of the operation—weapons confiscated, gunrunners arrested, nuclear material on its way for safe disposal—Ember felt very subdued as they headed back to the YDA on the motorway, completely outside all celebrations. Devlin's words confronted her with the fact that the fundamentals had not changed: her father remained dead, Max was still at risk of being accused of murder, and she couldn't clear her own name without implicating him. As much as she would like to pass the blame onto Devlin, knowing him capable of murder, it didn't mean he'd been responsible for this one. She had believed his shouted denials, even if Joe had not.

'I think I'd better go back to prison,' she murmured, mostly to herself.

Joe heard. 'What? Don't be a fool, Ember! You're not going back there.'

Damien must also have been listening in, as he chipped in from the driver's seat. 'Technically, she's right. She will probably have to go back before they officially release her.'

'That's not what she means, Damien. She's thinking of sacrificing herself again.'

'I don't know: when are you girls going to learn to think of yourself first, hey?' Damien glanced over at his girlfriend, who Ember had already gathered was one of the gentlest and nicest people she'd ever met.

'Damien thinks I lack an inner mean girl,' said Rose seriously. 'I tell him he's mean enough for the both of us.'

Ember smiled, even while feeling a tremendous sense of loss. She loved these people, Joe most especially, of course, but she couldn't see how on earth she could square the circle of seeing to her own needs while making sure Max remained free.

As a text came in, Rose checked her phone. 'Ember, I've a message from your brother. Oh.'

Ember realized that in the rush to get everything organized for the operation, she'd not called by Max's room to reassure him. He had to be wondering where they'd all gone. 'Is he OK?'

'Yes, I made sure someone was with him before we left, but the thing is, he's not stayed there. He's just texted to say he's gone to see Mrs Roe. She phoned him in some distress earlier, very confused about where you both were. He said you weren't to worry and that he'd sort it out.'

Ember closed her eyes briefly. That her vulnerable brother believed she was too busy to sort out a problem with their old nanny was her fault. He wouldn't know where to start.

'Damien—?' she began.

'I'm on it, Ember. I'll do a U turn at the next junction. Don't worry, he'll have his guard with him.'

When Damien parked the car in the driveway, the only lights on were in the annexe. The guard—Joe told her he recognized him as one of Isaac's most reliable men—was standing outside, keeping watch on the approach. He reported that all was quiet; only the old lady and Max were inside. Ember led the way to the little front door with its knocker in the shape of a fox, conscious of Joe, Damien, and Rose just behind her. That was a comfort. She rapped on the door.

'Nanny, it's me, Ember!'

With the sound of a chain being removed, the door opened.

'Ember love, thank you so much for coming. You and Max, both of you, such sweet children.' Nanny peered at the others. 'Who are these?'

Ember wondered why Nanny Roe hadn't commented on the fact that she should be in prison. Had Nanny lost it so much that she no longer remembered such things? What Ember had thought was age-related forgetfulness appeared to have bloomed into dementia without her noticing. 'Nanny, they're friends of mine—and of Max. Is Max here?'

'Yes, yes, he's inside just sorting out my television for me. I can't seem to make anything work these days. Come on in. I'll put the kettle on.' As Nanny Roe went off to the little kitchen, Ember noticed that she was wearing mismatched slippers, one of her old ones and one of the new ones Max had bought her at Christmas.

Joe slipped his arm around Ember's shoulder. 'Is she always like this?'

Ember shook her head. 'She's much worse than usual. I'd seen the odd sign, you know, senior moments? But I hadn't realized it had gone this far. I thought she looked after Max, but it looks like since her heart attack it's the other way round.'

They found Max kneeling on the floor in front of the television as he fiddled with the leads from the satellite box. A mug of steaming hot chocolate sat on the edge of the entertainment centre, accompanied by a homemade biscuit. Patch lay at his feet, staring at the biscuit morosely, giving a good impression of a starving man being denied the last crumb. Max looked up and grinned. 'Hi. I didn't expect you to come. I've almost got it sorted.'

Damien crouched down beside him and gave Patch a scratch on the tummy to cheer him up. 'What's wrong?'

'These things are too complicated for Nanny. She takes out the leads when she's dusting behind the unit and never remembers how they go back in. I tell her to wait for me but she won't be moved from her cleaning routine.'

A rattling announced the arrival of Nanny with a tray. Joe rushed to relieve her of it.

'There you are, Ember, I've made you your favourite.' She handed Ember a second mug of chocolate and a biscuit. 'Now boys and you, young lady—what a lovely shade of auburn hair you have there. I'm quite, quite envious!'

Rose smiled at the old lady. 'Thank you.'

'Now where was I? Oh, yes. I didn't know what you'd like, so I bought some hot water in the thermos, hot chocolate, milk, and various teas. Help yourself.' She looked down at the tray. 'Oh dear, I forgot the sugar.'

'You sit down. I'll fetch it for you.' Joe went out in the direction of the kitchen.

Ember noticed Nanny hadn't provided any biscuits either but was afraid to embarrass her with another reminder of her forgetfulness. 'So, how are you, Nanny?'

'Feeling old, and tired.' She sagged as she sat on her sofa, no longer able to keep her spine ruler straight as she once had. 'But it's lovely to see you both again. Quite like old times. I wish things wouldn't change so fast. There used to be just one switch on the television, on or off. Now there're handsets and fiddly bits, leads and whatnot. I don't know how I can survive day to day without Max here to sort it all out for me.'

'You know you can ask me any time, Nanny,' said Max. 'There, all fixed now.' He switched on the television and a news programme came on screen.

'Reports are just coming in of a big customs haul at an airfield in Essex,' said the news anchor. 'Early indications are that arrests have been made, including that of Seamus Devlin, a man well known to the police and associate of Mick Lord, the murdered London businessman.'

'Hey, that's Uncle Seamus!' exclaimed Max, pointing to the picture on the screen. 'Nanny, Uncle Seamus has been arrested.'

'Good gracious! At least that means I don't have to deal with him myself—sending his men to scare you in the park like that! I've always said he's nothing but a bully. Come sit by me, Max. Bring your drink, and we'll see what they have to say about that nasty little man.'

Ember stood back observing two of the small number of people she loved settle down as spectators to an operation in which she had played a pivotal role. Isaac had promised that the details of the mission would not be made public before the trial so there was no mention of what the YDA had done. She preferred it that way. Nanny didn't seem able to cope with normal life any longer, so talk of nuclear waste and gun battles would distress her. What was Ember going to do with her? Nanny needed to move into some kind of sheltered accommodation, but then where would Max go? Could he stay at the YDA for the moment, at least until the court case was sorted out?

Ember rubbed her temples. Everything was in a terrible muddle. She had no idea which end of the string to tug first.

Joe searched through the kitchen cupboards looking for the sugar bowl and kept coming across items in odd places. He found a set of keys in the salad spinner and a pair of reading glasses with the teabags. He finally located the sugar on the spices shelf. Feeling hungry, he wondered if there were any more of the cookies that Nanny Roe had served Max and Ember. It was fairly miraculous that the old lady had managed to bake if her mind was wandering as much as the signs suggested. The cookies proved less difficult to find, being stored in a tin with 'cake' on the side. He levered off the lid and took a sniff.

What?

Picking one up, he broke it apart. A fragment of something white fell out. Touching it with the end of a moistened fingertip, he put it to his tongue. Bitter but not salt.

Oh my god. Joe's gaze went to the knife block. *Oh my god.* Dropping the tin back on the counter, he ran back into the living room. Ember had lifted the hot chocolate to her lips and was about to take a sip. 'Don't!' Joe snatched it from her. 'Damien, take the drink from Max—and the cookie.'

'What?' Ember looked at him in shock. 'You don't have to grab it. I'd've shared it with you.'

He put the mug down but out of her reach. 'It's not that. Ember, the cookie is laced with some kind of pill. Sleeping pills maybe.' He broke it apart so she could see the white grains he'd noticed in the batch.

268

Ember gave a shocked laugh. 'Oh no. God, I hadn't realized it had got that bad. She's mixing things up, but she could've . . .' It was sinking in. 'She could've killed us and herself.' Before Joe could stop her, she knelt before Nanny Roe. 'Nanny, darling, did you eat any of the biscuits earlier? You've got to tell me the truth now, as we might have to call an ambulance.' She looked round to Joe. 'Shall we call one just in case?' Another thought struck her. 'Max, you haven't eaten anything have you?'

Max was scowling at Damien, who was keeping him away from his hot chocolate. 'Yes, I tried a biscuit but it tasted funny. Even Patch didn't like it.'

Both Max and the dog had had a lucky escape.

'Oh lord.' Ember pressed a fist to her forehead. 'OK, OK, let's deal with this. Nanny, do you realize what we're talking about?'

Nanny nodded quite contentedly. 'Yes, dear. But you shouldn't worry. I gave you some before, remember, to help you sleep? I just wanted us all to go to sleep together.'

Ember stiffened. 'So you did it on purpose? You put your sleeping pills in our food?'

'I must've put too much in this time as Max didn't eat it earlier. That's why I made the drink for you both.'

Damien confiscated the second mug and carried both into the kitchen where he began looking for the empty pill bottles as evidence.

Joe didn't buy Nanny Roe's twinkly-eyed explanation that she just wanted them to sleep. He suspected she knew full well what would've happened if they'd finished the drinks. 'Mrs Roe?'

'Yes? Who are you, young man?'

'My name's Joe Masters. I'm Ember's friend, as she told you earlier. Mrs Roe, when you said you wanted all three of you to sleep, did you ever mean for Ember and Max to wake up?'

Her expression went sour. 'I'm not answering that. That's a horrible question. I don't like you. You aren't polite. You're just like that social busybody, telling me I couldn't look after Max any more. Why won't you all just go away and leave us in peace? I only want us to be together—just us, and dear Ember, of course, now she's here, but not you.'

Realization dawning, Ember stood up and moved closer to Joe. Rose took Max's arm, keeping him back.

'Nanny,' said Ember, 'Joe is being perfectly polite and he asked you a question. Did you mean to send us to sleep permanently?'

The old lady pressed her lips together.

'Mrs Roe, did you kill Mick Lord?' asked Joe.

The nanny's face suddenly crumpled. She wrapped her arms around her middle, rocking slowly. 'Such a lovely boy when he was small, my little angel, but he grew up so bad. It takes some of them like that and there's nothing you can do, can't discipline it out of them, they're just wrong inside.' She raised tear-glazed eyes to Joe, imploring him to understand. 'Then Mick threatened to take my sweet Max from me, put him in a horrible asylum with mad people. Max isn't crazy; he's perfect, kind, and loyal. I knew then Mick had to go, had to be put out of his misery, because he can't have been happy living like that, loving no one, could he? He even killed his wife, their poor mother, drove her to take her own life. I forgave him that but I couldn't let him hurt Max, not him too.'

'So you drugged Ember that night, and you had already put a listening device in her room?'

'Of course I had to do that.' Her voice firmed as she remembered her plan, feeling fully justified by the action she took. Her actions made complete sense to her, in the world

270

where she was Nanny and had final say over rewards and punishments. Joe didn't know what Ember was making of this terrible mental collapse in someone she loved so much. He wanted to comfort her, but they had to get the confession while the old lady was talking.

'Why?'

'I didn't want her to wake up and see what had to be done. It was my responsibility, not hers, to deal with my boy.'

So Kieran had been right: the video feed had been put there, possibly by Mick originally but certainly used by Devlin. The listening device had been placed by the amateur assassin, purchased from the kind of shops Nanny would be in the habit of using.

'Oh, Nanny, what have you done?' whispered Ember.

'I just wanted you to be happy, to be safe.' Nanny Roe turned to Max. 'I wanted to keep you with me always. If we could all just snuggle down together and go to sleep, none of this would matter.'

Joe reached for his phone. He had some calls to make: first Isaac, then the police. The night was far from over.

Chapter 18

A hot day in June and the sun was dancing on the waves of the Thames just below the terrace of the YDA where the graduation was being held. Ember sat proudly with Carol and Patrick Masters, Max beside her, to watch Joe step up to the rostrum to make the valedictory speech. Chosen unanimously by his year to speak on their behalf, Ember knew Joe had sweated long and hard over what he should say to the audience. She'd heard him practise it numerous times but couldn't help feeling nervous for him. Inside he would be trembling but no one would be able to tell that looking at his warm smile and confident poise. He really was the most gorgeous person alive and she was the lucky girl that he had chosen; she couldn't believe her change in fortune.

'Oh my,' said Carol, dabbing her eyes.

'He'll be fine,' Ember assured her.

'I know, darling, but I'm just so proud I could burst!' Carol gave her a watery smile and hugged Ember to her chest. 'Oh look at me, making you all rumpled!' Carol smoothed Ember's hair.

'Leave the poor girl alone, Carol,' rumbled Patrick good-naturedly. 'She'll miss the speech.'

Ember smiled back, not at all worried about being messed up a little by the lady who had rapidly become a new mother to her and Max since they all met a few months ago.

Up on the podium, Joe cleared his throat. He was speaking without notes. Ember crossed her fingers that he would not stumble. 'Ladies and gentlemen, mentors and students, friends and families, I am pleased, proud, and peculiarly daunted to be standing here before you all. The last few years that I have spent in the YDA have truly been a gift. Giving this address here, in the shade of Shakespeare's theatre, I think it only appropriate to express what I feel in a few words borrowed from him.'

Ember blinked. This wasn't the speech he had rehearsed with her! The wonderful underhand schemer had totally hoodwinked her. Their eyes met across the space that separated them and she felt his loving amusement warm her to the core. This new speech was primarily for her, she just knew it.

'"We happy few, we band of brothers" said Shakespeare. That's what we are taught to be at the YDA—a team of brothers and sisters. None of us would be graduating today without those around us. I do not exaggerate when I say that you, my friends, have saved my life on a couple of occasions, taught me a lesson when I needed pulling back in line, and filled my days in England with love and friendship.' Joe was now looking at Kieran and Raven, Nathan and Kate, and Damien and Rose, all of whom smiled back, their eyes full of shared memories.

'Shakespeare also said, "Strong reasons make strong actions." Our leaders here have always taught that we are to make sure our actions are founded on what is right and what is true. Never to abuse a weaker party, to use the minimum level of force required, to respect the different gifts of our team mates.' Joe turned to face Isaac, who was sitting behind him with the Metropolitan Police Commissioner who had handed out the diplomas. 'Colonel Hampton, Isaac, each one of us here would say you and your colleagues exemplify this quality. Thank you for your support and your wisdom.

'And finally, Shakespeare also said that "brevity is the soul of wit" so I will not run on and keep us all from the fine buffet I can see laid out in the canteen by our housekeeper, Mr Stone, and his great behind-the-scenes team. The last piece of wisdom I want to offer from my favourite writer is that, "we know what we are but not what we may be". My fellow graduates, we leave here as people of potential. It is still to be decided how we employ that in our future, but I am convinced the years spent here will ensure that each of us will make good choices as long as we keep to what we know now. You are going to be wonderful, a surprise maybe to yourselves and others, but you won't go wrong if you remember what you learnt here. I will sign off by saying a farewell from the same author, but in a gesture that I learned from a girl so special to me there are no words to sum her up: "So good night unto you all, Give me your hands, if we be friends."' Stepping down from the podium, Joe held out his hand to Kieran, who took it and then Kieran offered his free hand to Raven and so on until every student in the year was linked. Joe looked at the spectators and then back at his friends. 'I think maybe we should bow?'

The audience got to their feet, clapping and hooting, and in Patch's case, barking, as the graduates all bowed. Carol surreptitiously passed Ember a tissue to catch her tears.

'Wasn't he wonderful!' Ember whispered.

'Yes, dear, he was. Quickly now, he's looking for you.' Carol pushed her forward and Ember ran through the crowd to jump into Joe's arms. He whisked her in a circle as he loved to do, laughing in the sunlight.

'Did you like my speech?' Joe asked, dropping her to her feet.

'You rogue and villain!' Ember batted him on the chest. 'All that practising you made me do!'

'I couldn't resist. My friends encouraged me to keep you in the dark. Kate said you'd like the surprise.'

Ember's gaze sought out her best friend who was talking and laughing with her mother and stepfather while her little sister fed biscuits to the spaniel Jellybean. Nathan was nearby, arm linked with his artist mother as they contemplated the river scene, discussing from their gestures how best to paint it, while his father and mentor, Jim Rivers, looked on with pride.

'I did like it. It was wonderful. And you're wonderful, Joe. Truly, you are.' There was no more talking for a few minutes while they kissed.

When they broke apart, Joe leant his forehead against hers. 'So no second thoughts about coming with me to New York?' Joe was enrolling in NYU, majoring in law, but he was also going to help set up an American branch of the YDA. Ember had a place at drama school lined up thanks to Henry and his connections in the Big Apple, but she also had made it through the first round of auditions for an off-Broadway production of Romeo and Juliet, the next round coming up in a week's time. Ember had discovered that she loved acting, never feeling freer of all the burdens of the past than when she was on stage, casting the spell of make-believe over an audience. It was an exhilarating feeling, beaten only by Joe's kisses. She looked to see if she could spot the theatre director, her guest today, in the crowd: she had so much to thank him for. Henry was standing with Damien's Uncle Julian, the two men having a very loud conversation interrupted with guffaws of laughter and much waving around of champagne glasses. Damien and his parents were clustered around Rose, admiring her graduation present from them, which was a jewellery box in the shape of Tutankhamen's casket made by craftsmen in the Ugandan village where Damien's doctor parents worked.

'No second thoughts. I'll just miss our friends here, that's all.' Ember's notoriety in England hadn't followed her to New York. The people she had met so far were only interested in her talent. She would have to come back to testify at the trial of Szabó and Devlin, but it looked like Nanny Roe would be judged not fit to plead and would instead see out her days in a secure unit for dementia patients. She had now lost all sense of time and forgot who Ember and Max were; Ember didn't think she was suffering but she was gradually losing her grip on life little bit by little bit. A trial would be a waste of everyone's time. Ember had handed over all the information she had on her father's operation, including the Swiss bank accounts, to Isaac, who was busy rolling up what was left of the operation. Max and Patch were coming with Ember and Joe, of course, but would be living with Carol and Patrick who said they were missing having a youngster at home. Max was going to attend courses at a local art school.

Joe smiled at the scene around them of happy families and friends meeting friends. 'I'm sure there will be plenty of opportunities to call in specialist advisers as we set up the YDA over there. Cambridge has long holidays so Kieran and Raven should be free to visit. Damien and Rose have already said they're coming in September before they start at University College London.'

Ember smiled. 'Yes, Rose is in heaven at the prospect of going to college next door to the British Museum.'

'Damien is a clever and ruthless man when it comes to Rose; he wouldn't let her have anything but the best. And Nathan and Kate have promised to come at Christmas during their vacation from St Andrews.'

'So much to look forward to. Kate and I are taking you clubbing: we've already agreed that. Oh, and shopping.'

'At least I've got a few months to mentally prepare myself for that cruel and inhuman treatment. But do you know what?' Joe looped his arms around her waist and leaned back a little. 'Do you know what I look forward to most?'

She thought perhaps she could guess. 'What's that?'

'Seeing this view every day for the rest of my life. "I would not wish any companion in the world but you."'

'Nor I, you.' She smiled up at him. 'You've been practising your quotations.'

'Naturally. I'm a graduate of the YDA: I detected early on what I need to do to prepare for my most important mission: keeping you happy.'

'Well met in the sunlight, fair Oberon.'

'Lead on, my Titania.'

Hand in hand, Joe and Ember joined their family and friends to celebrate their dreams for the future in the sunshine of a midsummer's day.

Discover a thrilling world of romance with **Joss Stirling**

ALSO BY
Joss Stirling

Joss Stirling lives in Oxford and is the author of
the bestselling Savants series. She was
awarded the Romantic Novelists' Association's
Romantic Novel of the year 2015 for **Struck.**

You can visit her website at **www.jossstirling.com.**